Wendy Craig's

Nanny

Wendy Craig's

Nanny

by
Jean Bowden

GRANADA
London Toronto Sydney New York

Granada Publishing Limited
Frogmore, St Albans, Herts AL2 2NF
and
3 Upper James Street, London W1R 4BP
Suite 405, 4th Floor, 866 United Nations Plaza, New York, NY 10017, USA
117 York Street, Sydney, NSW 2000, Australia
100 Skyway Avenue, Rexdale, Ontario M9W 3A6, Canada
PO Box 84165, Greenside, 2034 Johannesburg, South Africa
61 Beach Road, Auckland, New Zealand

Published by Granada Publishing 1981

ISBN 0 246 11593 9

Printed in Great Britain by
Richard Clay (The Chaucer Press), Ltd,
Bungay, Suffolk

CHAPTER ONE

With her father's hand under her elbow, Barbara came out of the Law Courts into the Strand. Her divorce case had been heard on the 1st October, the very first day of the Michaelmas term in the Queen's Bench Division. It had almost seemed as if, after months of waiting, they couldn't get rid of her and her problems fast enough.

'Well,' Donald said with the awkward jocularity that masked affection, 'how's it feel to be a free woman again?'

'A free woman? Is that what I am?' Free for what, she wondered.

He gave her elbow a little hug against his side. 'Will be, when the decree's made absolute. So long as you don't throw your cap over the windmill in the meantime.'

The solicitor had explained it all to her. The decree nisi ought to go through to 'absolute' without trouble, so long as everyone was discreet. The King's Proctors were unlikely to concern themselves unduly with the divorce of an obscure Watford cinema manager and his wife. Nevertheless, everything would have been much safer if there had been no lies. 'Collusion' was what the Proctors were supposed to be so hot on – and there had been collusion in Barbara Harris's divorce.

All because of Archie's starry-eyed romanticism. If he'd allowed Helen to be named as co-respondent, everything would have been out in the open. But oh no, that would put a stain on Helen's character, she'd be talked about even after they got married, it was unfair on her to drag her into the divorce.

Fair . . . it never seemed to bother him that it was unfair on Barbara to break up her marriage. It hadn't been a particularly marvellous marriage but, as the saying goes, it was the only one she had. It had lasted ten years. You don't throw away ten years of your life without pain. And if Helen wanted Archie so much, it seemed only fair that she should pay a little too.

But no. The chivalrous Archie Harris wouldn't have that. 'It's bad enough that she's expecting my child,' he said. My child . . . He invested the words with a special sonority. From the way he'd talked about it, you'd have thought all he'd ever wanted in the world was to have a family.

Barbara had been unable to give him that. Though they hadn't talked about it much, it had been Barbara who wanted children. Then after four or five years she'd come to accept that they'd be a childless couple. It seemed a shame, because she loved children, was good at being Auntie to other people's. Strange that it should be the coming of a child which finally wrote 'finis' to her marriage.

Her father was trying to get a look at her beyond the veil of her pert little hat. Poor girl, she was trying so hard not to show how much she was hurt by all this. That weak little bastard Archie . . . Donald could just picture how Helen had wept and wheedled and finally faced him with the dreadful news of her pregnancy. Otherwise, of course, there'd have been no divorce. For there'd been other girls before Helen, though whether Barbara knew of them Donald wasn't exactly sure.

He was never exactly sure of things between himself and Barbara. She was so self-contained and efficient. Well, she'd had to be, hadn't she?

'Come on, duckie,' he said in a too-bright tone, 'let's go and have a sticky cream tea at the Corner House.'

'Wouldn't you rather go home?'

'Seems a bit tame, doesn't it? We ought to celebrate. Come on.'

He took her across the busy street on his arm, to the bus stop. She knew very well that he'd rather be going for a drink but it was too early for the pubs to be open and he couldn't take her to his club, the Imperial and Overseas, because it wasn't a ladies' day.

The traffic was very heavy. Coming down from Fleet Street were the usual convoys of newspaper vans surging out with the editions of the evening papers, the *Star,* the *News,* and the *Standard.* At the entrance to the Temple the paper-seller was chanting his refrain: 'Sta-New-Stana.' They all used the same order, they must be poets at heart to catch the cadence so exactly. In the editions later this evening, her own divorce wouldn't even be mentioned, Barbara thought with wry acceptance. A cataclysmic event in her life, yet not worth a line of print to anyone else.

They were still waiting for a number 11 bus when a taxi singled itself out of the threads of vehicles and drew up alongside. Felicity Leschallas put her head out of the window, framed by handsome fox furs. 'Darling, there you are!' she cried. 'I've been trying to catch up with you! Hop in.'

Barbara was about to explain they were waiting for a bus. Her father, always the opportunist, opened the taxi door and pushed her in, tumbling in after her as the driver hurried on to the frenzied hooting of cars behind him.

'I'm sorry I didn't get here in time to be in court,' Felicity said, falling back on the leather seat and pulling Barbara down with her. 'I was driving in, got a puncture at Slough. So I had to get a tow to a garage and leave the car and catch a train and then a taxi from the station but here I am.' She drew breath. 'Darling, how was it? Ghastly?'

'Where are we going, miss?' inquired the driver through his glass partition.

Saved a reply by the question, Barbara let her father explain they'd been going to Lyons Corner house for tea.

'Oh, nonsense,' Barbara said. 'Driver, the Savoy!'

In almost no time at all they were set down in the forecourt of the hotel. Barbara followed her father and Felicity into the welcoming chintziness of the lounge. A waiter hurried forward; Felicity said in a little rush: 'Tea and scones and things, little cakes, you like Indian tea don't you, Mr Gray? Then I'll have that too – for three, waiter.'

It always amazed Barbara to see how much Felicity had changed since their nursing days in the War. Then she had been brisk and calm and rather quiet. Since her marriage to Peter Leschallas she had gradually been adopting another facade, one more suited to the life she led.

Felicity, as everyone was fond of saying, had done rather well for herself. Her marriage to a younger son of a substantial landed family took them all by surprise because, quite candidly, most of their nursing colleagues had thought his parents had a better match in mind for him. He'd come to know Felicity through one of the doctors at their hospital, a friend of his. There were those who were unkind enough to say Barbara only accepted Archie Harris because she was afraid of being left on the shelf after her best friend captured the handsome young lieutenant of the Oxfordshires.

But that was untrue. Barbara had really loved Archie. In 1917, when the war seemed to be turning into an endless blood bath, love was heightened by the fear of never seeing each other again. She hadn't hesitated a moment when he asked her to marry him before he went back to the trenches from his leave.

Strange that something which had begun with so much passion and hunger should end with a few dry words, like crumbs thrown for birds, in a courtroom.

'Well, darling, what are your plans now?' Felicity demanded, unfastening her furs and pushing them back from her shoulders. 'Got anything in mind?'

'I haven't had time yet. I suppose I ought to get organized.'

Her father glanced anxiously at Barbara. It was so unlike her not to know what she intended to do.

'Early days yet,' he said. 'Plenty of time to make plans. You should have a holiday first, I think – don't you, Felicity? She ought to go away, have a bit of a fling.'

Barbara made no response. As if written in the air above her head, Felicity could see the words: 'Using what for money?'

The waiter came with the silverware and the cake-stand.

Another appeared behind him bearing the tea. Felicity busied herself pouring it. Her thoughts were on the problem of what to do for Barbara.

She'd never really liked Archie Harris – selfish, self-satisfied little nobody! On only two occasions he'd come with Barbara for a stay at Dowers Farm, where he'd been like a fish out of water. Of course Felicity hadn't expected him to have much in common with the county types numbered among her friends, but he might at least have made an attempt to conquer his uneasiness. Now Barbara was different; Barbara had fitted in without difficulty. But then Barbara had that kind of outlook; perhaps it had something to do with having been brought up in India, this ability to seem at home anywhere.

'Have a scone, darling,' she urged, passing a plate to Barbara.

'I'm not really hungry, thanks.'

'Do try to eat something. You're much too thin.'

It was true. Barbara's fair hair, neatly dressed in the medium bob now fashionable, hung against cheekbones that were too prominent. Her eyes, always one of her most appealing features, looked huge now in her pale face.

'Oh, if I had Archie Harris here . . .' thought Felicity. What on earth had possessed the man to get a girl in the family way? Surely he had sense enough to prevent that? But there, you never could tell. Perhaps this Helen person really fancied him and wanted to force his hand with the news of the forthcoming babe. Well, the more fool she, thought Felicity with savage satisfaction. She'd find out before too long that Archie Harris was no great prize.

The wonder to Felicity was that her friend had stood him for so long. Barbara had never admitted it, but the two must have been drifting apart for years. Archie with his absurd enthusiasm for every tuppeny-ha'penny film that he put on at his cinema . . . The Bioscope, she remembered it used to be called. How proudly he had shown her round it when she went on her first visit to them after their marriage. Now it had been remodelled and renamed all ready for the talkies, which Archie had said would change the face of the entertainment industry. Felicity's father-in-law had been to a talkie on a visit to New York, a film called 'The Jazz Singer'. He said it was terrible, everyone spoke with a Yankee accent. That just showed how silly it was of Archie to expect great things of the talkies.

Donald Gray was enjoying the scones and jam and tea. He'd have preferred a pink gin, but even the Savoy couldn't supply that outside licensing hours. He lolled a little in his armchair, pleased with his surroundings despite the fact that his daughter looked so unlike herself.

Fact of the matter was, he told himself as he buttered another tiny scone, she'd have to get a job. Damned shame. Not a good time to be job-hunting. Unemployment was pretty bad and Barbara, let's face it, wasn't a young girl any more. Still, always a job for a nurse, surely.

If he'd only been able to put a bit of money by . . . But he'd never really adjusted to being back in England after the good old days in India. Somehow you couldn't seem to live in the same style on the same money. And of course he wasn't getting any younger, felt the cold, liked his comforts. Only another year to go in the office of his engineering firm and he'd be at retirement age. Pension was all right – better than most. All the same, it wouldn't be enough to support him and Barbara *and* Dottie.

And in any case, Barbara didn't like Dottie.

So really it was a case of her having to find herself a new niche in life. Well, she'd do it all right. A sensible girl, always equal to whatever life threw at her. But she really ought to apply to her old hospital to see if they'd take her back.

'Eileen didn't come?' Felicity commented, sipping her tea.

'No, she and Jimmy had a trip abroad fixed up – staying with some people in Cannes. They couldn't really change the date after we heard the day for the hearing.'

'Of course not.' Privately Felicity thought they could. She

was fairly sure Barbara's sister would have wanted to. But Jimmy Letts probably had some great scheme going whereby he had to make contact with somebody or other in Cannes who would give him a tip, or offer him a share in a deal, or some other fairyland pot of gold. Jimmy Letts was another man for whom Felicity hadn't much time. But he was a little better than Barbara's husband because he at least didn't drop his fork at the dinner table. Still, the Gray sisters had had no great luck in choosing their husbands, Felicity thought.

'You're staying with your father?' she asked.

'Yes, but it isn't very convenient. Dottie's gone away to work in a hotel in Bournemouth for the time being but now the season's ending she'll be back.'

There was a fiction politely maintained in the Gray family that Dottie Fleming was Donald Gray's housekeeper and that she occupied a separate room in his Bayswater flat. When Barbara had had to move out of her Watford home, there had been nowhere else to go but to her father. Dottie had obligingly packed up and gone for a seasonal job at the seaside – with the greater goodwill because she and Barbara didn't get on very well. Barbara meanwhile had acted housekeeper for her father.

It had been some slight solace to her to keep busy doing chores. She had caught up on the jobs Dottie had let slide – taken down curtains and had them cleaned, put buttons on all her father's shirts, darned all the socks with holes in, given him a much-needed variety in his diet. She'd even tried to cut down his consumption of spirits, with a little success, for Donald was ashamed to drink too much in front of her.

Barbara didn't fool herself that she could stay there forever. She knew her father would give a sigh of relief when she left, fond though he was of her. Already he was weary of living to standards that were higher than his own. Already he was looking forward to the lax management of Dottie. By mid-October Dottie's job with the Royal Sussex Hotel would be over and Barbara ought to vacate the room which Dottie officially occupied in the Bayswater flat.

But where was she to go?

'You must come to me,' Felicity said, chiming in exactly with her thought. 'I've been thinking, you need a holiday and the country is lovely at this time of year. Just throw a few things in a case and come, Barbara. You know how we are – quite informal.'

'Oh yes. Informal. Short silk dresses before six and long silk dresses afterwards.'

'Don't be absurd, darling. We don't dress much, except at weekends – especially while the shooting season's on. The men come in so tired – it's all they can do to struggle into a dinner jacket. Barbara, I really mean it. Do come. You could laze about and sleep and go for walks and get some food into you. And the children would love to see you.'

'And I'd love to see them.'

'So you'll come?'

'I don't know, Felicity. I'm not very good company at the moment.'

'Who's asking you to be? Darling, you needn't speak a word to anyone if you don't want to.'

'That wouldn't be much fun for you, though –'

'Oh, you'll talk to *me*,' Felicity said, laughing. 'Has there ever been a time when we haven't been able to talk? But if you're grumpy I'll leave you alone. Heaven knows I've enough to do to keep me occupied so don't think I'd be worrying about keeping you entertained. And if you don't want to talk to people who come, I mean, at cocktails or anything like that, well, you can just look silent and intense, like Greta Garbo, and become a woman of mystery.'

Barbara laughed. 'Don't talk to me about film stars. I've left all that behind me in Watford.'

It was the first time she'd sounded like herself since Felicity had picked her up. They smiled at each other. 'That's more like the Barbara Harris I know,' she remarked.

'Mmm . . .' Barbara said. 'I've decided . . . I'm going back to being Barbara Gray. The Harris part of my life is behind me.'

'We love you whoever you are,' Felicity said with a wink at Donald. 'Tell her she's got to come to me for a stay, just to get used to being Barbara Gray again, Mr Gray.'

'Yes, dear, I think you should,' Donald said. He really did think so. It would be far better for her in Felicity's fine house with all the servants – much more agreeable than his flat. And besides, it would be so nice to have the flat to himself again, and not to have to come home from the Three Crowns at nine-thirty because he felt guilty at leaving her at home on her own.

'A couple of weeks in Oxfordshire in this fine autumn weather would be lovely, Barbie. Not as good as two weeks in Cannes, I'll grant you, but Felicity makes up for the lack of Riviera sunshine.'

'Two weeks? Who's talking about two weeks? She must stay as long as ever she likes,' Felicity scolded. 'No time limit. In fact, if you could stay until at least Hallowe'en, darling, it would be such a help to me, because for some mad reason I've got myself involved in giving a party for the children, and honestly, I don't know how I'm going to live through it without help from someone like you.'

It was odd how the idea of the children's party made it all seem so much more attractive. Barbara heard herself saying, 'Thank you Felicity, I'd love to.'

At once Felicity's organizing streak began to show; it was still there, overlaid though it might be by the gush and the 'darling' of her new persona.

'Well, now, don't let's hang about. Off you go and do your packing, while I telephone that garage and see if they've got the car ready. I'll meet you at Paddington in, say, two hours – is that long enough? Then we'll collect the car and be home in time for dinner –'

'Felicity, I didn't quite picture myself going off this very minute –'

'Why not? What reason is there to stay in London now the case has been heard? You agree, don't you, Mr Gray – the sooner she gets away for a change, the better.'

'I do indeed.' Oh, the bliss of being able to sit down to his gramophone records with his feet on the table and a bottle at his elbow . . . Peter Dawson singing 'The Road to Mandalay', Tettrazzini singing 'Les Filles de Cadiz' . . . and the prospect of a saunter down to the Three Crowns for a pie and a double . . . 'Yes, Babsie, I can't see any point in staying here a minute longer than you have to. I mean, it's convenient, isn't it – here's Felicity with transport to take you to the very door, whereas if you leave it to tomorrow there's all the bother of taking the train and having it met from the house . . .'

Barbara allowed herself to be persuaded. She wasn't putting up much resistance. The idea of getting away to the tranquillity of Oxfordshire, to Dowers Farm with its well-ordered regime and its comfort, was heaven.

'I shan't be able to pack some of my things – they're in the wash.'

'Good heavens, girl, I'll have them sent on to you.'

'But, Father, what about a meal this evening? Are you sure?'

'I'll be all right. Have a meal out, nice little Italian restaurant just round the corner, you know.'

'You promise you'll eat? Not just have a drink and a sandwich?'

'I promise.'

She knew he wouldn't keep the promise, but for the moment she didn't really care. All at once it had become urgent to get away, from him, from everything to do with her family, and just have time to herself to think things out.

She and Donald took the bus back to Bayswater while Felicity telephoned the garage in Slough. She packed quickly but sensibly, well aware that the two pairs of real silk stockings hanging damp on the little balcony at the back would be appropriated by Dottie.

Luckily, because the weather had turned suddenly cool after a long hot summer, she had got out her winter clothes and refurbished them only last week. She packed her three good wool dresses, her Welsh tweed suit, the best of her blouses, and her evening skirt. After consideration she put in a crêpe-de-Chine frock and a washable tussore. That was the best she could do for afternoon clothes and the six o'clock drink session. She and Archie had done little entertaining at that hour, because it was the time when the cinema always needed his attention, with the crowds coming in for the first evening showing. So if she was to do anything more elaborate in the way of evening wear, she'd have to go into the long skirt. Perhaps Felicity wouldn't mind if she used the sewing machine in the nursery to run up a couple of evening blouses – she had enough money to buy a few yards of pretty material.

Donald went out to summon a taxi for her. She let him carry down her suitcase, let him give directions for Paddington. When he kissed her, she clung to him for a moment and was surprised at the fervour with which he returned the embrace. 'Look after yourself, dear,' he muttered against her ear, snuffling a little with unwonted emotion. 'Put that rotten little squirt out of your mind and find someone else among Felicity's rich friends, eh?'

'No fear,' she said. 'Once bitten, twice shy. Now you will have a proper meal, won't you?'

'Yes, yes – get in, dear, he's blocking the road.'

'Goodbye, then. I'll write to you to let you know I arrived safely.'

'That's right, do that. I'll send on those things.'

''Bye, Father. 'Bye.'

''Bye, dear. 'Bye.'

He stood on the pavement for a moment after she'd gone, sorry now that he'd let her go. But then he brushed up his moustache, turned, and hurried back to the consolation of gin and bitters and 'The Road to Mandalay'.

The garage had brought the car to Slough Station to meet Felicity. Barbara couldn't help noticing with some envy how easy everything was if you had money. They got in and drove off into the late evening light of October, with a drive of about thirty-five miles between them and dinner. Barbara, who didn't drive, thought thirty-five miles was rather a long way, but not at the rate Felicity covered the road. The smart little tourer which had been bought for Felicity's use as a run-about brought them into the long lane leading to Dowers Farm by just after seven.

The housemaid opened the door as soon as the headlights showed. Clearly Felicity had phoned from the Savoy to let the household know she was bringing a guest.

'Good evening, madam. Good evening, Mrs Harris. How nice to see you again.'

'Good evening, Edith. Nice to be here.'

'Shall I show Mrs Harris to her room, madam?'

'Would you, Edith? I'll just run up and cast an eye on the children. By the way, it's Mrs Gray from now on.'

Edith led the way to the main staircase. Felicity hurried off along the hall and through a door at the far end, which led to the other wing of the house.

It always struck Barbara as strange that the children should be exiled to the farthest recesses of the place, farther away even than the servants, who slept on the top floor of the main wing. Once, when she'd queried it, Felicity had replied with, 'Well, we might want to ring for a servant in the middle of the night, but we certainly wouldn't want to ring for a baby!'

'But what if they cry and need attention?'

'Darling, that's what the Nanny is for!'

The room into which Edith showed her was the one she had been given on her two previous visits, but this time she was coming as a single woman. She thought she felt the maid cast a glance at her, but Edith was too well-trained to show open curiosity. 'Shall I unpack for you, Mrs . . . er . . . Gray?'

'Thank you, I can manage.'

'I'll run your bath then, shall I? Mr Leschallas said to serve dinner at eight so you'll have plenty of time.'

The ease, the orderliness! Felicity didn't have to rush about seeing to things when she came in. All the hard work had been done already. True, she'd hurried off to look at the children, but that was only because, for the moment, she was without a Nanny. Even so, the nursery maid would have bathed the children and put them to bed; Felicity was only going to check that it had been done and to kiss them goodnight should they still be awake.

Edith went along to the bathroom that served Barbara's room, returning in a moment to ask if there was anything else she could do. 'No, thank you. Dinner at eight, you said?'

'Yes, madam. Drinks fifteen minutes before if you're ready, but the master said not to rush yourself.' Hesitating, she gave a little smile. 'It is really nice to see you again, Mrs Gray. I hope you're going to be with us for a while.'

'Thank you, Edith.'

When she had bathed and dressed and made herself presentable for dinner, Barbara was still a little ahead of the timetable. She could have gone downstairs at once, but as always she was seized with a desire to see Felicity's children.

Felicity hadn't wasted any time when her Peter came back from the war. When he came home from Mesopotamia in 1920 she had flowered into motherhood, and now had four fine children: Peter Junior, known as Petey, John, Cecilia known as Ceecie, and Alan. Their ages were six, five, three and one. Petey would be going to prep school next year but the hope had always been that their Nanny, Mrs Lewis, would stay with them until the youngest child went to school.

Alas, Mrs Lewis had been offered a post by a minor crowned head during the summer, and had just left. Poor Felicity didn't know whether she was on her head or her heels, as far as Barbara could gather. It didn't quite seem credible to Barbara that a family with so much domestic help couldn't handle four children, yet it seemed that the departure of Nanny Lewis had been a catastrophe.

The nursery maid, Mildred, was holding the fort until another experienced Nanny could be engaged. From Barbara's recollection of her she was a steady, reliable girl, if unimaginative.

It was all the more surprising, therefore, to go along the passage then up the stairs in the east wing and be greeted on the nursery floor with the sounds of uproar. Even from the staircase Barbara could hear the roars of Petey, the complementary shouts of John, the wails of Ceecie, and the fretful background chorus of the baby.

Barbara actually ran to the night nursery, expecting to find that the ceiling had fallen in at least.

'What on earth's happened?' she exclaimed, throwing open the door and hurrying in.

'Who – ? Oh, Mrs Gray! I'm sorry, could you close the door? The sound might reach – '

'I should think it will,' Barbara agreed, advancing into the room.

The noise was deafening. It had ceased for a moment as Barbara came in, to give the children time to see who was there. But as soon as they realized it wasn't Mummy, they had resumed their uproar.

Mildred had the baby in her arms and was attempting to soothe it by walking about – rather too smartly – while she appealed to the others to stop crying. 'Now, Master Petey, you're just being naughty. Lie down, there's a good boy. You're only setting a bad example to John. Please, Master Petey, lie down like a good boy!'

'Mummy!' shouted Petey at the top of his voice, sobs breaking on the two notes of appeal. 'Mum*mee*!'

'What's happened, for goodness sake?' Barbara asked, going to the cot and taking Ceecie into her arms. The little girl, her face smeared with tears and dribbles, paused in her cries for a moment then subsided into whimpers that actually shook her body as she breathed.

'It disturbed them when Mummy came in to see if they were all right. They haven't been sleeping well since Nanny Lewis left, I don't know why, I'm sure I do all that she did for them,' complained Mildred, looking bewildered and spent.

At the name of the beloved Nanny, John began to roar louder than his elder brother. 'Lou-Lou,' he wept. 'Where's Lou-Lou!'

'Why didn't Mrs Leschallas stay till they went to sleep?' Barbara asked above the lamentations.

'Oh, she couldn't stop forever, madam! Cook gets so wild if dinner is delayed too long. It was ordered for eight o'clock and really it would be unfair to her to keep it hanging about, I'm sure you'll see. So she had to go, I mean Mrs Leschallas, she had to go and get dressed.'

'Mummy!' wept Petey. 'Mummy didn't stay . . . !'

'Lou-Lou!' moaned John. 'I want Lou-Lou . . .'

Ceecie shuddered with repeated sobs in Barbara's arms. The baby wailed.

'Oh, dear,' said Mildred, and burst into tears.

Barbara stared at her in horror. How could someone given the care of four children retreat into childish tears herself? She said sharply, 'Stop that this minute, Mildred!'

'I . . . c-can't help it!' wept Mildred. 'Th-they're such a h-handful since Mrs L-Lewis went away!'

'Lou-Lou!' roared John. 'Where's my Lou-Lou?'

'Now that's enough,' Barbara said. She put the little girl into the cot for the moment, disregarding her renewed outcry, and went to the nursery maid's side. She took the baby boy from her, leaned him against her shoulder so that his cries were to some extent muffled, and faced Mildred. 'If you don't stop crying this minute I shall slap you, Mildred. It's against my principles to hit children, but you're a grown up!'

Mildred stopped crying, pressing her lips together hard and putting her fists to her eyes to scrub the tears.

'There,' Barbara remarked loudly. 'Mildred can stop. You see, grown-up people can stop if they want to. I expect someone as grown-up as Petey could stop too.'

Petey, hearing this in mid-roar, swivelled his head, looked at her, and let the shout diminish a little. He was standing up on his bed with the lower half of his sleeping suit descending round his bottom. He sat down suddenly, and began to make snuffling sounds into the cuffs of his Chilprufe top.

'There now,' Barbara said admiringly, sitting down on the side of John's bed with so much emphasis that the bed shook, tumbling John down from his outstretched wailing stance. 'Isn't Petey a clever boy? He can stop crying too, just like Mildred. I bet you couldn't do that, John.'

'I could!' John wept. 'I could if I wanted to!'

'Let's see you do it. Look, Ceecie is watching to see if you can.'

Ceecie, told that she was watching John, immediately began to do so. To watch the better, she stopped screwing up her eyes and screaming.

'Pick her up,' Barbara commanded Mildred.

'But, Mrs Gray, Madam says they shouldn't be picked up once they've been put down.'

'Pick her up,' Barbara said through her teeth. 'They've all driven themselves into a state of hysteria and they need to be comforted. Pick her up!'

With a little blink at the tone of command, the nursery-maid obeyed. The three-year-old burrowed her face into Mildred's bosom, wound her arms about her neck, and bade fair to strangle her with the desperation of her reaction. But she stopped crying.

The two boys had now quietened down, engaged in being each more grown-up than the other. The baby in Barbara's arms, hearing quiet prevail, stopped crying and began to breathe more normally.

Something like peace descended.

'Well,' murmured Mildred, 'thank goodness for that. I don't know what got into them.'

'I'll tell you some time,' Barbara said in a low angry tone. 'But not now. Now we're going to wash their faces and tidy their beds and put them back into them. And then we're going to sit with them until they're asleep.'

'But, Mrs Gray, dinner –'

'Oh, the devil with dinner!' Barbara said. 'Now go along, fetch a face cloth and a bowl of warm water and let's tidy them up.'

Five minutes later the four children had been washed, had their sleeping suits or gowns straightened, their pillows plumped and their bedclothes straightened. They were lying like slightly damp angels in their beds.

The baby, exhausted by his efforts and the late hours he was keeping, fell asleep at once. Ceecie, cuddled up with her favourite soft toy, began sucking her thumb and making sleepy sounds. The two little boys had beds parallel to one another with a chair in between. Mildred sat down on the chair, Barbara took the old nursing chair by the fire. The two women sat in silence. The fire glowed dully behind its bars. There was no sound except the breathing of the people in the room. Then there was a rustle as John snuggled down and pulled the cover up to his neck for sleep.

Petey was the last to give in. He put out a hand to touch Mildred's skirt, making sure she was there. But his grasp slackened, the hand fell away.

Barbara got up softly. She put the hand under the sheet.

'Goodnight, Mildred,' she said scarcely above a whisper, and tiptoed out.

She even had the presence of mind to go up to her room and tidy her hair again before presenting herself in the drawing-room.

'Hello, there, Barbara,' Peter Leschallas said, glancing at his watch. 'Hungry, are you? I think dinner's just about ready.'

As they went into the dining-room rather hastily Barbara saw it was ten minutes past eight. She had made them late for dinner and probably put Cook out.

But she didn't really care. She felt she had been doing something much more important than eating dinner on time.

CHAPTER TWO

Dowers Farm wasn't like any farm Barbara used to imagine as a child in India. Picture-books then had displayed the Farmer, a stout figure in a bowler hat and leggings, and the Farmer's Wife, an equally stout figure with an apron over a sprigged dress and carrying a basket of eggs. Around these two had cavorted calves, lambs, brown hens and clean pigs.

At Dowers Farm the only animals to be seen were dogs and horses. Of these there were plenty, and when Barbara awoke next morning it was to the sound of hooves on the forecourt. It took her some time to understand where she was. Tumbling into bed last night, she'd forgotten to draw back the curtains so that the room was in opaque darkness. She felt about on the bedside table for a lamp, switched it on, discovered it was eight o'clock by the little carriage clock, and sat up. After a moment of yawning and stretching luxuriously she got out, pulled back the curtains, and looked out.

Below a small group of riders was gathered. A groom was holding a handsome little bay mare. As she watched, Felicity came out, was helped to mount, and they trotted off, two men and two women.

Barbara went back to the bed, smothering a grin. She recalled Felicity soon after her marriage, confiding her terror of horses. But determination can do a lot. Felicity had learned to ride and though she would never aspire to join the hunt, she could join the early morning riders now with confidence and enjoyment.

Barbara had been told to ring for breakfast when she woke.

'You're not to get up for it,' Felicity had warned. 'We breakfast early, because Peter likes to get out and about with the men, and I often go riding. But you're to rest and take things easy.'

It seemed a wicked luxury to have breakfast in bed. All the same Barbara obeyed. She rang, there was a delay of perhaps five minutes until a girl came in to make a tidy job of opening the curtains and switching on the electric fire. She then disappeared, to be replaced within another five minutes by Edith bearing coffee, toast, scrambled eggs, honey and marmalade.

'If you'd prefer tea, I can easily fetch it,' Edith remarked. 'Mrs Leschallas said she forgot to ask last night which you preferred for breakfast.'

'It's quite all right, Edith.' Yes, last night . . . Drugged with fatigue, exhausted by the events of the day and suppressed emotion, Barbara had tottered upstairs quite early. Now, after ten hours' sleep, she felt like a new woman. And, she told herself, a new woman is what you've got to be. No more sitting about feeling stunned over the divorce. No more looking helplessly about wondering if everybody knew she'd been thrown out by her husband.

She didn't really enjoy breakfast in bed. Crumbs seemed to get everywhere and despite the fact that the tray had dinky little adjustable legs, it seemed impossible to get it to sit straight over her lap. If she put it on the bedside table, she had to twist round at an unnatural angle to eat and drink. By and by she compromised by taking her last cup of coffee to the little armchair by the fireplace, where she curled her bare feet under the hem of her dressing gown and contemplated the day ahead.

She was so unaccustomed to leisure that she was almost at a loss. When she looked back, it seemed to her that all her life she'd had tasks that demanded her attention. Since she was seven, when her mother died, there had always been something to be done and which it was her duty to do.

The years before seven were bathed in a rosy glow. India, with its hot sun and rich scents – flowers, fruit, animals, people – yes, even the people remained in her mind as having a smell of their own, compounded of dust, sweat, fragrant oils, spices. The houses in which they had lived must have been quite small compared with Dowers Farm, bungalows provided by the engineering firm who employed Donald Gray, yet they remained in her mind as spacious, airy, echoing, limitless. Perhaps it was because they had big gardens in which she had spent most of her time, attended always by the smiling, endlessly patient ayah.

Because they moved around with her father as his work demanded, schooling had been difficult. Until the age of six she had spoken Urdu almost as readily as English. It had come as a surprise to her at her first school to discover that when it came to reading and writing, you had to use English exclusively. Luckily her father had at that time been engaged on a bridge in hill country; they had stayed in one place for over a year, so she'd had a good grounding from a strict English schoolteacher. Then there had been six months in a plains town, remembered mostly because of the great slow river that dominated the landscape. After that, a kaleidoscope of places – small villages where the headman came out to greet them on their arrival and where the only other British were the Assistant District Commissioner and a few other engineering families concerned with the dam. Then Dacca, where the men wore turbans and the buildings had beautiful tall minarets and the smell of jute was everywhere. Then Bangalore, another great city, with steam trains chugging not far from their bungalow . . . They had stayed there, she and her mother, while her father went off to supervise the bridges on a new road stretching out into Mysore. Then Madras, then other small villages, and finally the never-to-be-forgotten town, Kharaghoda.

That was where her mother had died. They had been on their way to Navanagar for the Bombay packet, but the ferryboat ran aground at Kharaghoda, or was in a collision – Barbara had never really discovered what had happened. It was all blotted out in the greater tragedy of the premature birth of her sister, Eileen, followed by her mother's death.

Most of the time she couldn't remember the events of those days. But now and again, sometimes in a dream but sometimes when she was awake, she would see again her father's stunned face – her father, younger, fair hair and moustache bright against his tanned face, his eyes full of horror at having to give her the news. 'Mummy's gone to the angels . . .' Absurd nonsense. Lasi, her ayah, had explained to her that when people died, they went away for a time to prepare for their return in some other form, depending on how good they had been in this life. Since Mummy had been very good, she would return as a princess or a queen, with a crown and lots of jewels, so Lasi said. It was comforting to know this.

Most people would have expected Donald Gray to send his motherless children home to England. Luckily – or so Barbara thought – grief had made him cling all the more to the two little girls. Besides, Eileen had been delicate; it was impossible to risk the long sea voyage home in her first year.

Lasi, a simple and loving woman, had gone with them wherever Donald's work took them. At first he had kept strict control over her, but as time went by the first sense of loss, the first impulse of remorseful responsibility, began to wane. Although Lasi did her best, it was Barbara who began to take over control of their household. Eileen was often unwell, and it was Barbara who ordered the doctor to be sent for. It was Barbara who remembered to send ahead for servants to their new quarters. It was Barbara who urged her father to have friends in, to give dinner parties, bridge evenings, to accept invitations to picnics and outings.

She was helped, of course, by kindly neighbours, wives of other company employees, schoolteachers, missionaries, and some excellent Indian servants. She had never felt herself burdened. Yet she had never been free, as Eileen had been, to live from day to day without thought for tomorrow. She had always had responsibility.

When she was eighteen, her father was ordered back to

England. She was old enough to realize that it wasn't a promotion. For the last year he had been kept at head office in Delhi instead of going out on site. She had sensed his lack of concentration, his self-indulgence. Drink had always been something of a problem – but then drink was so much part of the British way of life in India that it was difficult to draw the line between social drinking and dependency. She had been pleased at the idea of a complete change in his way of life, excited at the thought of 'going home'.

The England of 1913 was a shock to them all. Luckily for them, they arrived in summer, the fine hot summer of pre-war Britain, but the sun seemed almost powerless compared with the one they had left behind in Delhi. Their flat, obtained for them by Bolt Engineering, seemed poky and grey. No garden – it seemed incredible to Barbara that you could live in a dwelling from which you couldn't walk out into a butterfly-haunted garden.

Eileen hated it. Still only eight, she had cried herself to sleep every night. They had had to leave the faithful Lasi behind, their last picture of her likely to distress them for weeks – abased in the dust in front of their garden gate, her sari thrown over her head, wails of grief rising from her. 'Oh my children, oh my darlings, what will become of Lasi without you? Don't leave me, take me with you!'

That had been impossible. Letters from other returned Britishers had warned how difficult it was for an Indian servant to fit into the new way of life. Besides, Lasi was old – or at least she had seemed old to Barbara. Looking back now, she supposed poor Lasi was only about the age she was now, thirty-three, having come to the family when Barbara was a baby and she probably about fourteen or fifteen. But Lasi had always seemed old, and the suggestion that they should take this old Indian woman to Bayswater with them was over-ruled as soon as Eileen put it forward.

Until she left home to settle down with Archie after the end of the war, Barbara had always been very close to Eileen. She had done her best to shield her sister from the worst effects of coming to live in cold, cheerless London. But nothing could diminish the hardships of Britain under blockade as year succeeded year and the casualty lists grew longer and longer. And, since patriotism had taken Barbara into a nursing career in 1914, there were long hours when Eileen didn't see her. Their father, at forty-nine, had been given a new lease of life and a sense of responsibility by undertaking the construction of roads to training camps for the army, but it meant he was often away.

Barbara had divided her life between the hospital and looking after Eileen. There had been one or two boyfriends, but only occasional dates until she met and married Archie on one of his leaves in 1917. She knew some of the other nurses thought she'd married so suddenly because she felt lost without her friend Felicity, but it was untrue. At twenty-two she had been passionately in love, for the first time.

Now it was all gone, all changed. Archie had found someone else. Eileen had hurried into marriage with the first exciting man she met to get away from the home that seemed so empty once Barbara had gone. Their father had found consolation with Dottie Fleming.

No one needed Barbara any more. She was free to do just what she liked.

And she found it scared her.

Jumping up, she got ready for the day. The weather was still fine and cool. She put on a tweed skirt and sensible shoes, then went downstairs. Edith offered her a note left by Felicity 'Darling, back for coffee about ten then alas, boring committee meeting about church restoration but see you lunchtime and we'll make plans. Have fun.'

Fun . . . The thing to do was get out and about. 'I'll be back for coffee, Edith,' she told the maid. 'I'm going to get some exercise.'

She marched briskly out of the front door, down the drive, and along the lane. Only afterwards, when she had learned her way about the estate, did she realize she could have got much better walking by going across the near paddock and over the stile into the woods. But country lanes were still a novelty to her, so she walked along between the Oxfordshire hedgerows enjoying the berries on the hawthorn, the old-gold of the chestnut trees, the strange misty scarf of some as yet unidentified plant growing along the bushes which she later learned was Old Man's Beard.

A quarter of an hour's walk, during which she met no one, brought her to the village – a linear village grown up along a coaching road and called Hurford. Here there were signs of activity and, in the post office-cum-store, actually a group of people. Mindful of her promise to write and let her father know she'd arrived, Barbara went in to queue up for some penny stamps.

The other customers, two middle-aged women, an old man, and a young woman with a baby, eyed her for a moment with open curiosity.

'Good morning,' Barbara said. 'Lovely morning.'

'Yes, it's fine enough, but 'twon't last.' This was the old man.

'Won't it? Why not?'

'Moon's changing. New moon in two days' time.'

'Oh, I see.' She didn't really, so to change the subject she admired the baby. He was a plump child, in his mother's arms, his mouth turned into a blue button by a dummy stuck in it. 'Hello, lovey,' she said to him. 'There's a lovely boy.'

His mother gave a bashful grin.

'How old is he?'

'He's nigh two.'

'Is he now? Come on, sweetie, let's take the dummy out and you can say hello.'

The mother put out a hand to prevent it. 'Don't you do that,' she said in rebuke, 'he'll cry if you do.'

'Oh. Sorry.' The middle-aged woman at the counter completed her purchase and moved back. It wasn't Barbara's turn but it seemed everyone wished to defer to her. She went to the counter and asked for four penny stamps.

'There y'are,' said the formidable lady who presided there. 'Staying at the Dower, are you?'

'That's right.' My word, news travelled fast here. But no doubt the servants mentioned it to tradesmen and the tradesmen told the villagers.

'Staying long?'

'A fortnight or so, I think.'

'Hope it keeps fine for you.'

'Thank you,' Barbara said, although there was a tinge to the way these words were spoken that made her wonder how they were intended. She smiled and took her leave. As she struggled to close the door after her she heard the conversation break out.

'That's the divorced lady . . . Down from London . . .'

The divorced lady. There was a stigma attached to divorce. Innocent or guilty, it didn't seem to matter. People looked askance at a divorced woman. To get a divorce was legal but not moral, it seemed.

Hurt a little at what she had heard, she walked on to the other end of the little village street, then realizing she'd get lost if she struck off across fields, was forced to turn back. To walk home along the same narrow lane didn't strike her as very appealing. She was therefore quite pleased when she heard a car behind her and a little toot as it passed then slowed to a stop.

A shaggy head came out of the window. She came alongside and saw a broad, fresh-complexioned face. 'Hello there. You must be the Leschallases' guest.'

'That's right. Mrs Gray.'

'I'm Bob Dexter. How d'you do. Want a lift, or are you out for exercise?'

'I've had the exercise, thanks.'

'Hop in.' He leaned over to open his other door and she hurried round to scramble in. 'Heard from Felicity you'd come to stay,' he explained as he put the car in gear. 'She rides with my wife most mornings. Do you ride?'

Barbara shrugged. She'd learned to ride fat little ponies in India as a child, but wouldn't trust herself on an English thoroughbred.

'You should. Nothing like it.'

As they went slowly through Hurford's main street, Barbara saw the customers come out of the post office to watch their passage. She could just imagine them saying to each other: 'Told you so – a fast woman, picked up somebody's husband right off.'

Bob Dexter caught the turn of her head, and grinned. 'They're interested in you,' he said. 'Something new to talk about, y'see.'

'You can't mean you're so short of topics of conversation that you have to talk about me,' she protested, laughing.

'Well, there are worse topics,' he said, with a glance that asked for approval of the compliment.

In no time at all they were at the front entrance to the drive. She told him coffee would probably be available and invited him to come to the house, but he said with regret that he was off to Oxford on business and would have to say no. 'See you later,' he said. 'I'm coming to dinner tonight, I think.'

She waved him goodbye then set off up the drive. Shrieks of mock terror in the shrubbery told her that the children were out to play. She was halfway to the house when a small figure with a feather in its hair and a bow and arrow in its hands leapt out before her.

'White squaw, Running Deer is going to kill you!' it cried.

'Oh, Running Deer!' cried Barbara, backing away in fear and trembling. 'Do not kill me, spare my life!'

'No, no, Running Deer never spares anybody,' explained Petey, and shot the bamboo from his bow.

It hit Barbara about mid-skirt. She crumpled at the knees and fell to the ground. Petey executed a dance of triumph, flapping a grubby hand in front of his mouth to make a war cry.

'Good gracious, Master Petey, what have you done to poor Mrs Gray, she'll catch her death on that damp gravel!' called Mildred, hurrying up with Ceecie in tow.

'I killed the white squaw,' Petey explained. 'Get up, Auntie Barbara, your skirt's all dirty.'

She rose, dusting herself down. The gravel wasn't really damp. She said to Mildred, 'They slept through the night, did they?'

'Like lambs.'

'That's good.'

'Mrs Gray,' Mildred said with anxiety, falling into step beside her as she made for the front door, 'are you going to mention anything to Mrs Leschallas about . . . you know . . . ?'

'Mention it?' Barbara was puzzled. 'Why should I?'

'Well, I was in a fluster. I admit it. I shouldn't have let them get so out of hand. Nanny Lewis never would have.'

'But Nanny Lewis had years of experience, Mildred,' Barbara pointed out. 'Besides . . .' She hesitated. 'I'm not so proud of last night's episode myself.'

'But, Mrs Gray, you were marvellous! You quietened them in no time flat!'

'But I shouldn't have spoken to you the way I did, and especially not in front of the children. I was wrong to say I'd smack you. I apologize.'

'Oh, Mrs Gray . . . Honestly . . . I think I deserved it!'

'That's not so. After all –' She broke off. She'd been about to say, You're only eighteen, what do you know about handling children? But she couldn't say it out loud. Mildred was insecure enough.

'You know what you said, Mrs Gray?'

'What?'

'About explaining why the children were acting up the way they were?'

'Did I? I don't remember.'

'You said you understood it.'

'Oh . . . Well, yes, I do.'

'You said you'd explain it to me.'

'I suppose I could. I think it's a bit complicated, though.' She knew Felicity was waiting for her in the drawing-room, anxious to have her coffee and then get away to her committee meeting. 'Could I come and have a chat later? About eleven?'

'If you would, Mrs Gray, I'd be ever so grateful.'

'Where will you be?'

'Out here, if the weather keeps like this. We go in for our lunch at twelve, then it's naps till two, and after that playtime till tea.'

'I'll come and find you about eleven.' She paused at the door to bow to Running Deer. 'Great warrior, off you go to the Happy Hunting Ground. By the way, where's John?'

'He's looking at a spider.'

'A spider?'

'Yes, he's found a nice one on a laurel bush.'

'I see. Well, see you later, Running Deer.'

'How!' said Running Deer, and backed away with palm upright.

'Been out, darling?' Felicity greeted her as she came in. 'That's good. Where did you go?'

'Walked into the village, bought some stamps. A man called Bob Dexter gave me a lift back.'

'Trust him,' Felicity said, pouring coffee. 'He's a terrible Don Juan, Barbara. You watch out.'

'Ah. Perhaps the turning heads in the village were for him, not for me.'

Felicity laughed with a flash of white teeth. 'For both of you, you can bet. Nothing goes unnoticed in these parts.'

'He said he's invited to dinner this evening.'

'So he is, *with* his wife. She'll keep him in order. I've invited Brian Sethard for you.'

'In what sense for me?' Barbara inquired, amused.

'Well, one can't have odd numbers at dinner, darling, can one? Brian's nice, you'll like him. But don't get attracted,

Barbara, he hasn't a penny.'

Barbara promised not to form any attachment to this man she hadn't even seen as yet, then went on to inquire if Felicity had enjoyed her ride. The conversation was deflected on to more general matters. Felicity hurried off to drive to the parish hall for the committee meeting and Barbara, after finishing her coffee more at leisure, went in search of Mildred.

She heard the children before she saw them. They were on a lawn at the back of the house, in the midst of a furious quarrel. Mildred was imploring them not to wake the baby, who slumbered peacefully in his pram nearby. But John was belabouring Petey, while Petey fended him off in a lordly, Indian Chief way.

'What on earth is the matter?' Barbara demanded.

'He took my spider!' shouted John. 'Tell him to give it back!'

'Running Deer capture heap big spider,' agreed Petey. 'Little Deer must obey big chief Running Deer.'

'I won't, I won't, this is a stupid game, give me back my spider!' John raged.

'Give back his spider,' agreed little Ceecie, pummelling Petey from behind with small fists.

They were all set for another sobbing match. Barbara said quickly, 'Where does Big Chief keep prisoners?'

'Running Deer won't tell secrets to white squaw.'

'Then Little Deer must show what a clever Indian he is by tracking another big spider,' Barbara suggested. 'Tell me, Little Deer, where do big spiders live?'

'I don't want to be Little Deer, I want to be John, and the spiders make big webs across between bushes and they're ever so difficult to find unless the sun shines on them, Auntie Barbara.'

'See if you can find a web, then come and tell me so I can see it,' she said. 'I'll be with Mildred.'

'Little Deer go find spiders,' commanded Petey. 'Running Deer takes prisoner.' He began to dance round Ceecie, who sat down fatly to watch him with equable interest.

'You're marvellous,' sighed Mildred. 'I though there was going to be another big row just then. They get so cross with each other these days.'

'It's because they miss Nanny Lewis,' Barbara said.

'But she's been gone more than two weeks now, Mrs Gray!'

Barbara remembered how her little sister had cried for Lasi night after night when they were first in England. 'It takes a while,' she murmured.

'But children get over things so quickly.'

'Do you think they do? I wonder if that's true.'

'Well, everybody says so, Mrs Gray, so it must be true.'

'But perhaps they say it because they want it to be true. If you can convince yourself a child has a short memory and forgets people quickly you don't have to concern yourself about their unhappiness when someone leaves.'

Mildred stared at her. She had a round, smooth face, almost child-like, unmarked by experience as yet. She had had the responsibility of the Leschallas children thrust upon her by Nanny Lewis's going, but she was unready for it. When Barbara had said she'd explain why the children were misbehaving she'd expected some simple, practical explanation such as that they needed more greens in their diet or their beds needed flannelette sheets. These musings about loss and the strength of memory were no help to her.

'There's nothing to be done about it anyhow,' she said, a little put out. 'Nanny's gone, and that's that. I mean, you could hardly expect her to stay, could you? Offered a Grand Duke's nursery, I mean. She had to go, didn't she? To better herself.'

'Of course. And the children have got to get used to her absence. But that won't happen all at once.'

'I can't see why it should make them so naughty at bed times. It's always worse then.'

'Because that was when Nanny Lewis was most important, I suppose. Always there, if they were restless or had a bad dream.'

'But goodness me, they were all right last night until their Mummy came in. I mean, you can't understand why their own Mummy should make them cry.'

'I wasn't there so I can't say, Mildred. But perhaps if they were half asleep they thought it was Nanny Lewis, and then they woke up properly and found it wasn't.'

'It was that Petey. He can be so naughty sometimes! He set them all off.'

'Yes, well, he's only six.'

'He's old enough to understand Nanny had to go to another job. I explained it to him and he knew what I meant.'

'I suppose he did. But that doesn't make it any easier, to think she preferred someone else to him.'

Mildred was baffled. 'Children don't think like that, Mrs Gray. They haven't the brains for it.'

Barbara could see she wasn't doing any good. It was too early for Mildred to have learned that children have the brains for anything, although understanding may be limited by lack of experience.

Luckily John came hurrying up to say he had found a big web, with a spider still spinning. Barbara, who had no great affection for spiders, accompanied him to admire this beast. On the way she rescued Ceecie from Running Deer, who went off on a hunting trip among the laurel bushes. Peace reigned until lunchtime.

Felicity drove up as they were straggling back indoors, Barbara holding on Ceecie's head a wreath of rose-hips strung on a grass stalk and Mildred bringing up the rear with the pram. Felicity leaned out to watch them, and waved.

When Barbara had washed her hands and joined the Leschallases for a pre-lunch sherry, they were deep in discussion. 'I hear from Edith you've been keeping the kids in order,' said Peter Leschallas as he brought her her drink.

'We've been playing Indians and watching spiders.'

'This morning, yes. But last night I hear you put paid to a

fracas in the nursery.'

'Oh, that.' She paused. 'How did you hear about that?'

'Hear about it? Darling, I started it!' cried Felicity. 'I went in when we got here last night to see if everything was all right, because really they've been so naughty since Nanny went and Mildred just doesn't seem to cope. They all started to yell the place down and nothing I said seemed to stop them, and anyway I had to bolt because I knew Cook was holding dinner for us. It seems you quietened them all beautifully inside five minutes.'

'You seem to have quite a way with them,' Peter took it up. 'I've noticed it before when you've been here. They seem to take to you.'

'Well, I take to them. It's mutual.' Barbara had no idea how her thin face had lit up at the discussion of the children. Her friend, watching her, thought for the thousandth time that it was a pity she'd never had any of her own.

That had not been by choice. Barbara would have loved a family. Perhaps if she had had children Archie wouldn't have wandered. Too late now to remedy the past, of course. But Felicity wondered if Barbara might find some solace in spending time with the Leschallas brood.

It became an established thing that Barbara spent time with the children. She had few social engagements outside the house, except for an occasional friendly outing with Brian Sethard, who took quite an interest in her.

When the preparations for the Hallowe'en party began, it was to Barbara that Felicity turned for advice on whether the turnip lanterns would scare Ceecie and if they should have bobbing for apples for the older children.

Barbara had never had a Hallowe'en party in her own childhood; it was one of the things they didn't celebrate in India, although Christmas and Easter had been great occasions. So she enjoyed this affair almost as much as the little guests, and perhaps more. She ended the afternoon drenched, sticky with treacle, black with smuts from the writing-in-soot game, exhausted, but happy.

'I don't know,' Felicity said in wonder. 'Where do you get the energy from?'

'It's all done by witchcraft,' Barbara said, taking off the witch's hat she'd been wearing since four o'clock. 'And I think it will just hold out long enough to get me to that chair.'

'Well, thank goodness it's over. I suppose the next thing is, there'll be an upset at bedtime because they're over-excited.'

'No there won't,' Barbara heard herself say firmly. She stopped short and went red. 'I'm sorry. I didn't mean to sound bossy.'

'You don't sound bossy. You just sound as if you know how to get the children to bed at the right time even though they're in a state of wild abandon.' Felicity waved at her. 'If you can do it, off you go. I have to get down to the kitchen for a word with Cook. We've got an extra guest for dinner – I bet she'll hit the ceiling.'

Barbara went to the night nursery, where Petey and John were splashing in the bath. Ceecie had already been bathed and put into her Viyella nightie. Baby Alan, having taken no part in the Hallowe'en festivities, was already drowsing off. It was the two boys who were still over-awake and roused up.

'I've told them,' Mildred said, 'it'll only end in tears if they don't settle down.'

Nothing like telling a child it will only end in tears to start it crying, thought Barbara. Aloud she said, 'You know my witch's hat that I had on?'

'Yes?' Petey said, ceasing to fight John for the toy battleship.

'Whoever is the best and quietest child will get it tomorrow morning to wear until lunchtime.'

'I'm the best!' cried Petey. 'I'm the oldest!'

'But you're the one that's making the most noise so you aren't the quietest, are you?'

Petey cut himself off in mid-shout. He eyed Barbara.

'Is it a magic hat?' John inquired.

'Oh, of course, Whoever wears it will be able to fly on a

broomstick next Hallowe'en.'

The two boys took that in with wide open eyes. 'I want to fly next Hallowe'en,' said John.

'Me first, I'm the oldest,' objected Petey.

'It all depends on being good so as to get the hat, doesn't it? So let's see how quickly you can get into your sleeping suits and into bed.'

'You'll stay with us, won't you? Because,' confided John, 'there's witches flying about tonight.'

'They always fly on Hallowe'en. But they don't come into nurseries where good children are sleeping.'

The two boys were quiet and well-behaved as they were dried and put into night attire. They went to their beds like angels. Only John looked about a little apprehensively. In the midst of the excitement of the party it had been impossible to prevent other children from telling him scary stories about witches.

They lay down, Mildred tucked them in. Barbara patted each one on the shoulder. Mildred lowered the light. The two of them sat down in the places that had become their accustomed spots.

Within ten minutes the breathing of the children had become deep and regular. They were fast asleep.

Barbara tiptoed out to bath and change. Downstairs she found the Leschallas's waiting for her. 'Darling, the peace from upstairs is wonderful, I hear,' Felicity said. 'Edith reports complete silence.'

'Yes, they're all asleep.'

Peter exchanged a glance with his wife. 'Barbara, this only confirms us in something we've been thinking of. You've made no plans as yet, I gather?'

'No, but I must start doing so. I can't sponge on you and Felicity for ever.'

'Darling, it isn't sponging!' Felicity cried. 'You've been absolutely worth your weight in gold, the way you've quietened down the children! They were *so* out of hand before you came.'

'But now it's almost like having Nanny Lewis back again,' Peter ended. 'And that's what we wanted to put to you. Barbara, would you like to stay with us on a more or less long-term basis and give a hand with the children?'

'Me?'

'With Mildred to do the donkey-work,' Felicity put in hastily. 'She's a hard worker and very willing, but she doesn't seem to have got the touch yet. You'd be in charge, of course.'

'In charge?' Barbara drew back, alarm in her wide eyes. 'I don't think I've got the training to be "in charge" –'

'Training? How d'you mean, training? Nanny Lewis had no training – except that she learned from the Nanny she first worked for as nursery maid. She –'

'Exactly. She got a wealth of experience passed on to her.' Barbara made a little gesture of negation. 'I really know nothing.'

'That's what you say, but look at the difference in the children since you arrived –'

'It was just that they . . . needed someone who understood about –'

'That's it! You understand them! I don't think it's anything anyone could teach you – I think it's instinctive. You know, darling,' Felicity said earnestly, 'you were always good at it in hospital. You seemed to catch on at once when those men with hardly any voice wanted something – you knew without telling. And that's how it is with the children. Especially John and Petey. You have a magic touch with them.'

'But Felicity, be sensible,' Barbara protested. 'I don't know anything about children's ailments –'

'What do you need to know? If they over-eat, they get sick. If they come out in spots, it's probably chicken-pox. There's a doctor just down the road, darling. It's not as if you'd be on your own.'

Peter, heavy and impressive in his evening clothes, moved in front of the fire and took up the 'master-of-the-house' stance.

'I'm used to judging people, Barbara,' he said. 'I couldn't manage this estate without having some instinct for it. And I can tell you, I'd trust my four to you without a second thought.'

'Oh. Well. It's . . . very kind of you to say –'

'Not kind at all. It's true.' He studied her. 'You don't want to do it? Is that it?'

'Oh, I do!' she cried. 'I'd love it.'

'Good. I thought perhaps you had other plans.'

Barbara gave a rueful smile. 'What, for instance?'

Husband and wife looked at each other. Felicity hesitated then said in a neutral tone: 'Brian Sethard, perhaps?'

'Brian?' Barbara was genuinely taken aback.

'He hasn't said anything?'

'My dear,' Peter rebuked his wife, 'he really can't. I mean, he hasn't a penny. He couldn't offer a home to anybody.'

Barbara shook her head so vigorously the fair hair shook about her cheeks. 'I don't think he has anything like that in mind. I certainly haven't.'

'Then, can we take it – it's settled? You'll stay as unofficial Nanny?'

'Until you can get someone better.'

'No one could be better, Barbara.' This was Peter, speaking in a measured tone that was more complimentary than Felicity's sometimes gushing words.

'Thank you. Then . . . I accept.'

Nothing had been said about salary. It didn't even occur to Barbara to make an issue of it. There was something so attractive about the thought of staying here, in this lovely house, to spend most of her time with the four heart-catching inmates of the nursery.

CHAPTER THREE

The situation had its problems, though. Entered into so impulsively, the relationship was beset with pitfalls. Was Barbara a friend or an employee? Should she be included in all social engagements, or not? How was she to be introduced? 'Mrs Gray, our Nanny.' 'Mrs Gray, a great friend of mine from my nursing days.' 'Mrs Gray, who's staying with us for a while to lend a hand with the children.' All these, and other variations, were in use according to whom Barbara was meeting.

'It's difficult to know whether you're servant or mistress,' Brian Sethard joked one evening, bringing her home from a theatre visit in Oxford. 'When I ring the house and ask for you, I'm never sure whether to say "Mrs Gray" or "Nanny".'

'Does that bother you?'

'It's a bit irksome. After all, Barbara . . .'

'What?'

'You're a lady.'

'You mean that people who look after children are usually working class?'

'Well – aren't they?'

'I suppose so.' She paused. 'Isn't that odd? People with money unhesitatingly hand over their children to servants to look after. I've noticed, looking at the other families we meet, that they seem to make almost no check at all on what's happening in the nursery. For all they know, the Nanny might be feeding the children on bread and water and selling the furniture for her own benefit, and they wouldn't know.'

Brian wasn't interested in the problems of other people's nurseries. He had stopped the car just inside the gates of the Dowers Farm drive. He took Barbara's hand. 'If only I could find a decent job,' he sighed.

'I wish you could, Brian.' She meant, for his own sake. The recession was having a terrible effect on the careers of able men and Brian had made a hundred applications, with no success.

'I could take you away from all this,' he said, unconscious of cliché.

She looked at his square, trustworthy face in the dimness. He was so kind, so dependable. So unlike Bob Dexter, who had to be watched like a hawk. Barbara heard that the debs had a category of escorts they called NSIT, meaning Not Safe In Taxis. Bob Dexter most decidedly came into that class; moreover he was not safe in conservatories, in corridors, in the darkness of theatres if you were sitting next to him, nor anywhere else if he happened to catch you alone.

But Brian was totally honourable. In fact, he was so honourable as to be almost dull. Barbara liked him but when he kissed her goodnight, as he was now about to do, no sparks were struck, no fireworks lit the sky.

'Can I take you out next week?' he begged. He meant on her next evening off, the Thursday of every week, when Mildred held the fort in her stead.

'That would be lovely.' They would drive to Oxford in his father's car and have an inexpensive meal in one of the cafes that catered mainly for students. They had gone to the theatre tonight because two free tickets had come Brian's way, explained by the fact that the touring company playing *The Constant Nymph* wasn't very good.

Brian set the car in motion, deposited her at the door. Barbara always went in by the front door. But that was no clue to her status because so did most Nannies, she had observed. It was something to do with being in charge of the children of the house - some non-servant prestige was conferred by that, enough to make the front door available whereas even Edith, superior servant though she was, used the back door.

The Leschallases generally went to bed early, for Peter liked to be up and out by six in the morning. But tonight there were lights in the drawing-room. Barbara put her head in before going to the stairs.

'I'm back,' she announced unnecessarily.

'Hello there. Was it a good play?'

'Very weepy. I don't think Brian took to it much. You're up late?'

Peter was sitting in an armchair by a dying fire, a whisky glass in his hand and the decanter, the liquid level significantly lowered, on a table by his elbow. It was so unusual to see him soaking it up that Barbara came further into the room.

'Anything wrong?' she inquired.

'Not more than usual,' he said. 'The wheat situation just doesn't improve.'

'But you had a fine harvest, Peter.'

'Ha.' He took a swallow from his glass. 'So did every other farmer in Europe, America, and Australia. Trouble is, America harvests ahead of us because they have those long hot summers on the wheat plains, and they bring in bumper harvests . . . Can you picture it, Barbara, mountains and mountains of wheat in the silos?'

'But that's a good thing, isn't it?' she asked. 'It's what every farmer –'

'There's a glut of the damned stuff,' Peter said bitterly. 'There's been a glut for the past two years. It's hardly worth putting the reaper and binder on the fields. Before we cut a single stook, the price has gone down below what it costs me to bring it in.'

'Oh, Peter . . . I'd no idea!'

'It's the same with everybody. Not just me. But I hate to make a mess of running the estate. I ought to change over to some other form of farming but we've always raised grain. It's a big decision to take, to go into dairying . . .'

So that was what it was about. He was drinking to blur the sharpness of the decision.

'What does Felicity say?'

'She says she trusts my judgement.' Peter laughed without

mirth. 'She's marvellous, you know. Nothing really worries her. She's so immersed in all her good works and local improvement committees, she doesn't have time to read the papers and see what a mess things are in.'

Barbara went over, took the empty glass from him, put the stopper in the decanter, and put them both on the tray on the drinks table. 'Go to bed, Peter,' she urged. 'You're not helping anything by getting tight.'

'No.' He got to his feet, stretching and yawning and a little unsteady. 'You said that just like my old Nanny telling me "What can't be cured must be endured".'

She laughed. 'Get along with you,' she said, consciously taking on the tone of the Nanny shooing her charge to bed.

He went, treading rather heavily. She stayed a moment to make sure the fire was safe and to put out the lights. When she went upstairs she checked, as always, in the night nursery. The children were asleep, Ceecie with her rabbit clutched against her cheek, Petey with half the clothes kicked off, John with his hands folded just under his chin like an angel on a reredos.

She gently took the rabbit out of the little girl's hand, put the covers back on Petey. After a last look round, she went to bed. It didn't occur to her that, like Felicity, she was too immersed in what she was doing to think seriously about the outside world.

She had spent a year already looking after the Leschallas children. It had sped past. As she made her pillow comfortable and got ready for sleep, she was conscious only of contentment. She didn't exactly tell herself that she'd be happy to spend the rest of her life in just this way, but the thought was there.

When Brian called for her the following Thursday evening, he was in a state of great excitement. 'I've something marvellous to tell you, Barbara,' he said. 'Great news!'

'What?' And then she guessed. 'A job?'

'Yes, Uncle Herbert got a friend of his to offer me a post. It's got some drawbacks but some great advantages. I'm over the moon about it.'

'I can see you are,' she said. On an impulse she took his arm and pressed it affectionately.

He turned his attention from guiding the little Austin along the dark country lanes to cover her hand with one of his and give it a squeeze. He smiled. But he had to go back to his driving.

Instead of the cheap little meal she'd expected, it turned out to be a celebration in The Mitre with a bottle of rather good wine. Brian's father must have given an advance on his son's future expectations.

When they had chosen their meal - and even with all this good news Barbara took care to keep to the less expensive dishes - Brian began his report.

'It's a job on a fruit farm in South Africa,' he said. 'Oranges, not apples.' His father made most of his money from extensive apple orchards. 'But I'm keen to learn and not too old to do so. They know all about my background so that's all right. I go in as a trainee manager at first and if I make it I get a farm to manage on my own.'

'South Africa?' Barbara echoed. 'Did you want to go abroad?'

'Well, my dear, there are more chances abroad in the Colonies than at home. And this really is worth the move. The prospects are very good. And what makes it even better -'

They were interrupted by the waiter bringing the soup. Brian waited until the man had gone before resuming. 'Barbara, the prospects of promotion to manager are better for married men!'

'What?'

'They like the managers to be family men. They find married men are more stable. There's quite a scattered community, you see - big distances between the farms. So bachelors are a bit of a risk. They like their managers to have wives to keep them in order.' Brian twinkled at her to let her see this was his little joke. 'So how about it, dear?'

She was about to say, in bafflement: 'How about what?' But luckily understanding came to her in time.

Brian was proposing to her.

'Why, I . . .' She was *not* going to say, 'This is so unexpected.' But it was. She had been going out with Brian more or less regularly over the last three or four months, but only for the companionship.

Making friends had been rather difficult for her in the environment of Dowers Farm. Most of Felicity's friends were nice to her, but they had the problem that always seemed to get in the way. How were they to regard her? Was she only a Nanny, or was she something more?

Male friends were scarce. There was the irrepressible Bob Dexter, always trying to get a smeary kiss behind a door or pinching her bottom as she passed, but he was a married man so it would have been impossible for him to invite her out – and she'd have said no if he'd done so.

Brian had been the nearest thing to an all-purpose friend that she had. She had always felt safe with him. She knew that, because he was out of a job and unlikely to get anything in the current economic climate, he couldn't be thinking of marriage. And being Brian Sethard, an honourable man like Brutus, he couldn't be thinking of anything else.

Now it had all been knocked sideways. Brian was proposing.

'I know it's a bit of a shock,' he said, eager to do away with the pause that was developing. 'I had no idea until yesterday that I was going to get this. But it changes everything, of course. Now I can offer you a home and a decent life.'

To him it was quite straightforward. They had been going out together for a while, and before that they had met over a period of six months or so at Felicity's. A courtship of about a year seemed right. It was time for them to get married. They were about the right age for each other, Barbara was a sensible girl who would make a good home for him in their new surroundings, and he needed a wife if he was to do well in his new career.

Barbara glanced across the table at him. 'Eat your soup, Brian, it's getting cold,' she said.

She sounded as if she were talking to young Petey.

'When do you have to leave?' she inquired.

'In a month. They want me there by Christmas, and as the voyage takes about a month . . .'

At the words she pictured the shipboard life when she, her father and Eileen came back from India. The instant attention of the crew, the long lazy days, the dance band in the big saloon at night . . . How lovely it would be to go back to that life. And South Africa – surely life out there must have some of the comforts of India. Plentiful servants, ample houses, sunshine . . .

Suddenly it was tremendously tempting.

'As trainee manager,' Brian was saying between spoonfuls of soup, 'I have to live in temporary accommodation at the farm where I'm learning, but Uncle Herbert's friend – Gracebrigg – says it's quite nice, quite suitable to take a lady to. And it would only be a year there. It's near Pietermaritzburg, or at least not too far – about thirty miles, I think.'

'It does sound nice, Brian.'

'Oh, I think it is. I think the climate's good, and Gracebrigg says the people are friendly enough although . . . But they wouldn't have to know about your divorce, after all.'

'Does that mean that they're Dutch?'

'Well, yes, and a bit strict. But the other fellows don't seem to have any problems fitting in and, after all, it's a long time since the South African War and they must have forgotten all that anti-English thing by now.'

He talked on, sharing with her all that he'd learned about the job, the place, and the prospects. When they had finished their meal they went into the lounge for coffee, but that proved to be a mistake since there was too much noise to make quiet conversation feasible. 'Let's go for a walk,' Brian suggested.

They got their coats and went out into the quiet streets of Oxford. The full moon touched the mellow stone of the colleges with silver. They turned out of the High into Catt Street and then by shadowed alleys and footpaths to the Cherwell. The river slid by, full after several days of rain, and with branches of willow carried on its rills.

Brian put an arm about her. 'Will you come with me, Barbara?'

'I – I never thought of leaving England again, Brian.'

'But you'd like it, I'm sure you would.'

'It would mean leaving my family. My father rather needs someone to keep an eye on him.'

'Eileen could do that.'

Barbara didn't say no to that. Brian hadn't met her sister so couldn't know how unlikely it was that she would take on the responsibility of Donald Gray. She'd been only too anxious to get away from him, and now she was embarked on a marriage with a very successful young man, she wasn't going to let herself be hobbled by problems from her father's way of life.

'If you really think he'd miss you, we could bring him out to join us by and by,' Brian suggested. 'I don't think my income would be up to it for a year or two, but he's retiring soon, you said – he'll have a pension, I suppose. If he could bring that with him, and live with us . . . We could manage, I'm sure.'

'It's awfully kind of you, Brian.' Not many men would be thinking of family arrangements like this. Brian was so utterly dependable. He'd make a marvellous husband.

The night air was very chill and damp. They turned back. Before they moved away from the riverbank he kissed her with an unusual urgency, and she returned the kiss. Then they walked back to where they had parked the Austin.

On the drive home he went over the good points in his plan. The job, the promotion prospects, the house that went with the job, the climate, the new start . . .

'I can see it's taken you by surprise,' he said. 'Think it over. I'll come and see you tomorrow.'

'Oh, not tomorrow, Brian. I've got to take Petey to the dentist.' Petey should have started at prep school the previous month, but a tooth abscess had made it necessary to put that off for the time being. The dentist had taken a look, swabbed the infection, and asked to have Petey brought on another day for the extraction.

'Oh, well – the next day, then. In the afternoon, while they're having their rest?'

'That would be best.'

'Righto then. See you Saturday.'

He dropped a kiss on her nose and helped her out. She went on up the drive, turned to wave as he drove off quietly so as not to disturb the household.

It was still quite early. Peter and Felicity were still in the drawing-room with friends. She put her head in to announce her return but didn't dally. Next she went, as always, to check the night nursery. Mildred was coming out and silently slipping the door to as she came along the passage. The maid put a finger to her lips.

'Petey woke up. He's gone off again now, after a bit of a snivel.'

'Visit to the dentist is worrying him.'

'Prob'ly.'

They were speaking in whispers.

'Had a nice evening, Mrs Gray?'

'Yes, thank you.'

'Goodnight, then.'

'Goodnight.'

In her own room Barbara sat on the stool before her dressing table and regarded herself in the mirror. Mrs Brian Sethard . . . If she liked, she could be that in three weeks or so – just as long as it took to call the banns.

Oh no – they couldn't be married in church. She was a divorcée. It would have to be a registrar's office. She pictured herself in a light-coloured costume, powder blue, perhaps. A small hat with a net veil. Beige? Grey? Grey suède gloves and shoes.

There wouldn't be much time to get the outfit. Had she

enough money put by to pay for something really good? She must tell Felicity tomorrow – not exactly give notice, because there were no conditions of that kind between them, but still, she must warn her to find another Nanny.

Leaving the children would be a wrench. But still, this was quite a good time for a change. Petey would be going to school, leaving only three in the nursery. John might actually get on better without Petey dominating him. But he would miss Barbara. Still, Mildred would be there to provide continuity.

Her mind went on, examining the situation from every angle. As she cleaned her teeth and brushed her hair, she settled one little problem after another. Her father, Eileen, Felicity, the children . . .

Next morning, after Felicity had seen Cook about the day's meals, Barbara went into her sitting-room. The children were in the grounds with Mildred.

'Felicity, could I have a word?'

'Is it about the dentist? I'm afraid I can't drive you in after all, Barbara, but Wentworth has agreed to do it.' Wentworth was the gardener and odd-job-man.

'That's quite all right, but it wasn't about that, as a matter of fact. Felicity . . .' She came into the room to stand face to face with her friend, who had turned on the chair at her writing bureau to look at her. 'Felicity, Brian asked me to marry him last night.'

'What?' Felicity stared, then leapt up. 'Darling!' she shrieked, and threw herself on Barbara's neck.

They hugged each other, then the questions poured out. How was Brian going to afford marriage? Where were they going to live?

Barbara explained Brian's plans, Felicity was at first astonished and then delighted. 'Darling, it sounds lovely! A new beginning! Oh, if anybody deserves it, you do! How splendid! I'm so pleased.'

'The thing is, Felicity – about the children . . .'

'Yes, I see. Yes, you'll be leaving them. Well . . . You know, darling, when Petey goes it will be less of a job. Mildred might be able to manage, mightn't she?'

Barbara was a little surprised. Mildred had come on a lot in the year since Barbara had been here, but it had never occurred to her that Felicity would confide her family to a girl so young.

'You don't think she could do it?'

'I suppose she could. I just hadn't thought of it.' She hesitated. 'You had, though?'

'Well, you see,' Felicity said, colouring a little, 'we had talked about it.'

'But why? I hadn't imagined I'd be leaving.'

'Oh, we always thought you and Brian would be a love match,' Felicity carolled, with rather too much enthusiasm. 'It's lovely, I couldn't be more pleased. Have you decided when you'll tie the knot?'

'Oh, no, we haven't got anywhere near as far as that. In fact, I haven't given Brian an answer yet.'

'But you're going to say yes!'

'I suppose so.' Yes, she supposed so. After all, why not? It was a very suitable arrangement. Brian wanted a wife and Barbara was the wife he wanted.

'Darling, do try to put a little more enthusiasm into the words,' Felicity laughed, her curvy bosom heaving. 'He's quite a catch. If he'd had more money every girl in the neighbourhood would have been after him. Pity there were two more sons ahead of him in the apple-orchard stakes. But he'll get the hang of growing oranges in no time, I'm sure of it, and be the Head Orange before long.'

They began to giggle, as they used to do when they were trainee nurses. 'Let's have a drink to celebrate!' cried Felicity 'It's not every day you get engaged.'

'No, I mustn't, Flick. The dentist will think I'm on the bottle if I go breathing sherry.'

'Oh, hang the dentist.'

'No, I mustn't. It's time to be setting out, really. I'll have it when I come back.'

'But I'll be at the meeting to arrange the point-to-point course by then.'

'This evening, then.'

'But we're dining with the Lawsons.'

'So you are. Well, tomorrow, then. There's no hurry.'

She went to fetch Petey to tidy him up for the trip to Oxford. He came with reluctance. Poor child, his world was full of threats these days – the dentist, prep school, separation from all he loved.

Mr Woolley, the dentist, soon dealt with Petey. 'He really doesn't seem too fit. A bit run down, is he?'

'It's a difficult time for him, Mr Woolley.' She didn't want to go into details with Petey, very distressed, listening to every word. Poor child, he must be feeling rotten, what with one thing and another; he thinks his entire environment was against him. 'I think his tooth has given him a lot of trouble. Soon better now, though.'

'Well, keep him in bed. Watch his temperature – it may go up a degree or so. Paint the gums with this tincture and if he has much pain give him half an aspirin. And no solids until the swelling dies down – arrowroot, bread and milk, jelly, that kind of thing.'

'I'll see to it.'

Petey sat close against her as they were driven back to Dowers Farm. He wasn't crying, but he looked weepy. He allowed himself to be put to bed without protest which, in itself, showed he was under the weather.

Barbara and Mildred took turns sitting with him during the rest of the day. After the other children came to bed, he became restless, and disturbed them now and again, but on the whole he had quite a good night and sat up next morning looking more himself.

He complained at not being given toast at breakfast but when Barbara knocked one of the crusts against his plate and asked him if he thought he'd like that against his 'sore tooth', he agreed perhaps not. He didn't want to go out to play. Barbara stayed with him in the day nursery to help with a new jigsaw.

Not until they had gone down for their afternoon nap did it occur to her that Brian was coming for his answer in about half an hour – and she hadn't given a moment's thought to it.

She left Mildred knitting in the day nursery, hurried to her room to take off her pinafore and to brush her hair. She dabbed powder on her nose. 'Thank you, Brian,' she rehearsed, 'I'll do my best to make you a good wife.'

Edith came in search of her. 'Mr Sethard is here, Mrs Gray. Shall I send him to the day nursery?'

'No, thanks, I'll see him in the drawing-room.'

Edith didn't exactly shrug, but there was something in her withdrawal that said she didn't approve of Nannies having access to the drawingroom. After a moment or two to settle her butterfly-fluttering stomach, Barbara went down.

'How nice you look, Barbara,' Brian said, coming to take her hand. 'I've been dying to get here and hear you name the day.' He gave her a little kiss on the cheek.

'Sit down, won't you.' She gestured to the sofa, and took her place beside him, but when he tried to take her hand she evaded him. 'Thank you, Brian, for thinking me the right kind of person to be your wife. But I have to say no.'

She was quite astonished to hear herself say it. Until that moment she hadn't the least idea she was going to refuse him.

'No?' Brian repeated, his square chin dropping. 'No?'

'No.'

'But why?'

Why? She hardly knew. The upper part of her mind, a moment ago, had been rehearsing her speech of acceptance. But some other part of her consciousness had been at work ever since he proposed, and had been telling her it was no good.

'I'll try to explain,' she said. She didn't want to hurt or

offend him. He was a good man. He didn't deserve rejection.

'We talked it all over the night before last,' she began.

'Yes, and if there was anything you objected to you only had to –'

'Brian –' she held up a hand, 'do you remember that conversation?'

'Of course I do!'

'The word love was never mentioned once.'

He stared at her. He had blue eyes, rather fine. They were filled with amazement. 'But you know all that,' he said. 'I thought that was taken for granted.'

'That you loved me? Or that I love you?'

'I . . . well . . . both.'

She suppressed a sigh and shook her head. 'I don't love you, Brian.'

'But . . . but . . . of course you do.'

'Why of course? Because we've been out a couple of times and held hands? I like you a lot – a tremendous lot. But I don't love you.'

If ever it had been going to work, he ought now to have grabbed her, held her close, and told her he had enough love for both of them. But all he said was: 'But you're fond of me – surely that's enough?'

'No, Brian.' Not by a long chalk. She had loved Archie, really loved him, but that had been too little to save their marriage. Because Archie had not loved her in the same way. She could not, dared not fall into that trap a second time.

Perhaps Brian was fundamentally a better man than Archie. But that made it all the worse to short-change him. He ought to have a woman who thought the world of him, eager to devote the whole of her life to making him happy. Barbara knew all at once that she could never make her life revolve around Brian; perhaps it was a failing in herself, but she sensed that at some time, and in the not too distant future, he would have come to bore her.

They talked for perhaps another fifteen minutes. Brian refused to give up without a struggle. He had envisaged Barbara as the perfect partner in his new life: attractive, capable, well-bred in speech and manner, educated but not intellectual . . .

Besides, the firm had let it be known they preferred married men. He had counted on Barbara as one of the stepping stones to promotion. He was like a traveller who had felt the stepping-stone wobble in mid-stream.

When he said goodbye he was hurt, baffled, and beginning to be vexed. 'I shan't come back and argue it over again,' he said, rather stiffly. 'I hope you'll change your mind and if you do, all you have to do is ring me.'

'Thank you, Brian, but I shan't change my mind.'

'Oh, very well,' he said, and went out. She watched him get into his little Austin Seven and drive away without a backward glance. He was affronted. He would never forgive her.

Felicity was aghast when she came home from a bridge party to hear the news. 'You must be out of your mind!' she cried. 'Refused him? Why? Just explain why!'

'I don't know if I can. Perhaps it's simply that I don't want to be married again.'

'Oh, nonsense! What else is there for a woman to do? You can't go on playing with other people's children for the rest of your life, now can you? And you don't want to go back to hospital nursing. What else is there, except some dreary office job?'

Barbara had no answer to that. It posed a lot of questions which she had been avoiding. For the moment she defended herself by saying simply that she didn't love Brian enough to marry him and had felt it would be unfair to accept him.

The atmosphere was cool towards her over the rest of that weekend. She went to church next day with the Leschallases, taking Petey and John as usual, but there was none of the usual easy small talk.

But the next day was Monday, 28th October 1929. Something happened that day that made personal matters fade into insignificance.

That was the day of the Wall Street Crash.

CHAPTER FOUR

The news began to come through in the evening of that day, because of course America was five hours behind Britain in time. The radio gave the news without too much comment at first. Next day the newspapers were more explicit – millions knocked off the value of shares, the New York Stock Exchange in turmoil.

Not until two days later did Peter Leschallas begin to look really worried. The coolness towards Barbara had by then been swept away in this new anxiety, so she was having drinks with them on the Wednesday evening about six o'clock.

'Forgive me if I've got it wrong,' Barbara said, looking at the headlines in the evening newspaper just delivered by the paperboy on his bicycle, 'but does it actually mean very much to investors? I mean, I can see it's terrible for dealers, who make money by buying and selling. But unless you actually want to sell the shares, does it make very much difference if their value on the Stock Exchange goes down for a while?'

'The key words are "for a while",' Peter replied. 'Things aren't going to pick up quickly after a crash like this. I mean, the market's still going down. Everybody says it's not going to change for a long time. It means companies will go bankrupt. Banks will close. You see, Barbara, banks make money from investing on the Stock Exchange – and the money they invest belongs to people, and firms, and trusts, and so on.'

'Yes . . .'

'But if you want my personal viewpoint – yes, it's important to me at the moment because I just set in motion the selling of some shares to finance the change-over to milk production. I think I'm going to lose a packet.'

Felicity glanced up quickly from the game of patience she

was playing. Barbara could see by the sudden alarm on her tanned face that she hadn't understood until now that it was so serious.

'Oh, Peter!'

'We'll have to wait and see. Everything's in a state of chaos. But the thing is, Dad's in a mess too.'

Peter's father was in banking. The family had always been important in finance. To Barbara it seemed impossible that they could be threatened.

But as the days went by it became clear money had just been oozing away through some crack in the market floor.

Barbara's sister, Eileen, rang up in a panic. 'Barbara, it's just *awful*! Jimmy doesn't know what to *do*!' The familiar sweet, light voice ended in a wail of dismay. Barbara could imagine the tears welling in the grey-blue eyes, the long blonde hair no longer carefully dressed into its pretty flat curls. Eileen tended to go to pieces in a crisis.

Jimmy Letts was one of those men who made his money by cottoning on to 'tips' about shares, and buying while they were cheap so as to sell when they went up. He dealt 'on the margin', which meant he seldom had to put down any real money, because he tried to buy and sell at a profit before ever he had to pay for the shares in the first place. Now he was caught in the general collapse, brokers demanding that he pay for shares he had dealt for and unable to sell so as to make the money to pay.

But he had to pay, or face a fraud charge. He was selling everything he and Eileen owned to meet his debts.

'We're trying to sell the lease of the flat,' Eileen said. 'But who wants to buy it, with everybody losing money as fast as we are?'

Barbara couldn't offer any advice. The money markets were a mystery to her. Only two or three weeks later, when Peter said his father was mounting a rescue operation for a group of businessmen, was she able to throw a lifeline. Eileen's husband clutched at this thread and by using the prestige of the Leschallas name and a little money he had got from a property in Cannes, was able to survive.

In the midst of all these greater problems, the matter of Brian Sethard faded into insignificance, so that it was without emotion except mere friendship that she was able to see him when he came to say goodbye.

'Everything seems to be going to pieces here,' he said, gloomily and yet with that muted pleasure which comes from knowing you're staying in one piece yourself.

'Yes, it was a good decision, to take that job. And I'm sure you'll have a big success with it, Brian.'

He hesitated, as if he were about to say that he'd have more success if she would come too. But she went on: 'And I'm sure you'll find another girl, someone who deserves you more than I do.'

There was no answer to that. He couldn't say: No one deserves me more than you do, because that sounded conceited. Nor could he say, I'm sure I shall, because that was to suggest he was going straight off to look for a wife to help his career. So he contented himself with muttering that he would miss her, shook her hand fervently, and left.

Her father came to see her on her day off, and took her out for a meal in what was now coming to be called a 'roadhouse' – a newish pub catering for the people who had cars and liked to drive out for a meal.

'Well, Barbs, what d'you think about Jimmy and his affairs, eh? Got caught with his hand in a vice, didn't he?'

There was some satisfaction in his tone. He didn't much care for Jimmy, whom he thought too clever by half. Archie he had rather liked at first – a man who paid for a drink and knew a few pretty girls. Jimmy wasn't interested in girls, only making money. But Archie had proved a cad and Jimmy was now looking like a worried little bank clerk.

'I think Peter's hand has been a bit nipped too, Father.'

'What? The great Leschallas family? Feeling the pinch?'

'They're not having any fun, that's sure. He and Felicity

were even discussing whether they could afford to send Petey to Vannings after all.'

Mr Gray tugged at his moustache, to hide his alarm. 'Not send him to school? What about Eton and Oxford and all that, then?'

'That's just the point. To get into Eton he's got to go to a proper prep school so in the end they decided to go on with sending him to Vannings.' Barbara gave a wry smile. 'Being hard up is a comparative term.'

He nodded. 'It's times like this I'm pleased I'm on the verge of retiring. Though, mind you, the old pension's not going to be as safe as I thought. Dammit, when money's put by for you in a bank, you think it's safe as . . .' He broke off, laughing. 'I was going to say, the Bank of England!'

'Well, that's safe, thank heaven. No matter what happens, the pound will always be worth twenty shillings and a golden guinea twenty-one. How's the cottage?'

The cottage was where her father was retiring to. Like many a home-going Anglo-Indian, he had had this dream of a cottage in the country with roses round the door, and a nice old-fashioned pub down the road in the village, within walking distance. Donald Gray had been lucky enough to find it, the cottage with roses – Fairlight Cottage, on the outskirts of Banbury, not so very far from Dowers Farm as the crow flies. The White Lion in the High Street suited him beautifully. He was in the process of furnishing the cottage and having a few improvements done.

'It's coming along fine. Dottie's having a whale of a time, choosing prints for kitchen curtains and all that kind of rubbish. D'you know, Barbara, there's a fellow two or three fields away who keeps bees? You can buy honey from him.' He closed his eyes and opened them again. One of the dreams in India had been to sit in an English garden under an old cedar, and have honey for tea.

'I'm sure it'll be lovely,' she said. She was beginning to wonder if she might not have to ask to be put up at Fairlight

Cottage. She was too sensitive not to realize that the Leschallases were going to be hard-pressed for money. Already they had reduced the household staff by dismissing a kitchenmaid and there was even some talk of letting Wentworth go and having a jobbing gardener by the day.

When she looked back, she saw that Peter had already been thinking of economy measures even before the Stock Exchange collapse. He and Felicity had been very pleased, very eager, about her marriage to Brian. She knew now that they had seen it as a way to dispense with her without actually asking her to go.

For the last few days she had been wondering what she ought to do. Her impulse was to say she felt she ought to leave. But several things prevented her. First there was her anxiety about Petey. It was bad enough for him that he was going to leave home and start at school, after minimal preparation – a few lessons each week with the Trackworth children and their governess. Then there had been the minor tragedy of his infected tooth. If she were to announce that she was leaving suddenly, she felt sure it would upset him very deeply – upset all the children, but Petey most of all at this crisis in his life.

Moreover, the Leschallases would ask her what she intended to do with herself. She would have liked to have a job to go to. But as Felicity said, what was there for her except going back to hospital nursing or a dreary job in an office? Felicity wouldn't want her to leave without some alternative ready. She couldn't claim she was going to keep house for her father because Dottie would do that, and there simply wasn't room in the little cottage for two women.

It wasn't as if she could even go and stay with Eileen for a time. From what she heard, Eileen and Jimmy were having a hard time keeping their heads above water. They didn't want an elder sister hanging round their necks like the Old Man of the Sea, increasing their expenses and adding nothing to their income.

An idea had been forming in Barbara's mind for some two or

three weeks now, but lack of money made it impossible to bring to reality. She'd already made inquiries, sorted out possibilities, found out how much it would cost – and the cost was what put it outside her range.

She said nothing of all this to Donald. She let him chat about the cottage, about the charms of the White Lion and the clients he'd already met on flying visits there. 'You must invite me to a meal,' she said. 'When you've got it more or less in shape, I mean. Preview of the new ancestral home.'

'That's a date,' he said.

He took her back to Dowers Farm by taxi, kissed her goodbye, then was taken off to the station for his train to London. Barbara went indoors prepared to do her usual act, putting her head in at the drawing-room door to announce her return and then making herself scarce. She could hear by the sounds that Peter and Felicity had friends with them.

'Barbara!' cried Felicity as her head appeared. 'Come in! Darling, we have the most stunning news for you!'

Barbara came into the room, bewildered. From Felicity's tone it was good news – but good news had been so scarce recently that she found it almost incredible. In the *Times* that very morning, the financial report had begun with the words: 'The Stock Exchange closed in cheerful mood. Yesterday passed without the report of any default', as if it was a marvel, and indeed it was, so many firms had gone to the wall.

So what could all the beaming smiles be about?

Felicity's guest was Bob Dexter. Barbara's heart sank a little at seeing him. As the financial situation got worse and he felt the need for a little comfort, he'd become very troublesome to Barbara. The time was coming when she would have to slap his face – and that would be very embarrassing for everyone.

'Well, Miss Barbara,' he said playfully, 'aren't you going to give a little kiss to the friend who's bringing the good news?'

'I . . . er . . . hello, Bob,' she said. Then, rather crisp, 'Perhaps I'll defer the kiss until I know what the news is.'

'Oh, you'll like it! It's spiffy! Remember that follow-through bet you made?'

'What?' Barbara thought, then shook her head.

'Oh, *you* remember! The day we all went to Sandown Park.'

Now she was having a vague recollection. It had been a family picnic in honour of Peter's birthday. They had packed everybody into the Armstrong-Siddeley and attended the races – at least the men had watched the horses and the women had watched each other, admired the clothes and enjoyed the picnic food.

At one point Bob, as usual, had got Barbara alone for a moment and tried to make an arrangement to meet her in Oxford. To distract him she'd begun talking about the races, so it had ended with her asking him to place a bet for her. She had given him ten shillings, which seemed a lot to hazard on a horse.

Later she discovered her horse had won. But, instead of giving her her winnings, Bob had said, 'Listen, Miss Nanny, why don't you leave it with me? I'm going to do a follow-through bet on Gordon Richards this season. He's been champion jockey for two seasons now and I've a hunch he'll pull it off again this year. What say we bet on Gordon Richards every time he's riding?'

'Oh, Bob, I couldn't. I'm not interested enough in racing to know when he's riding.'

'No, no, leave it all to me. I'll do it. Might make a nice little packet by the end of the flat.'

'You mean,' she said now, 'it's about that Gordon Richards thing?'

'That's it! It paid off! I knew it would – didn't I say it would, Peter?'

'You mean we've actually won some money?'

'Darling,' Felicity said, coming to her with a cut glass goblet containing brandy, 'I should sit down if I were you. You're going to get a very pleasurable shock.'

Barbara obeyed, taking the glass. She couldn't help noticing that Bob gave a pleased grin at the expanse of silk-stockinged knee exposed by her handkerchief-hem evening dress.

'I have pleasure,' Bob said, 'in presenting your winnings.' He handed her a fat envelope.

She set down her glass, took the envelope, and looked inside. It seemed to be stuffed full of the white banknotes that meant at least fivers, if not tenners.

'But . . . but . . . this looks like a fortune!'

'Twelve hundred and eighteen pounds, two shillings and threepence, to be exact.'

'What?'

'Isn't it splendid, darling?' crowed Felicity. 'Absolutely splendid?'

Barbara blinked, cleared her throat, then desperately picked up the glass and gulped some brandy. It went down the wrong way, and she choked. Bob came to pound her on the back.

'I say, old girl, don't kill yourself off by choking to death now! A rich woman, you are! Quite a windfall!'

'But . . . but . . . I can't take this –'

'Why not? It's yours. And it's quite legal.'

'But I did nothing to deserve this –'

'Who did, except good old Gordon?'

'But d'you mean to say you made all this money by merely putting on my pound every time Gordon Richards was riding?'

'No, no,' Peter put in. 'Contrary to what the newspapers try to imply, Richards didn't win every time he was up. But Bob's a bit of an expert. He held back when he didn't fancy the horse, doubled your stake when he thought the horse was good, put a bit extra on when the odds were right – and there you are.'

'Bob's your uncle!' laughed Bob. This was one of his favourite jokes.

'But – the money belongs to you.'

'Not a bit of it! That's from your pound. I did nicely for myself, thank you, with my own money.'

'But – I really feel . . .'

'It's all right, Barbara,' Felicity assured her. 'People trust other people to make their bets all the time, and think nothing of collecting their winnings. You mustn't think there's anything special in it. Gordon Richards has turned up trumps for a lot of people this year and you just happen to be one of them.'

Barbara looked at the envelope in her lap. Twelve hundred and eighteen pounds, two shillings and threepence. She could even see the little silver threepenny piece tucked into a corner of the envelope. She took another swallow of brandy, feeling a sense of celebration at last.

She had money! She could take a step for herself at last! She looked up at Bob. 'I can't thank you enough,' she said. 'I never dreamed you were bothering with all this.'

'Oh, always ready to bother myself for *you*, Barbara, you know that,' he said. 'If you like, I'll do the same for you over the steeplechase season.'

'Oh, no thanks.'

'Come on, you've got money now, and an expert to guide you. I could make your fortune for you.' He was laughing, his heavy face alight with pleasure and self-importance, his shaggy hair on end. There was an undertone of meaning in the words which he imagined was noticeable to Barbara alone, although Felicity was well aware what he was up to.

'Let the poor girl get used to it,' she said. 'I know I'd be staggered if I suddenly found myself the owner of a sum like that. Come on, now, one last drink to make a toast to the lucky ones, and then it's time we got to our beds.'

Peter did the honours, and proposed the toast: 'Here's to Lady Luck, may she smile on us all now she's got back to the habit.'

Bob took hold of Barbara's hand in the hall as they were exchanging goodnights. 'You'll let me talk to you about spending a bit of that windfall – on having some fun?' he inquired.

'Well, I've certainly got plans for it,' she murmured.

'Plans that include me, I hope,' he whispered as Peter came

with his coat.

When he had gone out to his car Peter smiled at Barbara. 'You're going to find it even harder to fight him off,' he said. 'He feels he's got a right, now.'

'Poor old Bob,' Felicity said, yawning. 'But what are you going to do with that money, Barbara?'

'Do you mind if we talk about it tomorrow? I'm all in a daze for the moment.'

'You're right. Come on, Peter, lock up and let's get to bed.'

Barbara's first call was to make sure everything was all right with the children. They were softly asleep. The weather had been stormy but mild, so the fire had been allowed to die down. There was no moon; only the starlight twinkled at the window.

She went to it and stood for a time looking out, seeing the vague outlines of the trees now almost bare after the strong winds of November. From the distance came the sound of the mail train chugging towards London. Her mind seemed empty.

As she turned to go, baby Alan made a snuffly sound and wriggled in his cot. He had a slight cold. She stooped over him to check he wasn't going to wake. He made a sound of muffled, sleepy annoyance, then cuddled down again.

She went out, along the passage, and to her own room. There she put the light on and sat for a long time opening and shutting the clip of her evening bag which contained the envelope full of money.

Then she got up, looked on the table at her bedside, and found a nursing magazine she had been reading last night. She found the page she wanted easily – she had turned down the corner while she was reading it, although how she had thought she could ever want to use the address she couldn't explain. At the time the money problem had been an insuperable barrier.

She got writing paper and ink and pen from the cupboard in the corner. On her knee she wrote a brief, businesslike letter. She put it in an envelope, addressed and stamped it. She was going to tiptoe downstairs with it to leave it on the silver tray in the hall for the post, but stayed her hand.

She might change her mind overnight. She would leave it, sleep on it.

She woke early next morning as she always did, but this was earlier than usual. The letter was where she had left it on the bedside table.

She washed and dressed quickly, pulled on a coat, put a torch in her pocket, and took the letter with her as she went out, light-footed so as not to disturb anyone. Peter was probably up and about already but Felicity was asleep and the children too, she hoped.

She walked through the hall and out of the front door without pause to look for Peter in the breakfast room. It was a clammy, moist day. She walked briskly down the drive, into the lane, and down to the spot where it met the traffic road. There a postbox was fixed into a wall. She shone her torch at the timetable on it. The indicator told her the first post had not yet been collected.

She stood for a long moment looking at the red box. Then, with a nod of affirmation, she popped the letter in. She heard it fall inside.

Then she turned and walked back more slowly. Her decision was taken. Now she would tell Felicity and Peter.

Felicity always had breakfast in bed, a good deal later than Peter's start to the day. Barbara went along to the night nursery to find the children stirring, then Mildred came to help with the morning chores. When at last they were all sitting dutifully in the day nursery starting on porridge and boiled eggs with bread and butter soldiers, Barbara nodded to Mildred to keep an eye on them then went to Felicity's room.

Her hostess was sitting up in bed with a quilted dressing-jacket folded about her ample bosom and a pink lace boudoir cap still tied over her hair to preserve the marcel wave. 'Hello, darling, you're early on the move,' she said. And then, recollecting as she raised her coffee cup: 'Oh, of course –

couldn't sleep for thinking about all that lolly, eh?'

'I slept very well, in fact,' Barbara said, with some surprise. 'I suppose it was because I'd really made up my mind what to do before even we broke up the celebration last night.'

'You had? Do tell, darling!'

'I've applied to be taken on at the Hogarth Training School for Nursery Nurses.'

Felicity put down her coffee cup carefully. Her dark eyes were fixed on her friend in astonishment.

'You did what? What's the idea? Are you going to go there as a housekeeper, or office bod?'

'I've applied to take the training.'

'The training?'

'To be a Nanny. A proper Nanny.'

'Take the training?' Felicity clutched at the sides of her pink lace cap. 'At your age?'

'I'm only thirty-four Felicity. Lots of Nannies are about my age.'

'But they've ten years of experience behind them at that age. Good God, Barbs, you don't want to go back to being a student at your age?'

'I wish you'd stop saying "at your age" as if I was past it. I've still got all my faculties, you know.'

'Oh, darling – I didn't mean that!' Felicity was contrite. She pushed her tray aside, swung herself out of bed, and came to engulf Barbara in a hug. 'Of course you've got plenty of time to do anything you want to do, but really, darling – is it the best use for the money? I mean, Peter and I were saying last night, as we got ready for bed . . . I mean, there are one or two men we know who sort of fancy you, Barbara. With a bit of money like that, you could do a season – you might get yourself quite a catch!'

Barbara freed herself gently from her friend's arms. 'I don't want a catch. I could have had Brian, remember? I realized then – marriage isn't a sort of last resort you run to when you can't do anything else. It ought to be something you want to do before everything else. Like you and Peter. No, I'm going to train properly to be a Nanny. I've had it in my mind for quite a time – ever since you and Peter began to look a bit white around the gills over money.'

'Oh, *darling*!' cried Felicity. 'We would never have –'

'I know you wouldn't, that's the whole point. You would have let me stay with you, when you really couldn't afford it. I've given it a lot of thought. Mildred is pretty confident now, she could handle the three when Petey goes. I admit Petey will still domineer over them when he comes home on school holidays but perhaps John will get a bit more tough with him as he grows older.'

'You know what will happen.' Felicity groaned. 'Just as Mildred's got a bit of experience and is beginning to hold it all together, somebody'll come along and woo her away with more money. That's what happened with Nanny Lewis.'

'I suppose it will.' Barbara hesitated. 'It was Nanny Lewis's departure that made them so naughty a year ago. They were very upset.'

'They'll be upset when you go.'

'I know, and I hate it. But I think it has to be. Yet even if Mildred goes too, some time in the future, you can help keep things happy in the nursery, Felicity.'

'Me?'

'Yes, you. You're their mother. You should be the mainstay of the children's life. In fact, if things really got difficult about money, I don't see why you shouldn't take charge of them with only a maid –'

'Don't be silly,' Felicity broke in, almost with sharpness. 'As Peter's wife I have to play a part in the community that can't be avoided. I can't look after three children and be at committee meetings, open fetes, chair concerts, and all the sort of thing that's expected of me.'

'No, I suppose not.' Barbara thought a moment. 'I don't ask you to change your way of life. I see that would be too difficult. But I can't help knowing that you could be a bulwark to your children against any changes of staff in the nursery. If you saw more of them, if you let them know you'd always be there no matter who else might come and go –'

'But they know that, Barbara.'

'Do they? Well . . . Anyhow, where I'm concerned the change has to come. I feel it's time to stop marking time with my life. This last year's been a Godsend, Flick – you've given me a safe place to go and lick my wounds after the divorce, but that's all behind me. I have to do something constructive. And Bob's money has made it possible to do what I've sort of known I want to do for weeks now.'

'Poor old Bob,' Felicity said, with a sudden giggle. 'He's going to be a bit dashed when he finds he's given you the chance to whisk yourself out of his range!'

'It's a good thing. I was about at the end of my tether with him. But I reckon he'll soon lose interest if he has to pursue me to the hallowed halls of the Hogarth College.'

'Darling, it sounds like doom!'

'Not a bit,' Barbara said, although she had no way of knowing whether it was charming or nasty. 'It has a marvellous reputation and it's where I'm going.'

She broke off, thought for a moment, then added: 'If they'll have me.'

CHAPTER FIVE

That began to seem dubious from the very outset of the interview with the Director of the Hogarth School.

'My dear Mrs Gray,' said Mrs Stepps-Astley, inclining her iron-grey head, 'I had no idea from your letter that you were such . . . er . . . a mature person.'

Barbara, in her good navy blue coat with the small persian lamb collar, felt like a tweeny-maid being interviewed. 'Is that a factor?' she inquired.

'Well . . . ah . . . most of our students are under twenty. The oldest is twenty-one.'

'I should have thought it was an advantage, in dealing with children, to have some maturity.'

'It is also an advantage to be near them in age either in fact or in attitude, Mrs Gray.'

'Well,' Barbara said, with an attempt at a smile, 'I can be as childish as anyone else if I put my mind to it.'

The joke didn't go down well. Mrs Stepps-Astley didn't exactly frown, but her strong features took on an added coolness.

'It seems rather late in life to be taking an interest in children, if I may say so?'

'I've always had an interest in children. It's just that I feel I'd like to have proper training.'

'That is certainly laudable.' The Director glanced at the letter in her hand. 'You are a widow, I take it?'

'No.'

She was surprised. 'Your husband is living?'

'Yes.'

'My dear Mrs Gray, it is not usual for a Nanny to wish to find a post where her husband can also be employed.

Housekeeper and butler – yes, that is quite common. But Nanny and . . . What category of staff does he come into?'

'My husband doesn't come into it.'

'You are not with him?'

'No.'

'You can't mean,' said Mrs Stepps-Astley, scarcely above a whisper, 'that you are a divorced woman?'

'Yes, I do.'

'Mrs Gray!' Mrs Stepps-Astley rose, tall and imposing, like a battleship hoving over the horizon. 'This is impossible. It is quite out of the question that the Hogarth School should accept a divorcée.'

'But why?' Barbara said, refusing to rise and be ushered to the door. 'I am the innocent party. I have done nothing wrong.'

'But a divorced woman! We have never accepted a divorced woman!'

'Is there any reason why you shouldn't?'

'A hundred! The families to whom we send our gels have the highest expectations of us –'

'I'm not likely to fall short of their expectations just because my husband went off with another woman!'

'But the remnant of a broken marriage –!'

Barbara felt like saying, 'I am not a remnant!' But she could see the older woman was genuinely upset at the revelation, so she said instead, 'Mrs Stepps-Astley, I assure you I am a woman of good principle. I was born in wedlock –'

'Mrs Gray!'

'Baptized, confirmed, and have attended church regularly.' She thought it unnecessary to add that she had generally disagreed with the sermons she heard, but was pretty sure Mrs Stepps-Astley was the kind to disagree with sermons herself. That strong nose and firm chin told her so. It was for this instinctive reason that Barbara was fighting back strongly against the first reaction of shock. She felt Mrs Stepps-Astley had a mind of her own.

'If you inquire of Mrs Peter Leschallas, she will tell you I have been caring for her four children for the last year and given the utmost satisfaction. Before that, I looked after my younger sister, ten years my junior – you might say I almost brought her up.'

'Indeed. And what became of her?'

'She married a Mr James Letts, has two charming children, and lives in Holland Park.'

'Ah.' Mrs Stepps-Astley was not unimpressed by this narrative. 'Nevertheless, what are we to say when the prospective employer asks for references?'

'Does the prospective employer usually ask if a woman has been divorced?'

'Certainly not! Such an idea would not cross their minds.'

'Then what's the problem? They'll take it for granted I'm a widow, as you did.'

'But that would mean going under false pretences.'

'Mrs Stepps-Astley, the only pretensions I shall have are that I can look after children. And I can. I know I can. All I want is the proper training to feel sure of my decisions.'

'Hm,' Mrs Stepps-Astley said, 'even the best training in the world cannot make you feel sure of every decision where a child is concerned. So much of it is instinct.'

'And are young girls of eighteen more likely to have that than I am?'

'Well . . . It would be untrue to say that, I agree.' For a moment the Director looked softened. Then she said: 'It is for your own sake I tell you this would never do. We have had older women before as students, but it has never been a success. How should you feel, settling down to study with gels a little over half your age? For you are, if I'm any judge, in your thirties.'

'I am thirty-four.'

'There. Some of the gels here are, as you mentioned, eighteen. Do you really feel you could study and work with gels of that age?'

'Might I not have to work with girls of that age, or nearly so, in a household where I cared for the children? Many families have girls about to come out and children still in the nursery. Surely it can only be an advantage to spend time with girls in their teens?'

'That is quite different, Mrs Gray. If you were a Nanny in a family with gels – or even boys – of seventeen or eighteen, you wouldn't be on the same footing. You would be a superior – a guardian. Here, you would have to fit in with the others at their own level.'

'I think I'm adaptable enough for that.'

'But – forgive me, Mrs Gray – have you the educational suppleness? Your school days are some way behind you, after all. And the course here is rigorous.'

Barbara thought with regret of her odd schooling in India. How helpful it would be at this moment if she could say, I am a product of Roedean, or I went to Cheltenham Ladies College. But all she could do was be honest.

'Mrs Stepps-Astley, I had a very mixed schooling. I went to school in India.'

'Ah?' said the Director, resuming her seat behind her big oak desk. She was reassured. In her view, anyone who had been a child of the Raj must be of superior stuff. She herself had relatives in British India, had visited them, and rather envied the almost vice-regal splendour in which they lived. If Mrs Gray had been brought up in India, then her background was of the best.

She couldn't know, of course, that Barbara's father had not been one of the top-rank Civil servants, but one of those ragamuffin engineers regarded as somewhat beyond the pale.

Yet wherever Barbara had been educated and whatever her background, she was older than the usual applicant and divorced to boot. Mrs Stepps-Astley hardened her heart.

'Mrs Gray, I must tell you plainly that I cannot accept you. I can tell that you are enthusiastic, and might do your best. But I feel sure you couldn't keep up, and your presence among so many young gels would be disruptive. I –'

'Disruptive? In what way disruptive?'

'I . . . er . . . you wouldn't fit in.'

'I jolly well would,' Barbara said, 'or die in the attempt!'

Despite herself, Mrs Stepps-Astley laughed. 'Well, you know your own mind, that's clear,' she said. 'Believe me, I rather admire you for your initiative. But I have to think of the school. And I think it would be difficult for all of us – gels and instructors alike.'

'I don't see how. To the instructors I'll just be another face sitting in the classroom – an older face, I grant you, but I won't make an issue of that if the instructor doesn't. As to the girls . . . well . . . there's no guarantee about that. They might find me embarrassing. But if I'm prepared to risk it, why can't they?'

'No, no. I really think . . . Mrs Gray, why don't you choose another career and go elsewhere for training? Secretarial college, for instance.'

Barbara leaned forward, her big eyes full of earnestness. 'The career chose me, Mrs Stepps-Astley. I felt I had to do something with my life and it came to me that to be a Nanny was a good thing, a worthwhile thing. I don't want to train to be a secretary.'

'No, well . . .'

'Listen. I could walk out of here and apply for a job – I've seen dozens advertised in the *Times*. I could get a post as a "mother's help", a lady-nurse. I don't need a diploma, I could just apply and get something. But I want to be trained. I want to learn all there is to learn about children. So much is coming to light. I've read little bits – about psychology, about kindergartens. I want to know all that.'

She stopped. There was a silence in the room broken only by the stolid ticking of the wall clock. It was a spartan room, smelling of beeswax and Jeyes Fluid. The big oak desk was bare of all except a few papers, an inkstand, and a telephone. The two chairs were straightbacked wooden pieces, as if they came from a schoolroom. Mrs Stepps-Astley herself had something the look of a schoolmistress; tall, clad in a dark grey flannel frock with white crêpe-de-Chine collar and cuffs and modesty vest edged with lace, a pince nez case pinned to her bosom.

'Ahem. Aha. Well, Mrs Gray, I see your point. Yes, quite see your point. It has been my view that much damage is done to children by ignorant women hired by parents equally ignorant – or unconcerned. Yes, indeed. Well . . .'

'Yes?' Barbara said eagerly.

'If I accepted you, you would have to agree to keep up with the studies on the same basis as everyone else. I mean, no allowances could be made for the fact that you are out of the habit of doing class work.'

'I wouldn't expect any special privileges.'

'And you must not cause any problems among the other students. If you fail to fit in, you have to go. Is that understood?'

'Perfectly.'

'Er . . . I have no idea what your personal life is like, but it must be understood that there can be no romantic entanglements.'

'I understand.'

'The autumn term is almost over. You would wish to start in the spring term?'

'After Christmas, yes.'

'That puts you at a disadvantage. There is an examination at Easter, by means of which we assess aptitude and ability. All the gels must take it. Those who fail are asked to leave immediately. There's no point wasting time on gels who have no real vocation.'

'I'll catch up, I promise.'

Mrs Stepps-Astley studied her, her head on one side. 'I believe you might,' she murmured. 'But I warn you, Mrs Gray, this is no easy path you've chosen.'

'I know that. I'm just grateful that you give me the opportunity.'

'Exactly so. The opportunity. I don't encourage you. I think you're making a mistake. And I must point out that the fee, paid in advance, cannot be refunded.'

'I expected that to be the case.'

'Very well.' Mrs Stepps-Astley rose again, and this time Barbara rose with her. 'Term begins the 6th January. I will send you a list of textbooks and other requirements. You are not asked to wear uniform during the first year but please have white blouses and dark skirts and flat shoes. Cosmetics are not encouraged, nor are polished nails. Aprons are provided for practical work but you must pay for the laundering. Please bring sewing equipment, notebooks and pens. We can supply those at an additional fee if you don't have them.'

'Thank you.'

'I will write confirming your acceptance and asking for the year's fees in advance. I should like a prompt remittance.'

'Of course, Mrs Stepps-Astley.'

'Goodbye for the present, then, Mrs Gray.'

'Goodbye, Mrs Stepps-Astley.'

As Barbara walked down the drive of the old house she didn't notice the cold wind lashing at the rhododendron bushes. When she got to the gates, out of sight of the windows, she executed a little dance of triumph. She was going to train at the Hogarth School, the best and most modern of the colleges for nursery nurses!

Fastening up her coat collar against her neck, she set off at a smart pace for Haslemere station. When she got to Waterloo she'd nip into the station buffet and buy herself a stiff whisky. She felt she needed it both as restorative and celebration.

Felicity heard her account with awe when she got back to Dowers Farm. 'She sounds a terrible old battle-axe. Like Matron at the Brixton General!'

'There's a resemblance. I shouldn't like to get the wrong side of her. But she's fair. Who was it of whom it was said, "He's a beast, but a just beast"?'

'Dunno. Judge Jeffreys?'

'Oh, he was the Hanging Judge! Mrs Stepps-Astley isn't exactly that. Still, I think she could be pretty ruthless if the good name of Hogarth's was involved.'

'I think you're mad, Barbara. Utterly mad! Fancy shutting yourself up with a gang of eighteen and nineteen year olds for – how long?'

'It's a three year course.'

'Three years! Darling, will Bob's winnings last you out for three years?'

'I'll manage. I'll try to get jobs in the holidays, if the money runs out.'

'But it sounds such a grind, darling!'

Yes, it did. And now that the first flush of triumph had worn off, she was wondering whether she really wanted to spend three years under the tutelage of Mrs Stepps-Astley.

Well, she could always change her mind when the official confirmation of her acceptance came, requesting her cheque.

Yet she didn't. She sat for a long time with her pen in her hand and her cheque-book open, hesitating, for it was an awfully large sum of money. But her reluctance had nothing to do with undertaking the course, it had to do with finance. Was she really going to be able to manage through three years without a proper income?

'Hang it, yes, I am,' she said, and quickly filled in the cheque blank.

After some thought she'd decided not to let the children know she was leaving. She felt young Petey had enough to contend with. If she felt a traitor when he chattered on about seeing her when he came home for the Easter holidays, she concealed it. She was due to leave for Hogarth's the very same day Petey was taken to Vannings.

It was a day she didn't like to look back on. Nor the night that preceded it. Petey slept badly, beset by nightmares. John, not quite understanding what was about to happen but affected by his elder brother's terror, kept clutching at Barbara for comfort. Ceecie was unhappy, though she didn't know why. Even the baby seemed upset.

Whey-faced, the little boy was put into his uniform and taken by his parents in the Armstrong-Siddely to be inducted into school life. Barbara finished her packing. Then she went into the nursery to say goodbye to the remaining three. 'I'm going away too, John,' she said, sitting down at the nursery table where he was cutting out with a pair of blunt-ended scissors.

'To school?' To John, anyone who left Dowers Farm must be going to school.

'Yes, as it happens, to school.'

'Back for the Easter holidays?' he inquired, for that seemed to be the natural train of events.

'Yes, dear, back for the Easter holidays.' She would come. She made a vow there and then. She'd be here when Petey returned from prep school eager to pour out the tale of his first term. It would mean having to say goodbye all over again – and whether that was a good thing or not she didn't know. But she had never denied it when Petey had taken it for granted she'd be here waiting when he came home, so she would manage it somehow. Even if it meant taking a day's leave of absence from the college, she'd be here.

Felicity and Peter returned in time for lunch. They were shaken by the parting. 'He cried, Barbara,' Felicity said. 'Poor little darling, he cried.'

'Felicity –'

'What?'

'Don't call him darling.'

'What?' Felicity said, staggered.

'You call everybody darling,' Barbara burst out. 'The merest acquaintances! It's meaningless.'

'Oh, now look here, Barbara,' Peter put in, taken aback by the vehemence of the reproach, 'everybody uses the word –'

'That's my point! Petey's your little boy – he's special. He needs to be spoken to as if he was special.'

'But we don't want to give him ideas like that. He'd only get spoiled.'

Barbara reined in the words she was going to utter. She gave a little sigh. 'I'm sorry. It's just that . . . children aren't fools, you know. They hear grown-ups talking. Petey knows Flick calls everybody darling – the Master of the Hunt, the vicar's wife, you, me . . . It just seemed to me that if you could let him know he was more to you than –'

'The vicar's wife?' Felicity put in with a giggle.

In a moment they were all smiling shakily, the two women perhaps on the verge of a minor hysteria. 'Come along,' Peter said 'if you're going to catch that train we'd best get going.'

When he came back from depositing Barbara at Oxford Station he murmured to his wife, 'Perhaps it's a good thing she's gone. Getting a bit too possessive about the children, d'you think?'

Barbara reached the Hogarth School in Surrey by a complicated system of a taxi across London from Paddington to Waterloo, train to Haslemere, and taxi from Haslemere to the school. She only had one large case and one small; the main bulk of her clothes had gone to be stored with her father. In the large case, as commanded, was a supply of light-coloured blouses and dark skirts together with newly-bought flat shoes. The small case held books.

There were only two other new students arriving. Most of the girls had enrolled last autumn. A tall, fair woman in a dark dress with sateen covers to protect her cuffs was sitting at a small table in the hall. 'Miss . . . er . . . Mrs Gray?' Barbara stepped forward. 'Ah yes. You are in room 12A. The porter will show you.'

The porter, small and stout, looked unwilling to pick up either of the cases. Barbara took the bag of books which was, in fact, the heavier. He hoisted up the other with great dramatic effect, to let her know it was a huge task.

He led the way across the hall, along a passage where all the windows were wide open to the blustery January wind and polished to skating-rink smoothness underfoot, up a staircase, and down a short corridor. The door of 12A stood open. He put her case just inside, made a gesture as if to say, 'Here you are,' and walked off. So far not a single person had said a word of welcome.

Barbara trudged through the doorway hefting her case of books. She stopped short. She stared.

There were four beds in the room.

It hadn't occurred to her to inquire about accommodation. She'd taken it for granted that it would be simple yet adequate. Certainly she'd had visions of a small room furnished with only the essentials. It had never come into her mind that she might have to sleep in a dormitory.

There was only one other girl in the room, a small, neat girl with light brown hair pulled back into a demure bun at the nape of her neck. She was wearing the obligatory light blouse and dark skirt. She was sitting on a bed taking clothes out of a case at her feet and putting them into the drawers of a dresser adjacent to the bed.

'Hello,' she said, turning her head at the thump of the case set down by the porter. 'You must be Mrs Gray.'

'Yes, that's right. I . . . I gather I'm sleeping in here?'

'Sleeping, doing written-work, and otherwise having your being. I'm Lillian Witherspoon, how d'you do? She held out a small hand.

'How do you do,' Barbara murmured, taking it. She set down the heavy books. 'Can I choose a bed?'

'Good heavens, no! The rest of us settled in last October and staked out our claims. I'm afraid you get that one.' She pointed to the one nearest the door. 'It's terribly draughty, as you'd probably guess.'

Barbara's heart, already sinking, now reached her shoes. She looked about her at the dormitory. It was a large airy room with three windows, at which hung bright chintz curtains. The bedspreads matched the curtains and the cushions which fitted the basketwork armchairs were likewise of flowered chintz. But that was the only sign of cheer in the room. The beds looked like hospital issue. The floor was covered in highly polished linoleum with tiny mats by the side of each bed. Barbara foresaw that if you had to get out of bed in a hurry in the middle of the night you'd inescapably go slithering across the floor on your seat.

There were four dressing-chests, more or less close to the bed whose occupant would use them. Each had a small square wood-framed mirror. Occupying the space of one wall was a long cupboard with sliding doors; this was presumably the wardrobe in which their pale blouses and dark skirts would hang communally. On top of the wardrobe there was space to keep books and personal items such as photographs.

Barbara didn't find the view encouraging. 'Are all the rooms like this?' she asked.

'Oh no. Some take three and some are singles. No doubles,' Lillian replied.

'Do you get a single room by paying extra?'

'No, it's done by some form of selection by Mrs Stepps-Astley, I gather. Though how she can tell at the beginning of a new term who's going to shake down with who, I can't tell.'

Barbara had a strong impulse to march downstairs, into Mrs Stepps-Astley's office, and demand a room to herself. It was utter sadism to expect her to live and sleep with three young girls – at her age! She looked at Lillian, who was studying her with open though not unfriendly curiosity.

'We were warned you'd be older,' she said. 'Are we to call you Mrs Gray?'

'Good heavens, no – my name's Barbara.' She broke off. By saying that, she was more or less accepting that she'd be staying in this room.

But it was such a disadvantage . . . How was she to study, how was she to read, surrounded by the chatter of three young girls?

All at once she knew that if she went to Mrs Stepps-Astley and demanded better accommodation, she'd be asked to leave. It was just the excuse the Director was waiting for. Clever old thing! Battle-axe, no – she was much sharper than a battle-axe.

Well, she wouldn't give her the satisfaction of getting rid of her at one stroke and on the first day. Barbara pressed her lips together, fetched her case from the door where the porter had left it, and plumped it on the bed which was to be hers. She opened the drawers of the adjacent dressing-chest.

'Need any help?' Lillian inquired.

'No, thanks. The others haven't arrived yet?'

'No, Agnes has to come up from the West Country so she won't arrive till afternoon tea. As for Janice . . .' There was a shrug in her voice. 'Janice is a law unto herself. She'll be here, though – she'll slip in just under the rope.'

Barbara was taking underwear out of her suitcase and placing it in the drawers. Lillian watched with interest. 'Is that real silk?' she inquired as a lace-edged petticoat was put away.

'As it happens, yes,' Barbara said. She had brought it to wear under the one pretty frock she had packed, for surely there must be occasions when she'd want to go out somewhere special.

Lillian held up a serviceable looking round necked petticoat in stockinette. 'Makes mine look a bit schoolgirlish,' she said wistfully. 'I sometimes wish I had spent a bit of time swanning around before coming here to train. But . . . well . . . the way things have turned out . . .'

Barbara guessed that the current financial depression had made it imperative for Lillian to get on with her training. 'You came straight from school?'

'Mmm . . . It's just like *still* being at school.'

'You find it hard going?'

'It's not easy.' Lillian pushed her clothes into a drawer and closed it emphatically. 'I was never good scholastically. They put a lot of emphasis on getting through the exams here. I can't help wondering if I'm going to make it . . .'

'There's an exam coming up?'

'Yes, just before the Easter break. Sorts out the sheep from the goats. I've an awful feeling I'm going to be a goat.'

'Cheer up. There's a long way to go yet.'

'Not so long. Only three months. Ah well . . . If you'd like to leave that, we can go down and get some lunch.'

'But it's too late for that, surely?'

'No, on account of the fact that girls have to come from all over the country, they serve a buffet lunch on the first day. Come on, we can still get a hot sausage and some rice pud.'

Oh dear, thought Barbara as she allowed herself to be propelled out of the door and down the corridor. Sausage and rice pudding. Even at school she had never had to eat such juvenile fare, for her Indian schools had served food more suitable to the climate. But, as it happened, she was hungry. She'd been too tense this morning for breakfast.

The dining-room was not very full, most girls having eaten and gone upstairs or into the sitting-room to resume old acquaintance. They went to a long side table and were served by a plump, beaming woman in a green wrap-over apron and a mob cap. 'Afternoon, Miss Witherspoon. Nice to see you back.'

'Afternoon, Trudie. This is Mrs Gray.'

The serving-lady gave Barbara a long stare. 'Afternoon, I'm sure,' she said, and handed her a plate of sausage and mash.

'That's Trudie,' Lillian explained as they found a place with knives and forks ready. 'She's a marvel – she never forgets a name although she must have seen hundreds of us come and go.'

'What happens next today?'

'Well, we finish unpacking then fetch our timetables. They'll be with Mrs Stepps-Astley's secretary, Miss Goodie – you probably met her when you arrived.'

'The one with the cuffs?'

'Yes.' Lillian grinned. 'We call her Goodie Two-Cuffs. The porter's Timpson – he's a lazy thing but the other man, Lowell, is much nicer. Then there's Richison, the maid for our floor – we have to make our own beds, by the way, but the floors are polished and the room is dusted by Richison.'

'How about the instructors?'

'You'll meet them after tea. There are three besides Mrs Stepps-Astley. Mrs O'Mara is ex-hospital – she lectures on medical topics and hygiene, that kind of thing. Miss Bell teaches the management of children.'

'Management?'

'Well, you know, like how to run the nursery, how to divide your attention among several children, how to keep domestic staff in order, and so forth. Then there's Miss Parrish, who is a dietician and nutrition expert. She gives instruction in exercise and physical energy and so forth. She's rather good fun, is Miss Parrish – had us clambering up a tree just before Christmas though I don't think Mrs Stepps-Astley quite approved.'

'And that's all?'

'There are visiting lecturers. You'll see on the timetable. I hear we get talks on psychology next year – Freud and Adler and that bunch.' Lillian said it with a dismissive wave of her fork. 'Can't make out what they're on about, myself, but there you are, Mrs Stepps-Astley thinks it's important so we have to listen.'

'I think that kind of thing is very important,' Barbara remarked, putting aside her plate. 'Is that all we get? I'm still hungry.'

'Well, there's still the rice pud to come, and you can always claim an apple. Mrs Stepps-Astley has a thing about an apple a day.'

'Keeps the doctor away?'

'No,' said Lillian, going faintly pink. 'She thinks it helps the bowels. We talk an awful lot about bowels here. Do you know, it was a word I had absolutely never used until I came here?'

'Really? We were always on about the bowels in the Brixton General.'

'Brixton General? Hospital?'

'Yes.'

'You were a nurse?'

'Yes.'

'Oh, thank the lord!' cried Lillian, leaping up. 'You can help the rest of us with this terrible medical stuff. None of us can make head nor tail of the anatomy lessons. Come on, let's get our pudding.'

Barbara followed her, secretly amused. She had realized she would have a value to her dormitory-mates. Perhaps she could wring some quid pro quo from them in return for help on the medical nursing lessons.

They finished unpacking and settling in. Lillian took her for a tour of the building, a handsome old country-house with no architectural pretensions but well-built. It suffered from the drawback of most country-houses, however. It was freezing cold the moment you walked more than a yard or two from the fire.

'In the evening,' mourned Lillian, 'if you want to listen to a radio programme or play cards or anything, you have to rush here immediately after dinner to bag a place by the fire, otherwise you perish of cold. Last comers find themselves in Outer Mongolia, furthest from the fire and almost unable to feel it at all.'

'What d'you do, wear all your outdoor clothes?'

'What we generally do is give up and retreat to the dorms. So long as you have a good supply of pennies for the meter, you can have the little fire on. It's quite cosy, really, especially if you can bribe Trudie to fill your Thermos with hot water before you come upstairs. Then you can make Camp coffee.'

To Barbara it had the sound of midnight feasts in the dorm at school, which she herself had never experienced but only read about. She had been a day girl at her various schools in India. In a way she had always felt a little envious of such boarding school escapades, but now that she was likely to experience them they had lost their appeal. She would have given almost anything to be back at Dowers Farm and its cosy nursery, with Mildred at hand to fetch a tray of cocoa when it was wanted.

As prophesied, Agnes arrived about four o'clock, rosy with the outdoors cold. She was a large-framed girl who looked older than Lillian but proved to be exactly the same age, eighteen. She brought her suitcase upstairs without the reluctant aid of Timpson and without apparently even raising her pulse rate.

''Lo,' she said in a soft voice with the trace of a country burr. 'You'll be Mrs Gray?'

'Barbara,' corrected Lillian. 'I say, Aggie, what d'you think? She's been a trained nurse –'

'Then why's she –'

'No, no, a hospital nurse! She knows all that awful stuff about veins and arteries.'

'Do you really?' Agnes said, giving Barbara a calm, appreciative stare. 'That's a turn-up, isn't it?'

'We were all sort of dreading having an older woman with us,' Lillian confided, 'but it's going to work out great, isn't it, Ag?'

'Might do,' Agnes said, and humped her case on to the bed where she began to drag out her belongings. By the looks of them, she had absolutely no idea how to care for them; everything looked as if it needed pressing and mending. 'Mother was busy,' she explained. 'We had trouble with the lambs –'

'Already?'

'Goodness, yes, lambs start arriving first few days of January. We meant to do all the mending but we just didn't get round to it.' A long account of all the work she'd had to leave undone on the farm followed; Lillian listened inattentively, making two neat piles of clothes, one to be mended or darned and one to be put away at once.

'You'd better get those blouses ironed,' she warned, 'or Mrs Stepps-Astley will put you in the corner tomorrow first thing.'

'Oh, she doesn't really –' began Barbara.

'No, no, of course not. But she can make her displeasure felt.'

'Yes, only some it doesn't bother,' Agnes said, looking with dismay at her fingers coming through the heel of a rayon stocking. 'Janice isn't here yet, I suppose?'

'You suppose right. What d'you bet she doesn't get here until lights out?'

'Which is when, exactly?' Barbara inquired.

'Nine-thirty in the downstairs rooms, ten o'clock in the bedrooms. Lowell always gives a blink on the lights before he throws the switch, so you have a couple of minutes to scramble back into your room if you're off somewhere else.'

'But suppose you can't sleep, or want to read?' Barbara suggested.

Lillian and Agnes exchanged a glance. 'Er . . . you're not allowed to read after lights out. And let me tell you,' Lillian said, 'you'll be ready to sleep once you get started on the course!'

By the time they retired that evening, Barbara was inclined to believe her. She was dropping with fatigue. She had been given her timetable, had met the resident teachers and had a short private interview with each, had listened to a welcome-back lecture from Mrs Stepps-Astley, and been introduced to about a dozen girls whose names she'd already forgotten.

As they prepared for bed the fourth occupant of the dormitory still hadn't shown up. 'She's for it,' Agnes remarked with gloom. 'Goodie Two-Cuffs will have her on the carpet in front of the Boss as soon as she shows up tomorrow.'

Barbara fell asleep on the hard bed almost at once. Some time during the night she woke with the impression that someone was moving about in the room but she was too drugged with sleep to follow the thought through.

When she woke next morning she couldn't think where she was. It took her a moment to remember she had started at college and was now in her dormitory there. She sat up, feeling for a light switch. But the bedside lamp didn't come on though she turned the switch.

'I shouldn't bother,' said a voice. 'They don't put the

current back on until seven o'clock.'

'Who's that?' Barbara said, in alarm at the strange voice.

A little battery-powered bedside lamp came on, giving a ghostly glow. In the bed unoccupied last night a dimly discernible figure was sitting up. Barbara could distinguish a head of dark curls, a slight frame in what looked like crêpe-de-Chine pyjamas.

'You must be the new inmate,' she said. 'Welcome to the booby hatch.'

'You're Janice?' whispered Barbara.

'That's me.'

'How did you get here? I thought the place got locked up at ten o'clock?'

Janice made a clicking sound with her teeth. 'You can always get in and out if you keep on good terms with Lowell.'

'But how are you going to account for your appearance? You didn't get ticked off on Miss Goodie's list yesterday.'

'Huh,' Janice said. 'Of course I'm ticked off. I saw to that before I crawled upstairs.'

'But what on earth happened to you? You were supposed to be here by tea-time.'

'Sweetie,' remarked the girl in the crêpe-de-Chine pyjamas, 'if you think I was going to spend a dull evening here when I could be out with my boyfriend in London, you must be even older than we were led to expect.'

Barbara lay back on her pillow and smiling, half-closed her eyes. Perhaps life in the dormitory was going to have its compensations after all.

CHAPTER SIX

Before classes began on that first day Barbara had time to write to the three people most interested in her future career. She wrote to Felicity telling her that she thought she might survive, but only just. To her father she said cheerfully that all was well. To her sister Eileen she was much less vague; she said firmly that the course was about to begin, that she had settled in, and felt she would soon find her feet.

Eileen was the one who had protested most at her plan. 'I don't know how you can throw that money away on an unnecessary scheme like that!' she had cried. 'You say yourself you could get a job with children without all this nonsense about getting qualified – can't you see that the money could be put to better use?'

By 'better use' Eileen meant that she should hand it over to Jimmy Letts to help him restore his financial base. It was never actually put into words, but Barbara sensed that Eileen felt she was being selfish, self-serving, by putting the windfall to the purpose of gaining a Hogarth School diploma. Barbara, always accustomed to hurrying to Eileen's aid, had had to steel herself against the silent begging. She had to keep reminding herself that Eileen had a husband to care for her, a home of her own. She, Barbara, had neither, and it was time now to make some provision for her future.

Her father disapproved of the plan to become a Nanny, but on more rational grounds. 'My dear, you could go back to hospital nursing – there's still jobs available to nurses.'

'Not for divorced nurses, Father –'

'Oh, come on, not every hospital matron is an old dragon with High Church principles. You'd find one that would take you on.'

'But the fact is, Father, I don't want to go back to hospital nursing.' She checked a sigh. She had seen so many men die in France and during her years at Brixton General. The aftermath of the War, the lung injuries due to gas, the influenza epidemic that came just after hostilities ended – it had made her almost run from the wards into Archie's arms when he came home demanding they should settle down into the home he would provide for her.

Donald Gray was willing to abide by his daughter's choice of spending the winnings. From time to time Donald himself had a flutter on a horse and he'd have thought it impertinence in anyone to tell him how to spend it. Besides, young Barbara had a right to try out her own plans. She'd had a bad enough time with that fool Archie, who'd wanted to live her life for her.

When she'd gone to stay with Felicity he'd regarded it as taking shelter. Now she was venturing out on her own. Good luck to her, was his view.

The notes she sent from time to time reported that she was getting on quite well. It was some weeks before he gathered that she was sharing a room with three other girls, which appalled Donald – but it seemed she only mentioned it because she'd at last come to terms with it.

She gave lively little word pictures of the teachers: Miss Bell peering at them through thick glasses, advising on the merits of hand-knitted vests versus Chilprufe; Miss Parrish, shepherding her students out for a run in the Surrey countryside, urging them not to care when their thick rayon stockings snagged on the blackberries; a visiting lecturer, writer of children's books, advising them how to deal with children's fantasies.

It was clear she was working hard. It also seemed she was enjoying it. Thank goodness for that.

On the whole Barbara found life at the college better than endurable. She had met the other girls in the first year class and also some of those in the second year. The third year group were an élite, off doing 'practicals' often out of the college or closely involved with children staying in the residential nursery. Children were taken in as boarders for various reasons and at various ages. The first year students could watch them playing or being taken out for walks by the third year students but were regarded as too inexperienced to have contact with them. From time to time a small group of the older children would be 'visited' – that's to say, while the children had their lessons or were told a story, the first and second year students would be allowed to join them in the schoolroom. But this was regarded as so unnatural that Mrs Stepps-Astley preferred the little guests to be left to the Nannies who had charge of them, exactly as if they were at home.

But, when you came to think of it, as Barbara remarked to herself, the only way to prove whether a girl is capable of looking after a child is to give her charge of one. And the only way to do that in controlled circumstances was to have child boarders who, poor little things, acted as guinea pigs.

'What happens if one of the third-year girls makes a hash of it?' Barbara inquired of Mrs O'Mara.

The former hospital sister gave her a cool glance from blue Irish eyes. 'And what makes you think anyone at Hogarth could ever make a hash of anything, my fine young lady?'

'By the law of averages, there must be failures, Mrs O'Mara.'

'Very few. We supervise at every stage. Let me tell you, my dear, we take a far greater interest in the Nanny–child relationship than many a mother does. If there are Nannies making a hash of things, they're far more likely to be in private households than here in the residential nursery.'

'But it's all so . . . clinical. It's not a bit like home to the child.'

'Agreed. Sure, no one's saying it's an ideal method. But the children who come here need a place to stay for one reason or another – mother's in hospital, family troubles, parents going abroad, oh, there's dozens of reasons. And you have to admit they get more attention here than they would almost anywhere else.'

'Attention, yes . . . I was thinking of affection.'

Mrs O'Mara folded her arms, leaned back in her chair, and shook her head at Barbara. 'And are you telling me you believe a girl can take sole care of a child for the whole length of its stay here – whether long or short – and not learn to be fond of it? Ah, I'm telling you, there's many a tear dampens a pillow on the night after the child leaves here, Mrs Gray.'

Although the teachers were wary of Barbara in class, where her questions sometimes took them at a loss, they weren't averse from a little conversation. Surrounded as they were by young girls, they found Barbara more on their own level. Yet she had to be wary about getting too friendly with them. Janice had remarked, rather acidly, 'It's not hard for you to be teacher's pet, is it?'

The reverse was probably true. In a reaction of trying to be completely fair to the other, less experienced students, the teachers were rather hard on Barbara. But that didn't prevent them from liking to chat with her – and that could give a wrong impression.

It was a bit like walking a tightrope. It was another complication in the life which she had chosen.

Barbara had had to pass exams to become a hospital nurse, but she hadn't enjoyed them. She wasn't academically gifted. Yet it was inevitable that she should have an advantage in some of the studies she was now undertaking. She found the facts began to come back to her from past lectures: 'During the first year the pulse rate of an infant is about 120 per minute . . . The rate of pulse is often less important than the volume . . . At the onset of acute disease the pulse may increase to 150 or more . . .' Or: 'The tonsils may be enlarged to such an extent that they meet, causing symptoms such as frequent sore throats, liability to the common cold . . .' Or: 'Anaesthetics are divided into general and local, the latter producing insensibility of one part of the body by acting on the nerve endings and are injected subcutaneously . . .'

Her dormitory-mates found her invaluable. When they had failed to get all the points down in their notebooks, Barbara could be invited to recite what she remembered so that they could make good the omissions.

They found her useful in other ways. With the exception of Janice, they turned to her for advice. Agnes usually wanted to discuss family matters: whether it would be best to take a post near her home when she left the College or whether Barbara advised a complete break (which Agnes was clearly reluctant to make).

Lillian at first asked about practical matters: where to buy shoes that combined comfort with smartness (impossible, since the current fashion was for high heels and very thin soles) or how to get starch to dissolve properly when one laundered collars and cuffs in the washbasin. But by and by something more personal came out. Lillian was incurably romantic, had been jilted by the boy she thought she was going to marry, and was now suffering – as she herself saw it – from a broken heart.

'You know what it's like to lose someone, Barbara,' she said one night over cocoa in the dorm. 'How long does it take to get over it?'

'It was different for Barbara,' Agnes put in. 'Her husband died.'

'No he didn't,' Barbara said, over the gasp of dismay this tactlessness caused in Lillian. 'I divorced him.'

'What?'

It was the first they'd heard of the divorce. Like everyone else who heard Barbara's title but noted her solitary state, they had taken it for granted she was a widow.

Janice looked at her with new respect. 'Well,' she said, 'good for you. What did he get up to?'

'I don't think it's suitable to talk about over mugs of cocoa.'

'Meaning that it needs champagne? A gay blade, was he?'

'I meant that it might give you wild dreams,' Barbara said, and heard the Nannyish tone in her own voice. She went on quickly, 'It was very dull really. He just preferred someone else.'

'And how about you, then?' Janice insisted. 'Did you retaliate?'

'Retaliate? Good heavens, no.'

'You mean it didn't occur to you?'

'Well . . . no.'

'Huh,' Janice said, 'I'd like to see the man who could walk out on me and not get his behind kicked as he went!'

'Janice!' shrieked Lillian, but in a muffled way so as not to have someone come in and complain about the noise.

'There's a lack of elegance about the words but I understand the sentiments,' Barbara confessed. 'But I didn't feel like that at the time. I was just perplexed and hurt.' She glanced at Janice, whose dark hair was pinned with Kirbigrips in a hopeless effort to discipline the unruly curls after a shampoo. 'I suppose you think that's spineless.'

'Hmm. I wouldn't say there's anything wrong with your spine. As to you,' Janice said, turning to Lillian and pointing an accusing finger at her, 'a girl with your looks doesn't have to sit around grieving for some sixth-form boy who went cavorting off. The world's full of fellows with more experience and more money than your Jonathan.'

'You don't understand,' Lillian said, with a sigh. 'He was different.'

'Oh yeah, as the Americans say in the talkies. Never met a man yet who was all that different from any other man.' Then, as Janice knelt to put her damp hair close to the fire to dry it, she gave a little secret smile. 'Not that I'm complaining, mind,' she ended.

As April came Barbara began to worry about two things. The examination was looming, at which the first year students had to prove they had taken in enough to justify letting them continue. And Easter was approaching, at which time Petey Leschallas would be coming home expecting to find her at Dowers Farm.

She telephoned Felicity from the coin-operated phone in the hall of the college. There was no problem about inviting herself to Dowers Farm for a day or two at Easter.

Or so she had thought. But oddly enough Felicity seemed strangely unwilling.

'Well, as a matter of fact, darling, we're having a lot of people to stay. The family, you know. Peter's parents, and his elder brother and sister-in-law and their two. It's a full house, you see.'

'But Felicity, I really did want just to be there . . . I could fit in somewhere, it wouldn't matter where –'

'I don't see where, darling. The house hasn't got elastic sides, like Granny's boots.' There was a weak laugh at the old joke. 'I really think we ought to leave it to some other time, Barbara.'

'But, surely you see, this time is the important one. Petey will expect me to be there – I promised him –'

'Well, you know, Barbara, I don't think the household can be organized on the basis of Petey's expectations,' Felicity said.

Barbara could hear an echo of Peter's tones in those words. She was touched by a finger of apprehension. 'Felicity,' she persisted, 'I do have to see Petey. It's important.'

'I don't see how, darling. Petey's quite big enough now to understand that you've gone away to get on with your own life. I'll explain it to him, don't you bother.'

'But I wanted to do that myself! I really only let him go to school without explaining because I thought I'd be there to tell him.'

'Of course. I see you feel it's got to be sorted out. Children do put a lot of importance on that kind of thing, I suppose. But I'll see to it, Barbara. Don't worry.'

'But Petey will –'

'Worry? No, of course not. Children forget things so quickly. In fact, by now he's probably stopped thinking about who's in charge in the nursery. Look, darling, I have people here for lunch, I must go.'

'But Felicity!'

'What, darling?'

'I really must see Petey.'

'Yes, of course, we'll fix up for you to come some other time when the house isn't so full. The summer holidays, perhaps? And of course, you're welcome any weekend you can get away – it's just that for Easter we have so many of the family coming.'

Barbara replaced the heavy receiver in its hook with a hand that trembled slightly. She understood what Felicity had been saying. She had been warned off.

She went upstairs to the dormitory instead of going into lunch. She didn't think she could talk to anyone, not just for a minute or two.

Why had Felicity been so determined not to let her come to Dowers Farm? It couldn't be that their friendship had become less. No, it was because either Felicity or Peter felt she was getting too involved with Petey. It was because Petey was to be home that she had been kept away. She was welcome at other times – Felicity had made that clear. But she wasn't to see Petey until the summer.

Instinct supplied the answer – a cruel answer. Peter and Felicity thought she was becoming too close to their eldest son. They resented it.

No, she corrected herself quickly, they were thinking of what was best for Petey. Perhaps they had understood what a wrench it had been for him to leave home for school – having to take him there and leave him in the midst of his distress must have shown them that. They were trying to spare him the hurt of seeing Barbara again, only to learn that she was no longer living at the farm.

Were they right? Was it better that Petey should come home and be told, simply, that Auntie Barbara had had to go elsewhere? She had wanted very much to explain it to him face to face – but was that only for her own comfort, to assuage her own sense of guilt at leaving him?

She didn't know. She had no idea whether she'd been right

to keep it from Petey that she wouldn't be there when he got back from school. There were a lot of things she had done that she wasn't sure of any longer. That silly fairy story about the witch's hat, for instance, it had calmed the children down, made them 'good' so that they settled to sleep. But though she'd thought of it as a jokey folk-tale, an instant invention, who could tell if serious little John had not believed it and would bother Mildred next Hallowe'en, asking to be given the hat so he could try riding on a broomstick?

No, nonsense, that was taking things too far. If you couldn't be quick and easy with children, if you couldn't be inventive at their own level but had to analyse every word before you spoke, the whole thing became impossible. So much of what she had done with the Leschallas children had been instinctive. And it seemed to have worked. That had been a happy year, for the children as well as for Barbara. Nothing could alter that fact – the children had been thriving under her care.

But she must resign herself to the fact that she wasn't to see Petey until he had 'grown out of' his need for her. Felicity or Peter – or perhaps Mildred – would explain her absence to him. She could only hope Felicity was right in her estimate of the effects – that he would shrug it off, too grown up now he was a prep schoolboy to care if a beloved figure had gone from the nursery.

Barbara got up from the side of her bed, blew her nose vigorously, blinked at herself in her wood-framed mirror a couple of times, and went down to lunch. No good would come of moping in her room and going without food, especially as the first item on the afternoon timetable was a nature walk with a local botanist to explain how to interest children in plantlife.

On the walk Barbara stopped off at Haslemere post office to send a greetings telegram to her father. Next day was his retirement day; Bolt Engineering would give him a slap-up lunch, present him with an onyx clock, let him get a bit too squiffy, and send him out in the middle of the afternoon with the contents of his desk in a briefcase to start a new life. She had no doubt he would foregather for a last party in the local bar before eventually getting back to the Bayswater flat.

Over the weekend he and Dottie would move to Banbury. The last pieces of furniture would be transferred by Pickfords. The lump sum which Donald would receive was to be invested in a small secondhand car so that he and Dottie could get around. It might end with a wedding; Barbara had a feeling her father was edging towards the idea that he and Dottie ought to regularize their somewhat casual relationship.

Barbara would have to write in a day or two to ask if she could come for Easter. It was either that or go to Eileen, now that Felicity had given her the cold shoulder. She had a feeling Dottie wouldn't be best pleased at having to offer hospitality in the tiny cottage but that was preferable to having to spend a week listening to Jimmy Letts talking non-stop about his money problems.

But before she faced the Easter holiday, she had to face the exams. And she was very scared about the exams. She always got exam nerves, which didn't help. Moreover, she disagreed so strongly with some of the things the instructors had been handing out as received truth that she didn't know if she'd be able to write the 'expected' answers which would gain marks.

In next morning's post came a letter from Felicity. At sight of her handwriting Barbara's heart leapt up – she'd relented about having her for Easter. But no, it was a loving little apology, somewhat shamefaced: 'You know we'd love to have you but really we'll be bursting at the seams, it's Pa-in-law's thirtieth wedding anniversary, we've got Ma-in-law a pearl pendant, we'll fix it for another time, good luck with the exams, love, Felicity.' The breathless style brought her friend before her mind's eye. Barbara felt a little stab of guilt at thinking badly of her.

All the same, the lesson had gone home. She had no rights over the children she looked after. It was something to remember for the future.

As so often happened with the approach of Easter, a spell of cold rainy weather set in. It even hailed. Trees round the college, which had come into bud, ceased their foolish activity. The drenched bushes in the shrubbery looked cowed and huddled. Girls walked round indoors repeating runes to themselves, or sat with tense attention over text books.

Barbara had to struggle hard to get time for her own revision. The other three in her room wanted her to go over and over the anatomy lectures but she needed to spend time on the subject known as 'child management' – a term which made Barbara's hackles rise at the outset. She went around with a copy of Dr Truby-King's book in her handbag, so that she could take it out and study. It was forbidden to take books into the dining-room, but they went everywhere else, even in the bathroom.

The examinations were to be held on the Thursday before Good Friday. There was one paper in the morning and one in the afternoon, after which everyone was expected to leave for the holiday except those few who lived so far away it was not worth their while to make the trip.

On Wednesday afternoon, Timpson the porter came into the library, also known as the silence-room, where a bevy of anxious girls was sitting over last minute revision. 'Mrs Gray?' he said in a loud whisper, looking about.

'Yes?'

He beckoned. 'Telephone,' he mouthed.

Blowing out a sigh, she obeyed the summons. What now? Perhaps it was Dottie with a good last-minute excuse to put her off from the Banbury visit.

It was, however, Eileen. 'Barbara? Thank goodness. Barbara, I just had a phone call from a man at the White Lion.'

'The what?'

'The White Lion. It's a pub –'

'Oh yes, down the road from Fairlight Cottage – yes, what?'

'He got my phone number from the operator – he

remembered Father mentioning my name.'

'Why should he need –?' Suddenly Barbara was alarmed. 'What's happened, Eileen?'

'I've no idea. This man – his name's Fisher, I think – he says Father and Dottie were in the pub a couple of nights ago and there was a long wrangle and since then Father hasn't been into the pub which is unusual, since apparently he goes every evening.'

'Yes, yes, I know that was the routine. But why is this man Fisher ringing you?'

'He thinks Father must be ill. Seems to go past the cottage on his way to and from work and says the curtains haven't been pulled back. And the milkman says no one took in the milk yesterday.'

'Oh, Lord!'

'This man Fisher . . . he wanted me to go and see what's wrong. But Barbara, I can't leave the children. And in any case, I haven't a key.'

'Neither have I.'

'Janey's got a sore throat,' Eileen hurried on, 'and my mother's-help has gone home for Easter already so I'm on my own, and I've a dinner party for two of Jimmy's important friends this evening.'

'But Eileen, I've got exams.'

'That's not till tomorrow, is it? You could nip down to Banbury and back before tomorrow.'

'But Eileen, I need the time to –'

'If you don't think it's serious, then that's all right. Only this man Fisher took the trouble to ask for my number and ring me up and seemed a bit worried so I thought –'

'They've just overslept and forgotten to open the curtains.'

'But the milk? I mean, Barbara, it's the middle of the afternoon. I could understand not wanting to open the curtains when it's pelting down outside and everything looks so miserable, but surely Dottie would take in the milk?'

Barbara wasn't even so sure of that. Trained in good

households and risen to the eminence of housekeeper so that she could if she wanted obtain good hotel work, Dottie nevertheless liked to relax totally when she was *chez elle*.

It was absurd to get in a state over nothing. 'I really can't go down to Banbury, Eileen. I have to do last-minute revision. If I fail the exam tomorrow I get thrown out.'

'Oh, you won't fail,' Eileen said, with blind faith in the ability of her elder sister to do anything. 'But if you're not anxious –?'

'Not a bit. I'm sure there's a simple explanation. They've probably gone away overnight.'

'But they're expecting you for Easter – they wouldn't go away –?'

'No, perhaps not. Still, I'm sure it's all right. Put it out of your mind, Eileen.'

'Do you think –? Only I told this Fisher that I'd see to it.'

'Well, you have. You've talked to me, and set your mind at rest.'

'All right then. If you're sure . . .'

'I'm sure, Eileen.'

'Righto. Good luck for tomorrow.'

'Thank you, dear.' She hung up, turned with purposeful manner, and headed for the silence room. But when she had got there and picked up the hated Truby-King, she found she couldn't concentrate. She pictured the cottage in Banbury, with its curtains still unopened at mid-afternoon. And the milk on the doorstep.

It meant nothing. They were a lazy pair, her father and Dottie.

If only they were on the telephone. It would be so easy to ring and make sure everything was all right.

A thought struck her. Presumably the man at the White Lion, Fisher, had knocked on the door. Surely he would have done that, just to make sure there was nothing wrong. Otherwise he wouldn't have taken the trouble to track down Eileen's telephone number. It stood to reason – you didn't pay for a telephone call to London unless you'd first done the obvious things.

Should she ring the Banbury police and ask them to check? But suppose the pair *had* gone away for a day or so and the police could get no reply . . .? Would they break in? If they did, she could imagine Dottie's indignation when she and Barbara came face to face over the weekend.

It was no good. She would have to go and see for herself.

There were no classes today; the day had been allotted for private study. She wouldn't be missed if she slipped away now. She could catch the bus at the top of the lane in fifteen minutes, be set down at Haslemere station, and be on her way in half an hour.

There was no point sitting here hesitating. Either she must go now or not at all.

She picked up her books and notebooks, walked quietly out of the library, ran upstairs, and was off down the drive in less than two minutes.

The rain beat down on her umbrella. She wished she'd had time to change into thicker shoes. The lane was muddy, her stockings soon became caked with splashes up to mid-calf.

The bus was crowded and steamy. She had to stand all the way to the station. Since she'd had to miss afternoon tea at the college, she filled in the time before the train by tussling with a chocolate machine on the platform, without success - it kept her twopence but refused to disgorge a chocolate bar.

Luck was with her in catching connections. Yet the two hour journey to Banbury from Paddington seemed to take forever. Dusk was falling as she set off in a taxi from Banbury station. She saw with some dismay that there were no lights on in the cottage when she alighted there.

She rang the newly installed electric bell. No reply. She rang again. Her foot hit something on the doorstep. She looked down. A bottle of milk.

She rang again then tried to peer through the glass panels of the door. Nothing was to be seen. She picked her way from the front to the back of the cottage, being clutched at by the twigs of rosebushes and feeling wet grass soaking her legs.

There was no bell at the back door but she knocked vigorously. No reply. She knocked with her fist, as hard as she could, so hard that she hurt her hand. But still nothing happened.

Now what should she do? Walk back into the High Street and find a policeman? And then what – what could he do?

Nothing that she couldn't do herself, she said inwardly.

She tried the handle of the back door and shook it, but it was an old oak door, far too strong to give under her efforts. But the front door had glass panels.

She went back there, picked up the milk bottle, broke one of the glass panels, put her gloved hand through the star-shaped opening she made, and turned the latch. The door opened. She cut her sleeve on the glass in withdrawing her hand but by now she was past caring about the damage to her clothes.

She stepped inside, feeling for a light switch. The little entrance passage sprang to life. She went to the room on the left hand side, the sitting-room, and put on the light. Sofa, armchairs, fireplace with ashes of a fire, drinks table with several empty glasses, an empty glass on top of the Bush radio set.

But no occupants.

She tried the room the other side of the passage. This was the kitchen-cum-dining-room. There were the remains of a meal on the table and some unwashed dishes on the drainingboard. Otherwise there was nothing remarkable to be seen.

Uncertain whether to be relieved or alarmed, she went up the steep oak staircase to the little landing. There were only two rooms upstairs: the one on the right was the main bedroom, the other was the guestroom. She put her hand on the knob of the main bedroom door. It swung open.

There was a figure sprawled on the bed, fully dressed. For one awful moment she thought her father was dead. There was something so totally lifeless about the attitude.

But then a small snore reached her ears. She rushed forward. Her foot hit an empty bottle. She looked down – a Booth's gin bottle. There was an empty glass on the bedside table. Cradled in her father's arm was another bottle, half full.

He wasn't dead, he was blind drunk.

At first she was so angry that she shook him. But it had no effect. Then her nurse's training came back to her. Yes, Donald Gray was drunk, but he seemed to have consumed at least one whole bottle of gin and half of another within the last few hours – and remembering the empty glasses downstairs, she wondered how much more.

There was such a thing as alcoholic poisoning. And though that was rather a grand name for a bender, that was what her father was suffering from. He had to be brought round. Moreover, she had to find out what had caused this outbreak, and prevent him from getting drunk again when the effects of this one had worn off.

It took her a long time to get him into a semi-reclining position on the pillows of the bed. Then she went down for a glass of mustard and water, at the same time putting on the percolator for lots of black coffee.

There was no possibility of returning to the Hogarth School in time for the exams.

CHAPTER SEVEN

By the early hours of the morning Donald was conscious enough to know that he was being helped into bed, and by whom.

'What you doing here?' he mumbled, gazing at his daughter. He looked much older, strangely vulnerable without his glasses, and quite ill.

'I'm looking after you,' Barbara replied. 'Come along now, under the covers.'

'God, I feel awful.'

'No doubt.'

He sank back into his bed. She brought the covers up to his chin.

'How long have you been here?'

'Since about eight o'clock last night.'

'Last night . . . What day is it?'

'Thursday, by now.'

'Umm.' He put up a shaky hand to his head. 'I've got a terrible headache.'

'Try and take these aspirins, then –'

'Ugh!' He turned his head away. She understood that the mere thought made him feel sick. 'I could do with a hair of the dog that bit me.'

'No, come along, you've had more than enough.' She had taken away the bottles, both empty and half-empty. But the room still had the smell of too much gin.

'I could take the aspirin if I had a drink to swallow them.'

'I'll fetch you a glass of water.'

'Barbara, I need a drink.'

'No you don't. You need some proper sleep and some food. Close your eyes and try to nod off.'

'I can't while my head's banging away like this –'

'Then take the aspirin.'

He groaned. She poured water into a glass, helped him to take two aspirins and a sip of water. She saw him looking about for the gin.

'I took it downstairs,' she said.

'Oh.' A pause. 'Off you go and get some sleep,' he said. 'The spare bed is made up.'

Oh yes. And the minute she closed the door of the other room he'd be off downstairs for the bottle. 'No, I'll sit with you,' she said.

He was really not well enough to argue. He closed his eyes and after a while, probably to his own surprise, he went off into a normal sleep.

When he woke again it was about eight in the morning. Barbara had slept in the chair by the bed but very badly, so that she'd been glad to tiptoe downstairs around six and make herself some tea. When she heard him stirring she came back up to his room.

'How d'you feel?'

'I think I may live.'

'Could you eat some breakfast?'

He grimaced, but after a moment said he thought he could manage some toast and coffee.

'I'll bring it up in two ticks.' She opened the bedroom curtains so he could see the daylight, then went to the kitchen. When she came back he was sitting up looking more himself. 'Now,' she said. 'What happened? Where's Dottie?'

He let her settle the tray on his knees before he replied. 'She left me,' he said in a flat tone. 'She said she didn't think she could stand country life and left.'

'Oh!' Barbara recovered from the surprise in a moment. 'It's only because the weather's been so awful. She'll be back.'

'No she won't. She's got the offer of a job in Bristol. She took all her things.'

'When was this?'

'What day's today?'

'Thursday.'

'She told me she didn't like the cottage on Monday evening. We had a bit of an argy-bargy in the pub. When we came home she suddenly came out with this about the Bristol hotel. I was furious, I can tell you – negotiating for a job behind my back!'

'So you had an even bigger row?'

'You might say so. We'd both had a drop, you know. I suppose I thought it would be all right again in the morning but when I got up, I found she'd gone. Her clothes were gone. I . . . er . . . I . . .'

'You had a drink to console yourself, I suppose?'

'Well, it was a shock, Barbara. I never thought she'd do that after all these years. I mean, we were even talking about getting married . . .'

So he'd been drinking practically nonstop for two days. No wonder he'd been in such a bad state. She watched him nibble dry toast and sip coffee, and couldn't help feeling a strong sympathy for him. Poor father . . . what would he do without Dottie?

One thing he mustn't do was get into the habit of drowning his sorrows in the gin bottle. He had always been fond of a drink, but until now he'd never lost himself in it so thoroughly.

After he had eaten he had another little doze. Then he said he thought he'd get up and shave. 'I feel like a haystack,' he said, scratching three days' growth.

Luckily he used a safety razor so wouldn't nick himself with his trembling hand. He came downstairs looking shaky but in command of himself. She had done the washing up and tidied the place, so she settled him by the fire with the radio while she got lunch going.

He ate quite well from the meal she provided – a plain omelette followed by a milk pudding. Afterwards she said she thought they ought to go out for some fresh air. 'Um,' he said without enthusiasm, 'I don't feel much like it.'

'Just a little stroll, Father.' She wanted to break up the day a little.

They were on their way back when a man in a sports jacket and baggy flannel trousers hailed them. 'There you are, Mr Gray. Haven't seen you for a bit.'

'Hello, Fisher. I've been a bit under the weather.' He nodded at Barbara. 'You haven't met my daughter, I believe.'

'Mrs Letts?'

'No, I'm Mrs Gray.'

'Oh, the other one. Everything all right?'

'Yes, thank you, everything's fine.'

'We might drop in this evening to see you, Fisher,' Donald said. 'Fisher works in the White Lion, Barbara.'

'Oh yes? Well, we might see you.'

Donald went in at the gate of the cottage. Barbara lingered to say thank you to Fisher. 'He was in a bad state. It's a good thing you got in touch.'

'Knew somebody'd turned up when I saw the lights on last night. Need any help?'

'Not just at the moment, but thanks for the thought.'

'Come on, Barbara, don't keep Fisher hanging about in the cold,' her father called.

She went indoors. The fire needed making up, and as she attended to it her father said suddenly, 'How did you come to be here last night, anyhow?'

'Fisher rang Eileen to say you hadn't been around. He was worried.'

'But Eileen didn't come –'

'Well, she has the children. It was easier for me.'

'You got in by breaking the glass? Is that what that hole is?'

'Yes, Father.' She scrambled up from her knees. 'We'd better get someone to come and put in another pane.'

'Um,' Donald said. He settled himself into an armchair with a shrug, felt about for his pipe. Then he said, 'Didn't you have an exam today?'

'Never mind that. What d'you think you'd like for dinner?

There's not too much in the larder – it'll have to be something out of tins.'

'Barbara – you did have an exam!'

'Yes, but it's not important. Let's think about dinner. If you can think of something you really fancy, I'll nip out to the High Street and get it. How about a piece of steak?'

'Do stop nattering about food, Barbara! What about that exam?'

'Well, I've missed it, haven't I?'

'Because you came here –? Oh, hell . . .'

'It doesn't matter, really it doesn't.'

'Yes it does. Stop burbling. You told me only a couple of weeks ago that if you failed it meant you'd be tossed out. What happens if you don't take it at all?'

'I've no idea. I'll have to inquire when I get back.'

'Why don't you hurry back now? It's still only early afternoon –'

'I missed the first paper. I don't think I'd be in time for the second. Don't let's bother about it, Father.'

'Oh, Barbara.' He leaned forward and took her hand. 'What a damned nuisance. The last thing I wanted was to get in your way like this.'

'It's not the end of the world, after all.' She gave his hand a squeeze and turned away. They had never been able to express emotion to each other. 'What about dinner? Shall I go out for some steak?'

'No, let's make do with what we've got. I don't feel much like steak.'

It was a pity, because if he'd agreed she could have gone out and while she was shopping she could have phoned the college. But she didn't like to leave him unless he sounded more himself. So she sat with him listening to the BBC Dance Orchestra and then a quartet from the Hotel Cecil playing 'The Wedding of a Rose' and other hotel-lounge music. He nodded off in his chair after a while. She left him to find something suitable for dinner, which she served early.

When they had eaten and she had cleared away, he said, 'Let's go down to the pub for an hour, Barbs.'

'Oh . . . I don't think . . .'

'It's all right, I'm not going to soak it up. It's just . . . I like it there. And I rather think I owe them an apology for causing a hoo-ha the other night.'

It was true that Mr Fisher, the barman, seemed to regard Donald as a friend. Perhaps it would do him good to be with people who liked him. 'All right,' she said, and was about to add, 'Just one drink, mind,' but thought better of it.

The saloon bar of the White Lion was a friendly place. Donald was greeted with nods and smiles by one or two regulars and with a broad grin from Mr Fisher. 'Well, what'll it be, eh?'

'I think I'll stick to pale ale tonight, Fisher. And a dry sherry for my daughter.'

When they had their drinks one or two acquaintances murmured that they hadn't seen Donald for a day or two. No one except Fisher seemed to know there had been any sort of crisis. 'He's a nice man,' Barbara thought to herself. Later, when he took the chance of a word with her, she explained that Dottie – Mrs Fleming – had gone, apparently for good.

'So that was it?'

'He was upset.'

'I quite see that. Well, well. That means he's all alone in the cottage then.'

''Fraid so.'

'And after him making such plans for his retirement an' all. That's rotten.'

'Makes it difficult,' she confided, 'because I don't think he's very good at being on his own.'

'Who is?' Fisher said with a rueful grin, and moved off to collect the empties.

When Barbara let it be seen that she felt they ought to go, Donald rose without demur. They walked home in the dark night of the country lanes.

'I used to quite enjoy this part of it,' he said, sounding mournful. 'It was nice to have Dottie clutching my arm.'

There was nothing to say to that.

They spent the rest of the evening reading, Donald with the evening paper they'd bought in the High Street, Barbara with a book. She made him go to bed early. He was being extremely good, extremely docile; she knew his conscience was troubling him. But how long would it last when he was on his own in the cottage?

She was preparing to lock up when the doorbell rang. Surprised, she went to answer it, to find the friendly barman on the doorstep. 'Mrs Gray,' he said, 'hope this isn't too late. I'm on my way home from work. I had an idea, y'see. Over what you said – about him not being good at living by himself.'

'Do come in, Mr Fisher. Can I get you a drink? Cup of tea?'

'No, thanks, the missus'll be expecting me. Look, Mrs Gray, I was thinking – he'll need someone to sweep and clean and that.'

'A daily help – yes.'

'I was wondering . . . how about my sister?'

'Your sister? Is she available for that kind of thing?'

'Well, she's out of a job, y'see. Worked at the egg-packing station but they've cut down. She and Mr Gray knows each other. They've met in the Lion. She . . . I mean, she quite likes him.'

'Oh yes?' Barbara said, trying to picture the lady.

'All above board, o'course. It's just he's bought her a drink or two. She thinks he's a real gent – which he is.'

'It's very nice of you to –'

'I wondered if I could tell her to drop around tomorrow, like? See if the idea of having her do for him is all right. She . . she's got a bit of sense, see. She wouldn't need it spelt out to her, about Mr Gray and Mrs Fleming.'

She couldn't exactly refuse. And in any case, perhaps it would be a help. 'Thank you, Mr Fisher.'

Lily Fisher arrived while they were eating breakfast next

morning. 'I know I'm early,' she exclaimed when she was ushered in, 'but I just wanted to inquire after you, Mr Gray. Ted said you were under the weather –?'

'I'm quite all right now, thanks, Lily.'

'Er . . . Thought I'd mention – the shops are closed today, being Good Friday. 'Cept the fish shop. I'm just going there, afore all the best bits go. Shall I fetch you summat for your lunch?'

'Oh, thank you, that'd be such a help.' The larder was beginning to look like the one in Hansel and Gretel.

'Shall I just buy what looks good?'

'Yes, please, enough for two. I'll give you the money.'

'Pay me when I've bought it.' She bustled off, looking like a plump green apple in her green mac.

'She's a good soul,' Donald remarked with a smile and a sigh. 'It's just like her to come hurrying round trying to be helpful.'

'You know her?'

'Oh, quite well,' he said. He went on to mention one or two anecdotes of getting to know the regulars at the White Lion. He had been dropping in there for quite a time before he moved into the cottage, making a point of visiting it each time he came to see how the renovations were getting on. Dottie's flight had marred his dream of settling comfortably into the neighbourhood.

By the time Lily reappeared with what she described as 'lovely bits of turbot' he had talked himself into thinking she was one of the main attractions of the place. He welcomed her heartily and when she said she'd be glad to help if ever there was anything she could do, it seemed a small step to asking if she'd like to take on the housework.

'Couple of hours a day,' he said coaxingly, 'suit yourself what time you come, morning or afternoon.'

Lily, who had been angling for just such an invitation, had enough sense to seem unwilling. 'Well, I dunno . . . They might start taking on at the egg station –'

'If they do, of course you'd go,' Donald said. 'Shouldn't expect you to do anything else – your own interests come first, of course. But meanwhile . . . it would be such a help to me . . . You see, my daughter can't really stay here for ever.'

'No, o'course, she's got her own family to think of.'

Barbara didn't disillusion her on that score. It ended with Lily offering to come next day from ten till two, thereby including the provision of lunch in her duties.

'Don't you worry your head about him,' she said in a whisper as Barbara was seeing her out. 'I'll see he gets at least one good meal a day, and if I can put something in the oven, or do a salad, he can have that in the evening, see?'

'Thank you, Miss Fisher, you're awfully kind.'

'Not at all,' Lily Fisher said, blushing a little. It was quite clear she was not at all unhappy at having the chance to look after Donald Gray.

Donald seemed to perk up quite considerably too at the thought of the new arrangement. 'Now you don't have to stop here worrying about me,' he said. 'Just you take yourself off to the college and see what can be done about those exams you missed.'

'I'll go first thing in the morning, then, if you're sure it's going to be all right.'

'Certainly, certainly. Goodness me, I'm not going to break my heart over Dottie, if that's what you're thinking. Ungrateful little minx! But it's no use being cross about it, the thing is to look to the future.'

Quite right. Barbara was pleased to see him so determined to make a new start. She left next morning with a certain sense of equanimity. Everything might settle down quite well.

But as she neared Haslemere the equanimity evaporated. She had yet to face Miss Stepps-Astley. She had put through a phone call yesterday, been greeted by the hall porter with the news that Mrs Stepps-Astley was at church, and had left a message of apology. Now she was going to have to explain her behaviour.

The college seemed almost empty when she walked up the drive. There were children playing on the lawn at the back of the residential nursery and three or four girls on duty looking after them, but the hall was deserted. Even Timpson was nowhere about.

She walked across the echoing parquet floor, aware that she was not looking her best. Her coat had got very wet on her journey to Banbury and needed a visit to Achille Serre to be pressed. Her shoes had not recovered either and looked as if they never would. She hadn't had a change of clothes with her when she hurried away so her pale blouse was rather grimy by now and her skirt was creased.

She tapped on the door of the office. 'Come in,' called Miss Goodie. She entered. The secretary looked at her with surprised disapproval. 'So there you are, Mrs Gray.'

'I rang yesterday and left a message. Did Timpson pass it on?'

'He did. Mrs Stepps-Astley found it rather incomplete.'

'Well, I didn't want to go into a long explanation with Timpson. There was a family crisis. May I speak to Mrs Stepps-Astley?'

'Wait here and I'll see whether you can be spared a moment.'

Miss Goodie got up, went to the door of the inner office, tapped, and went in. Her very back expressed disapproval. She returned after what seemed to Barbara a very long time.

'You may go in,' she said, holding the door open.

Barbara passed her and went into the presence. Mrs Stepps-Astley was sitting at her desk, on which the exam papers of Thursday were ranged in little piles. She was clearly in the middle of marking.

She raised her iron grey head, put on her pince-nez, and surveyed Barbara.

'Well, Mrs Gray? Explain yourself!'

Barbara had rehearsed it to herself on the train. 'I got a phone call from my sister to say that my father seemed to have been taken ill.' She explained about the unopened curtains, the milk not taken in. She described finding Donald unconscious. She refrained from saying that he had been dead drunk. There followed a brief summary of nursing him back to normality.

'And, pray, what did the doctor say was wrong?'

'I didn't call a doctor.'

'You didn't?'

'No.'

'So it was nothing very serious, after all. Would you explain why you didn't think fit to let us know where you had gone?'

Because I didn't like to leave him in case he went straight back to the bottle. But she couldn't say that aloud. 'The cottage is not on the telephone,' she said.

Mrs Stepps-Astley sniffed. 'And there is no other form of communication, of course – no letter service, no telegrams.'

'I'm sorry, I did ring as soon as I got the chance to go into the post office. But you were at church.'

'Naturally, since it was Good Friday. But by then, in any case, you had been gone for over twenty-four hours. And you had missed the exams.'

'I want to talk to you about that.'

'Do you indeed! There is nothing to say, however. You know the terms on which I accepted you for the college, Mrs Gray – you were to fit in in every way, you were to pass the exams. I'm afraid you've failed on both counts.'

'That's not true!' Barbara burst out. 'No one could say I failed to fit in with the other students. Have you had a single complaint?'

'From the students, no. But I have complaints of my own. No other gel would have rushed away without a word to anyone, on the very eve of her exams. No other gel would have failed to send word of her whereabouts. Did it not occur to you, Mrs Gray, that we would be worried?'

Barbara was checked. That had not occurred to her at all. 'But Timpson told you I had had an urgent phone call.'

'He did, quite so, but you left no word of any kind. Even a

note would have been a help.'

'I'm sorry. I see I should have done so, but I was in a hurry to catch the bus.'

'Leaving all that aside, there is still the matter of the exams. You have failed –'

'I have not!' Barbara interrupted. 'I haven't even taken them!'

Mrs Stepps-Astley fingered the gold pince-nez. 'Exactly. You have had a very good excuse to avoid them, have you not?'

'You mean, you think I made all this up?' Barbara was aghast.

'I don't say that. But you certainly didn't hurry back once your father had been taken care of. It seems very odd to me that you didn't summon a doctor.'

'I told you, that wasn't necessary –'

'No, because then you would have had no excuse to linger there. You could have come back in time for –'

'I couldn't. It was out of the question.'

'You are asking me to accept your version of the story without any proof at all, whereas to me it seems quite apparent that you rushed away –'

'I admit I rushed away. I got word from my sister that something had happened to my father.' Barbara almost banged the desk with her fist. 'Good gracious, what did you expect me to do? And what are we being trained for here? Isn't it to take responsibility?'

'That is quite true, but –'

'A trained Nanny ought to be able to deal with a crisis without darting from one person to another asking for permission. Supposing a child were to be taken ill, would you want me to consult the butler, the cook and the chambermaid before I sent for the doctor?'

'That is a very inexact comparison. You took it upon yourself –'

'Yes, I did,' Barbara cried, too tired and confused to rein in her anger. 'I took it upon myself to hurry off because I thought my father's life might be in danger. I –'

'But it wasn't –'

'No, but on the other hand he needed me. Things might have gone badly if I hadn't turned up. Don't let's go on about that, anyhow – that's over and done with. I assure you it won't happen again.'

'No certainly not, because you will have left the college.'

'That's unfair! Surely you would let another student go if her family needed her?'

'There's still the point about the exams, which you have failed.'

'How can I have failed when I haven't even taken them?'

'It's my opinion you haven't taken them because you knew you'd fail!'

Angrier than she had ever been in her life, Barbara leaned over the desk, twitched from in front of the Director one of the cyclostyled question papers, and read out the first question: Describe a schedule for a one-month infant and comment.

'The most usual schedule for an infant of one month is the four-hourly schedule,' Barbara recited. 'This is considered desirable whether the child is fed by breast or with a formula of cow's milk or other milk specially prepared. Breast milk is the food intended by nature for the infant so that if possible the mother should be encouraged to persevere even if there are problems at first. The infant generally digests a feed in the span of about four hours but on occasions crying, due to indigestion, has led to the idea that the infant requires another feed. It is therefore recommended –'

'Mrs Gray!' cried the Director, holding up a hand. 'That is of course very impressive, but it was quite easy to foresee what the first question might be and to prepare for that.'

'The child's wish for independence: Show examples and suggest how to deal with these, either by encouraging or discouraging. A child in its fifth or sixth year,' Barbara announced, having selected the fourth question at random, 'will wish to show that it can fit in with the world around it without help from parents or other guides. At this stage a child sometimes goes through a phase where it does not wish to be kissed. It may not wish to be dressed according to the taste of others, and may seem to enjoy getting dirty so as to show independence. Other expressions of this spirit are: determination to have its own way over such things as food, the choice of toys, the time to sleep. Certain questions are so serious that the child may not be left to judge for itself; for example, behaviour towards traffic in a busy street. But over such matters as clothes and toys, the building up of antagonism is perhaps a waste of energy. Lenience should be shown towards these –'

'Thank you, Mrs Gray,' Mrs Stepps-Astley said loudly. 'I believe you have shown you could answer at least some of the questions on the child-management paper. Whether you would do so well on the medical paper is another matter.'

'If you let me do them both, you'll find out, won't you?'

'Let you do them?'

'Why not? You haven't marked the papers yet, as far as I can see. If I can be allowed to do them today, surely –'

'You mean, sit alone?'

'With someone to watch over me, of course,' Barbara flashed, 'to make sure I didn't cheat.'

'My dear Mrs Gray,' said Mrs Stepps-Astley, 'naturally there would be an invigilator if you sat the exams. But it would be most irregular.'

'There's no law against it, surely?'

'No, not exactly.'

'Suppose someone was ill – there must be occasions when special arrangements apply?'

'Well . . . yes . . .'

'If I could take those papers today,' Barbara said, 'before you've finished marking the others – what difference would my having taken them separately make?'

'None, I suppose. But the question is, should I allow it?'

Barbara drew a deep breath. 'I hope you will,' she said, and waited.

Once more she heard the wall clock ticking loudly, just as she had done at that first interview with the Director. She stood looking at her dampstained shoes, not daring to meet Mrs Stepps-Astley's eye.

She heard the Principal clear her throat.

'Hm . . . Very well, Mrs Gray. Go upstairs and change. Lunch will be served in half an hour. I expect you to be ready to sit the exams at half-past one. Two hours is allowed for each paper. In fairness to you I will ask you to do the first immediately after lunch and the second after the afternoon tea break. If you prefer you can take the second after dinner, but in my opinion that is very late. What do you say?'

'I should like to take both papers in the afternoon.'

'That is agreed then. Miss Goodie will invigilate. Be ready at one-thirty.'

So at one-thirty Barbara found herself sitting in the ground floor lecture room, with Miss Goodie – minus her sateen cuff-guards – at a desk at the far end. The first paper was handed to her on the stroke of half-past one.

The odd thing was, she was so eager to show Mrs Stepps-Astley she could do it that she quite forgot to be nervous.

CHAPTER EIGHT

After the first surprise, there was an unexpectedly calm acceptance of Barbara's survival at the school.

'Good gracious, we all thought you'd get the push,' Peggy told her as they unpacked at the beginning of the new term.

Barbara explained that there had been a family emergency, that she had taken her exams after she got back with Miss Goodie on guard.

'Oh, we might have known they'd make special arrangements for you,' said Janice, still thinking along the lines of 'teacher's pet'.

The exam results had been posted to the students during the Easter break. Barbara had got hers at her father's cottage in Banbury to which she'd returned on Easter Monday. She had passed with rather good marks although Miss Bell had noted: 'Handwriting needs attention.'

Her father, she was pleased to see, was settling down quite happily in his single state, enjoying the ministrations of Lily Fisher. Barbara dropped in on Eileen on her way back to the school to report to her that Dottie had gone but that all was well.

'Oh, she's cleared off?' Eileen said, with obvious satisfaction. She had never liked Dottie.

The way seemed clear for Barbara to devote her mind to the rest of her training. This was just as well, because now it became more demanding. The 'practicals' became very detailed; they embarked on cookery courses to complement their work on nutrition, besides learning how to tempt the appetites of invalid and convalescent children.

There was also the laundry course, which began with plain soap and water then went on to all kinds of variations. The reasoning behind all this was explained to them: Nannies trained at the school were likely to go with families all over the world, where conditions varied wildly, wherefore it was necessary that the Nanny should be able to keep her nursery spick and span and her charges clean and healthy.

'That's all very well,' groaned Janice as for the seventh time she took a Primus stove to pieces for cleaning, 'but surely there would be servants to do all this?'

'You can take nothing for granted,' Miss Parrish interjected, having overheard this complaint. 'What if you were in the situation of a family I worked for in Kashmir, when all the servants ran away during religious riots? Let me tell you, hot food and clean clothes become very important to children when everything else is going to pot. So stop moaning and get that burner clean.'

'They'll be teaching us to light a fire by rubbing two sticks together next,' whispered Janice when Miss Parrish had walked on.

There was the same intense thoroughness when it came to needlework and dressmaking. Housework was a subject that never seemed to end. By the time the summer holidays came, Barbara was so tired of taking down nursery cots and putting them up again that she was prepared to run a mile next time she saw one.

Eileen had invited her to stay at their flat in Holland Park. They were between mother's-helps, one girl having finished her stint and gone home and her successor having failed to turn up.

Eileen was now in her mid-twenties but still looked about eighteen, much to her annoyance. It wasn't fashionable to look eighteen; the mode of the moment was for the sultry experienced woman of the world after the style of Greta Garbo, or the elegance of Gertrude Lawrence.

'You're far more in fashion than I am,' Eileen sighed as they put away Barbara's clothes in the wardrobe. 'How do you manage to keep so slim? It isn't fair! You used to tell me my curves were puppy fat, but I've stopped being a puppy and

I've still got curves!'

'Why don't you follow this new idea and go on a diet?'

'I've tried that. I'm sick of grapefruit! Oh well,' Eileen ended, 'perhaps curves will come back into fashion in the winter. I've arranged for us to get tickets to Harrods' show – I hear they've got lovely things by Patou and Germaine Lecompte.'

'Eileen, you can't afford to buy clothes by Patou.'

'No, but it costs nothing to look, does it?'

'I suppose not. But who's supposed to look after Janey and William while we're at a fashion show?'

'Oh, we'll manage. Florence will take them for a couple of hours.' Florence was a neighbour, with two children of her own.

So the holidays passed pleasantly, with occasional outings to the big stores which Eileen adored so much, and trips to the seaside with the children. 'A bit hard,' Jimmy sighed as they strolled along the sands at Bournemouth. 'If we hadn't had to sell that place in Cannes to raise cash, we could have been lying in the Mediterranean sun now.'

'But would the children have enjoyed it any the more?'

'Trust you to think of that, Barbara. I'm not thinking so much of the kids as myself. This Depression's making me curtail my activities an awful lot.'

Barbara made sympathetic noises. But she couldn't help thinking there were people in Britain whose activities were 'curtailed' more harshly than Jimmy's. Jimmy could still afford to drive his family to Bournemouth for the day, he still lived in a very pleasant building a few minutes' walk from a green and open park, his wife could stroll through Harvey Nichols in Knightsbridge and ponder on buying for the winter a ponyskin coat costing almost a hundred and twenty guineas.

Coming back to London had been a minor shock to Barbara. Out in Surrey, there had been less sign of the hardships of the Depression. Haslemere was a bit of a backwater – horses and carts were still more common there than motor lorries, and if men were out of work they had their little plots, their hens and fruit trees to help make ends meet.

But in the big city the misery was out in the open. In the poorer areas, men hung about on street corners sharing a Woodbine. You could see queues outside the Labour Exchanges. One of the things that had struck deepest into Barbara's heart was to see a group of men in threadbare suits, their boots cracked and mended but scrupulously clean, singing in the gutter for coppers. Their strong Welsh voices, raised in perfect harmony as they competed with the noise of the traffic in their rendering of 'Land of Our Fathers', lingered still in her memory.

Yet in Jimmy's household there was very little evidence of hard times. The cook-general still used butter wholesale in her cooking, the charwoman still came every day, there were still flowers in every room and the *Bystander,* the *Tatler* and the *Illustrated London News* still graced the coffee table.

'You have to keep up appearances,' Eileen explained. 'The worst thing is to let people know you're struggling. It's – like an infection. If once anyone suspects things aren't going well, they start to steer clear of you – at least that's what Jimmy says. So we have to go on just as we always did, as much as possible.'

'But what happens when the bills come in?' asked Barbara.

Eileen shrugged. 'We pay the ones we absolutely have to. But you know, Barbara – shops and things are struggling too. They don't want to lose customers. It's always possible to keep them happy by paying a bit on account and letting the bill run on.'

'Duckie, isn't it a bit nerve-racking?'

'I'd like it better if we had as much as we seem to have,' Eileen admitted. 'But Jimmy says things have got to improve soon.'

Prosperity is just around the corner . . . It was the rallying cry of the politicians and financiers. But the corner seemed to be so big that Barbara began to suspect they were really going round in circles.

On a bright September day Eileen and Jimmy had an engagement to go to the races with friends. Barbara had volunteered to take care of the children for the day. She was quite glad of the chance to be on her own with them. Although she loved her sister, she found her way of life not quite to her liking, and her husband struck her as being so sharp he was going to cut himself. So to have the pleasure of seven or eight hours at her own dictates was something she looked forward to.

Jane and William were small enough to need a nap after lunch. When they woke, she decided to take them for a stroll in the park. She put William in the pram, tied Janey's straw hat under her chin, put on her own hat and gloves, and set off. Already her mind was ranging forward to next term at the training school. The year began next week. They would go on from 'practical' to 'theory' – she looked forward to it enormously. At last they were going to come to grips with the new teaching on child character-formation; they would have lectures on Freud, Adler, Jung et al. She had been reading some Freud and found him very scary. Could it possibly be true that a small baby, unable to communicate except by crying, still began to have emotional responses to its mother?

She settled on a bench in the shade, took William out of the pram harness and let him sit on the grass with his teddy bear. Janey began to collect daisies. Another small girl joined her. Peace reigned.

'Good heavens,' said a voice, 'it's – Barbara!'

She looked up from the children. Her husband, Archie Harris, was standing at the other end of the bench in the act of raising his hat.

'Archie!'

'Fancy seeing you!' He hesitated, then sat down, easing the crease of his trousers as he did so. He had always been careful about his tailoring. 'You don't mind if I sit down?'

What could she say but 'No, of course not'?

She and her ex-husband had had almost no communication

since the divorce was made absolute. It had been necessary to give him an address to which any letters could be forwarded, and that address of course had been Felicity's. When she left Dowers Farm it had not occurred to her to let him know since nothing had been sent on after a few Christmas cards.

This wasn't to say she hadn't thought of him from time to time. She had seen the announcement of the birth of Helen's child and had felt a pang of disconsolate envy.

'How are you?' she said now, politely.

'Not bad at all, as you can see. You look well, Barbara.' He eyed her with approval, and she was suddenly glad she had put on her pale blue shantung dress and matching hat.

'I'm fine, thanks. What brings you to Town?'

'Award dinner of *Kinematograph Weekly* – best cinema manager of the year. Oh, not me,' he added as he saw her about to offer congratulations. 'I'm just up for the fun, really. And to meet a few fellow managers and hear how they're coping in these hard times.'

'Are you finding audiences are small?'

'Funnily enough, quite the opposite. Seems as if folk need the escape of a really good flick. Have you seen any of these big new musicals that are coming over? I get queues for the evening performances . . . No, it's not getting people in that's the problem, it's costs that are worrying me. But you don't want to hear about that.' He glanced at the children playing on the lawns. 'Your sister's?'

'Two of them are Eileen's. I'm staying with her for the summer.'

'You . . . er . . . haven't got married again?'

'No, I decided against it.'

'Had offers, you mean?'

As always used to be the case, she was irritated by the way he seemed to want to know everything about her life. He had always wanted to take charge. Why had it rubbed her up the wrong way? It was accepted that the man was the head of the household – she ought not to have found it displeasing to be 'looked after'.

She inquired after the baby and was told the little boy was now toddling. 'I think he takes after me,' Archie said, 'he's always on the go. But he's not as fit as I'd like . . . Well, kids go through a bad time when they're teething, don't they – everybody says so.'

'A lot depends on the baby,' she replied. 'Of course the gums are very tender but some children feel distress for only –'

'A lot you know about it,' Archie interrupted with irritation.

'Well, in fact, I do.' She was stung by the dismissive tone. 'As a matter of fact, I'm training to be a children's nurse.'

'You're what?'

She hadn't meant to tell him. It was none of his business. She'd meant to end the conversation as soon as possible because, no matter how much she'd thought she'd put it all behind her, it still hurt to think he had broken up their marriage.

'I'm at a training college for nursery nurses.'

'What, here?' He gestured around at the park and the neighbourhood.

'No, it's a residential college in Surrey. We're on the summer break at the moment.'

'A residential college?' He eyed her with amazement. 'You mean, like being back at school?'

'Yes.'

'Good Lord! What a funny idea!'

'It's not funny at all. It's a very good and interesting career when you finish the training.'

'No, but I mean, fancy having to train for it. I always understood it was instinctive with women, looking after kids.' His dark eyes were bright with interest. He was clearly intrigued by this new view of Barbara, embarking on a career when he had more or less written her off. 'You have to pay for this training?'

'Of course.'

'I don't understand it. I thought you learned how to look

after kids by doing it.'

'That used to be the way. But modern methods –'

'Modern methods! Listen to the girl! There's only one method of bringing up children and that's to keep 'em healthy and teach 'em sense.'

She laughed. 'Well, it comes to that in the long run, I suppose. It's just how you go about it, I suppose.' To turn the conversation she said at last, 'How . . . er . . . how's Helen?'

He shrugged. 'Quite well. She's expecting again, actually.'

Despite all she could do, Barbara couldn't keep an expression of polite interest pinned on her face at the news. She said, rather stilted: 'How nice. Are you pleased?'

'Of course. That's what I married for, after all, isn't it?' He must have realized how tactless this was because he went on, 'Helen wants a family, just as much as I do, but we're pleased about this one because it'll be a companion for Dickie.'

'Yes, that'll be lovely.'

'It was a shame about us,' Archie went on almost as if to himself. 'We wanted the same thing, really, didn't we? But somehow it never happened. You did understand, didn't you, Barbara?'

She had come to understand in the long days after she left Archie. He had felt his masculinity was called in question by their failure to produce children. He had always taken it for granted, when speaking of it, that Barbara was to blame, that she was unable to conceive; but behind it all, she understood now, had been the fear it was some lack in him that accounted for it.

Hence the proving of his masculinity with other women, and hence in the end the resulting pregnancy of Helen. Helen, in her own words, had 'been caught' – somehow it had always seemed to Barbara that she wasn't entirely delighted at finding herself an expectant mother but, since it was a risk that was always present in any love affair, she'd had to face the fact that there was a baby on the way.

Although Archie had been perplexed and alarmed, he'd been

pleased too. He was the father of Helen's child. He had proved himself as a man. Once and for all it was established that their childlessness was Barbara's fault.

So there had been a double blow for Barbara when he came asking for a divorce. There was the feeling of shock that their marriage had come to this – and there was the fact that another woman had been able to give him what he wanted, proving Barbara's inadequacy.

She thought she'd overcome all that in the months since the divorce. But now it all came flooding back at his words.

'It's all in the past, Archie,' she said in a shaky voice. 'There's no point in harking back to it now.'

'I suppose not. Only, seeing you again . . .' He let the words die away. He couldn't exactly say, 'I realize you're a damn pretty woman and I was a fool to let you go.' Even if it was true, he knew Barbara would break off the conversation at once and walk away. Her sense of honour would force her to do that; she'd feel he owed it to Helen to be loyal to her.

'How's Eileen these days?' he inquired. Not that he cared. He'd never liked Barbara's younger sister, probably because Eileen had never liked him. But it was a safe topic.

'Oh, as pretty as ever. Of course times are hard for Jimmy at the moment. Gambling on the Stock Exchange is a risky business.'

He glanced at the Brabingham pram, with its shiny coach-built appearance. He looked at Jane pottering about among the flowers in her smocked frock from the Army and Navy Stores.

'They don't look as if they're going without anything,' he observed.

'Oh no. They get along pretty well. They're off keeping up contacts with important friends at Sandown today – that's the way it's done, mainly.'

They sat in the quiet sunshine chatting until it was time to take the children home for nursery tea. 'I'll walk with you,' Archie said. 'I don't have to get ready for tonight's affair until sevenish.'

There was no denying it was rather enjoyable to stroll through the park with a handsome man at her elbow. She felt that anyone looking at them would think she and Archie were still married and that the children were theirs. She wondered if the same thought had occurred to Archie and knew it was so when he took her elbow crossing the road, almost proprietorial.

It seemed only hospitable to invite him in for a cup of tea once they reached the block of flats. First she took the children out of their outdoor clothes and gave them their meal, then set them to play with a selection of toys. She kept an eye on them while she poured tea for Archie.

'You're awfully good at it,' he murmured, with a nod towards the two scrambling about on the floor.

'Well, I'm training for it, after all.'

'It's not only that.' He fell silent, sipping his tea.

The time went past without strain. She wondered whether she ought to ask him to leave when bathtime came round, but decided it would be more civilized to offer him a drink at that hour. She settled him in the sitting-room with a whisky and soda while the children were got ready for bed.

'Night-night, God bless,' she recited for Janey, who had learned this from the char who sometimes acted as stand-in in the evenings.

The little boy did his best to mimic the words, then turned towards his pillow and was instantly asleep. She blew a kiss to Janey and tiptoed out of the room, which she had darkened by drawing the blind.

Archie put down the copy of the *Financial Times* he'd been reading. 'All serene?'

'Oh yes, they're very good children.' She looked at his glass. 'Can I get you a refill?'

'Only if you're going to have one yourself.'

She poured another whisky for Archie and a small one for herself. They sat down on either side of the fireplace, now filled with a great arrangement of ferns and early chrysanthemums. She asked about the cinema managers' dinner, took an intelligent interest again in something she'd put aside over the last long months.

All at once Archie set down his glass to come and sit beside her on the sofa. 'Barbara, it seems all wrong to be making small talk like this.'

'There's no other kind of talk for us these days, Archie.'

'Do I hear regret in your voice? Does it mean you've missed me?'

'What kind of a question is that?' she parried. 'We're strangers now.'

'No we're not, and it's no use pretending we are.' He leaned over her, pushing her against the corner of the sofa as if unintentionally, and kissed her.

'No, now look here, Archie,' she began, turning her face away.

'Don't say no to me, sweetheart! When I saw you again today I knew you still meant so much to me.'

He had one hand on the arm of the sofa and one arm along the back, so that she was trapped in the corner. His body was heavy against hers.

It was all so familiar, so right. After all, he was her husband. No amount of talk in a court of law could change the fact that they had been man and wife, that they still had an instinctive knowledge of each other's needs.

She found she had put her arms around his neck as he kissed her again. They were close against each other, his fingers working at the buttons on the front of her dress.

'We mustn't –'

'Why not? It's right, Barbara – you know it is.' And if she had wished to argue with this he stopped her by bringing his mouth down on hers.

A long time had gone by since last she felt a man's arms around her with the urgency in Archie's. If she had felt hunger, she had disregarded it. But now there was a keen longing to know again the moment of happiness at the climax of love-making. She had a right to it – she had learned the rewards of physical passion with this very man, and he belonged to her now as he always had.

There was no thought in her mind now of his new wife. She owed her no debt of honour. Her own needs had taken control of her now, and her pride, that he wanted her as much as she wanted him.

She heard him calling her by the little endearments that had always melted her heart. She felt herself responding with every fibre of her being. She had always loved him, she loved him still – that was the be-all and end-all of her life.

CHAPTER NINE

The thin wail of Baby William waking up brought Barbara to her senses. She stiffened and jerked away from Archie.

'What's up –'

'The baby!'

'He'll settle in a minute.'

'No, he –' She shoved at him with both her fists and scrambled up. Archie, taken by surprise, let her slip from his grasp.

The baby was apt to fall asleep with his face turned into his pillows. Usually he turned as he made himself comfortable for the night, but now and again he seemed to wake himself by becoming short of air, in which case he would wake up for a moment, frightened and at a loss.

Barbara hurried across the hall to the nursery. In the dim light from the sides of the window blinds she could see William, fists waving, fighting his covers.

She pulled the honeycomb-wool blanket away so he could see that she was there. 'All right, William,' she murmured. 'I'm here. Stay quiet, dearie, it's all right.' She pulled the sheet away too, tidied the covers deftly, and put them back over him as he struggled about trying to make up his mind whether he was awake or asleep. The conditions that had given him the bad dream were gone. He heard the soothing voice close by. The light was soft and faint. The hand putting his hair back from his damp forehead was gentle. He made a gurgling sound, wriggled once or twice, sighed, and went back to sleep.

Barbara stayed by the cot for a minute or so after he was settled. It was the sound of Archie coming to the door of the nursery that roused her.

'Come on, sweetheart, what are you hanging about for?' he

demanded.

She moved with quick soft steps to the door and pushed him out. She half-closed the door, so that they were in the hall. She didn't go with him when he tried to urge her into the sitting-room.

'No, Archie, we can't – writhing about on the sofa!'

'Which is your room, then?' He surveyed the doors opening off the wide hall.

'No!'

The vehemence of the word made him wheel to stare at her. 'What's up?'

'This is just . . . so cheap!'

'Oh, come on, don't get high-minded –'

'You'd better go, Archie.'

'Now, look here, you can't lead me on like that and then –'

'Lead you on?' She bit off the words then turned away. Had she led him on? When she thought about her actions, it looked very like it. She had let him go home with her, given him tea and then a drink. There were three stages at which she could have said a dignified goodbye, yet she had let him stay. She had even let him know Eileen and Jimmy were away for the day.

She had wanted him to stay. That must be the reason. She had wanted things to go exactly the way they did. She had got what she'd asked for.

She shivered. It was an accepted fact that no decent woman would behave like that – to lay herself open to a scene like that. Did that mean she had no moral principles?

No, of course it didn't. She rejected the thought as soon as it flickered into her mind. She had standards as high as anyone else. But she also had needs, although the rest of the world seemed to deny that fact. Her recent dipping into books of psychology had brought her some insight into the whole character of a woman so that she had begun to understand there was such a thing as female sexuality. Women had needs, just as men did.

But this was not the time to assuage those needs, and Archie was not the partner. It was no use telling herself she loved him and always had – that was only dressing it up to make it acceptable. She didn't love Archie any more.

But she still found him physically attractive.

That being so, he had to go. Now, at once, while she was still feeling the revulsion of that interlude interrupted by the baby. In her crumpled shantung dress and with her hair a mess, she felt shamed and a little sick. She certainly didn't feel like making love.

'I want you to go, Archie,' she said. 'I'm sorry, but this whole thing was a mistake.'

'Who do you think you're fooling? I know you, lovie – you wanted it just as much as I did.'

'That's not the point. This is not the time –'

'When? Can you come to my hotel later? The dinner will be over by about eleven.'

'I was going to say, this isn't the time to explain or make excuses. Nor is it the place. I'm here to look after the children, not to go to bed with my ex-husband in the sitting-room.'

'If it's the divorce that's bothering you, of course that makes a difference – but we always used to be good together, Barbara, and with Helen not feeling too good –'

That angered her just enough to push her into being downright rude. 'So that's it, is it? Number Two Wife doesn't feel like sex because she's pregnant so Number One Wife gets her share? Who do you think you are, an Oriental potentate? You'd better go, Archie, before I –'

'Before you what? What are you going to do? Scream for help?'

'Do I need help, now that I've made it plain I want you to leave?'

'You've got a hell of a nerve,' he said, the urgency going out of him. His face was resentful, almost ugly with his disappointment. He stalked into the sitting-room to get his jacket, then as he put it on spoke to her over his shoulder. 'You always were a bundle of contradictions! Nothing was ever straightforward with you.'

'Then you're just as well to steer clear of me, aren't you?'

'What the hell did you think you were playing at?' He swung round to glare at her, his fingers busy straightening his tie. 'You as good as asked me to take you to bed.'

'Perhaps I did. I'm sorry.' She was hot with embarrassment, for even though she thought she understood the reasons for this debacle she could never have brought herself to give them to Archie. He was an old-fashioned man with strong notions about a woman's place.

'You know damn well I'd never have tried it on if you hadn't –'

'I said I'm sorry!'

'It was the same when we were married. I never could read your mind, though you seemed to expect it. And how it came about that you were so good in bed when you couldn't have a baby – but perhaps that's why . . .' He studied her. 'Perhaps it's because you know you're not going to get pregnant that makes you give a man the come-on –'

'Listen, Archie, it's not as easy as that. Please don't let's go into a discussion about it.'

'It all seems such a waste!' he said sullenly. 'Why the devil couldn't you have given me a family? Then we wouldn't be here now.'

'I don't know. It was never sorted out.'

He let her usher him towards the outside door of the flat. 'You know what's behind all this Nannying lark?' he said as she put her hand on the doorknob. 'It's just a way to get the children you couldn't have yourself!'

He stepped out on to the wide stone landing. Without any other word of goodbye he set off down the long flight of steps to the ground floor. She heard his feet skipping briskly on the treads and then the more hollow echo as he reached the big tiled lobby. Then she heard the outer door open and thud back into place.

Slowly she backed into the flat and closed the door. She went to her own room, took off the crumpled shantung dress and put it in the laundry basket. She showered vigorously. She put on an unpretentious cotton print dress, did her hair, restored herself in all outward aspects to normal.

But something had changed. Archie's words had shaken her. Until now she had thought her intention to train and work with children was rather noble, but now she was made to see that it might be very selfish. Childless herself, was she trying to take away the children of others?

When she looked back to the episode with the Leschallas children, she wondered if she had brought the reaction of Peter and Felicity upon herself. She'd made such an issue of being there to greet Petey on his return from his first term at school, as if it were the most important thing in the world. It *was* important: she still thought it was harmful to the child to see first Nanny Lewis and then herself vanish from his world without any reference to his need of them. Yet perhaps if she had handled it differently Peter Leschallas wouldn't have been so firm about the first re-union.

She had seen Petey again, during the summer holidays. She and Eileen and Eileen's children had gone for a day to Dowers Farm, where they had had a big family-like party. Petey had been pleased to see Barbara, but rather off-hand. She had been hurt but had understood his view – it was no use rushing to greet and hug her, she'd be off again in a few hours. He was probably learning that you couldn't depend too much on anyone.

Perhaps that was all to the good. Certainly Peter and Felicity took that view. It wasn't the outlook Barbara was learning through her reading of psychology but who was to say which was right?

Yet now she came to look at it from the new standpoint of Archie's remark, she began to be very unsure of all her own reasoning. Peter and Felicity had undoubtedly felt she was getting too possessive about their children. Did she have a tendency to monopolize the affection of the children she cared for?

She tried to look back into her own childhood and her feelings for Eileen. At first her little sister had been the sole concern of the ayah, but little by little Barbara had begun to intervene. She'd always taken it for granted she'd done so because she knew better; that as she learned what the British community regarded as proper, she'd seen her sister becoming too Indianized in a household without a mother-figure.

But had she been trying to get from Eileen the affection she'd lost when their mother died? Had all her feeling of loss and bewilderment gone into the sort of over-compensating maternal feeling?

That might be so. Her father, she seemed to recall, had figured very little in the upbringing of Eileen after an initial and very deep concern when their mother died. Had he lost interest, or had she elbowed him out as she grew into her teens?

It was a shocking thought. If she had really been selfish, perhaps she had harmed Eileen by depriving her of a true relationship with Donald. It was certainly true that Barbara loved her father more than Eileen did. Eileen was sharper with him, less tolerant. But then Eileen had undergone the shock of coming home to Britain as an eleven-year-old, and having to put up with the ministrations of Dottie Fleming instead of the gentle, humble ayah.

Perhaps it was useless to wander back into the past in search of the truth. What was done was done, and Barbara was as she was. But for the future, she could change. If it were really true that she was looking for compensations for her own childlessness, she must be on her guard from now on.

She couldn't help knowing that Archie might be right. All the other students at Hogarth were young – their child-bearing years were still ahead of them so there could be no question that they were reaching out to other people's children in place of their own. It was she alone, Barbara Gray, who had a barren marriage behind her, a broken marriage. Any other girl, asked why she was training to be a nursery nurse, could respond innocently: 'Because I love children.' Only for Barbara did that reply have undertones of self-gratification.

When she had reached this point in her thoughts she'd made herself so miserable she was ready to throw herself face down on the bed and cry. But a glance at her watch told her that probably what was wrong with her was hunger. It was almost eight. She ought to get herself something to eat.

There was some cold meat in the larder. She made herself a salad to go with it. Normally Mrs Mitchell would have prepared dinner about now but this was her day off, so Barbara found solace in pottering about the kitchen. She ate there, enjoying the domesticity. It was a long time since she'd had this housewifely feeling; there was something safe and sheltering in it. Being a woman alone in the world gave an awful edge of insecurity to her existence.

Was that why she'd chosen the nursery as her sphere of influence?

'Oh, nonsense,' she said aloud to the cooker. She mustn't impute bad reasons to her every action just because Archie had thrown a scare into her.

All the same . . . The nursery was the safest place in any household she had known so far. At Dowers Farm she had heard echoes of bickering and intrigue from the servants' hall, but she had never had to concern herself. And so it would be, she was sure, almost everywhere. In the nursery, the Nanny reigned supreme. No one challenged her or questioned her. If there were changes in the household, the last person to suffer, or to be dispensed with, was the Nanny. It was almost unheard of for a Nanny to be discharged until the children no longer needed her, having grown up or gone to school.

It was a chastening thought that she was running for shelter. In a harsh world, she had chosen the softest spot. Like a snail she was withdrawing into a shell by choosing to work with other people's children, cut off from the fears and tragedies of the adult world.

Barbara made herself some strong coffee to round off her meal, then sat with it at the kitchen table. She was deep in her thoughts. It wasn't too late to change her mind – she could leave the training school and get a job at something else.

Jobs were scarce, though. Thousands of women who ought to have married and settled down to have families had been cheated of that life by the death toll of World War 1, so that now they were in the job market – factory girls, office workers, shop assistants, dressmakers, servants. Most women of Barbara's age had their niche by now; they had gone out to work after the War and were secure in their positions.

Barbara had no training for anything except hospital nursing. She'd been quite a good nurse but she still looked back on that period with horror. She had seen so much suffering. If she were to give up training to be a Nanny, she could not, would not go back to hospital work.

This was the stage she'd reached when she heard Eileen and Jimmy coming in. She went out to the hall to greet them, and found them in a state of mild exhilaration.

They'd come out almost even in their wagers at Sandown, had made a good new contact with a man who knew the investment possibilities in Brazil, had had a pleasant dinner with him at Overton's. They were merry, but not too much so. Barbara shushed them, reminding them that they'd wake the children. They became solemnly silent and went into the sitting-room.

'Matter of fact,' Jimmy said, 'if things go the way they might with this new friend, we might be able to afford a house . . . Not have to worry about disturbing the children . . . How'd you like that, Eileen, nice house in Chelsea?'

Barbara saw Eileen's eyes light up. 'Oh, it would be lovely. Better still would be to keep the flat, and have a country cottage.'

'Could be, could be . . . Well, had a nice day, Barbie?'

'Very nice, thanks.'

'Good ole Barbie. Always reliable . . . What'd we do without you?'

'You'd manage,' she said. Yet it was pleasant to be approved of, after the gloomy thoughts she'd been entertaining.

Next day Eileen got up late and had a bit of a hangover. It was certainly a day when she was very glad indeed she had an elder sister pleased to take the children off her hands. Barbara, sensing that Eileen was out of sorts, took Jane and William to visit small friends in Kensington in the morning, then in the afternoon went for a walk with them. By evening Eileen was herself again, happy to have company because Jimmy had gone to his club to play billiards.

'I hope something comes of this introduction to De Lopez,' she remarked. 'We really could do with a chance to get into something good.'

'I hope so too, Eileen. He seemed very optimistic about it, didn't he?'

'Yes, but Jimmy gets optimistic about everything . . .' She sighed. 'Well, it's up to him. I don't really understand all this wheeling and dealing. I was a bit surprised he and De Lopez got on so well together. We only met him by chance in the enclosure . . . Were we very squiffy when we came in, Barbara?'

'No, just a bit gleeful.'

'I'm sorry I've been so grumpy today. Port always makes me headachy.'

'That's all right. I haven't felt too bright myself today.'

'Oh? Why? Anything wrong?'

Barbara hesitated. Then she blurted out: 'I saw Archie yesterday.'

'Oh.' Her sister gave her a glance in which astonishment melted into sympathy. 'Did you speak to him?'

'He spoke to me. I was in the park with the children and suddenly there he was.' After a moment she added, 'I brought him back for a cup of tea. I hope you don't mind.'

Eileen looked as if she did mind, very much. She had never

cared for Archie. But all she said was, 'If you felt you had to be polite to him that was all right.' Natural curiosity brought the next question. 'How's he getting on with Helen?'

'She's expecting their second baby.' Then out it came: 'Eileen, he said I was only taking my training so as to clutch at other people's children because I couldn't have any of my own.'

Eileen sat up straight. 'The rat!' she said.

'No, Eileen, he –' Then the comicality of her sister's outrage hit Barbara and she began to laugh. 'Oh, sweetie, if you could see your face!'

'Well, who does he think he is handing out opinions like that? He only said it to hurt you.'

Barbara shrugged, saying nothing. After a moment Eileen got up and went to the drinks table. 'Come on, let's have a little drinkie. It'll make you feel better. He's really upset you, hasn't he?'

'I just wondered if he might be right, you see.'

'Clutching at other people's children –'

'He didn't exactly say that. That was just me.'

'Oh, I see. You're being hard on yourself because he's got you bothered.' Eileen poured a liberal slosh of brandy into a glass and added soda. 'Here, drown your sorrows.'

'I don't think they're going to be all that easy to drown. They're doubts, really. I mean, maybe he's right, dear . . .'

'No he isn't. You're not doing it only to replace the children you haven't had yourself. Look, Barbs, I've seen you with my two and with Felicity's. You've got a natural talent. Remember when Ceecie and Janey got at loggerheads in the garden?'

'Oh, that . . .'

'Yes, that. Felicity was completely at a loss and so was I. I couldn't see how to get Ceecie's hands out of Janey's hair short of cutting off all her curls. And let me tell you, if I'd had to do that, I'd never have forgiven Felicity. There was the makings of a right old barney just then. And in two minutes you'd got it all sorted out, and the two kids were playing hairdressers with an old hairbrush and cooing over each other. *I'd* never have thought of that.'

'But it's obvious, Eileen. If a toddler's got sticky fingers tangled in another kiddie's hair, there's no use yanking and scolding. The only way to get them separated is to make a game of it.'

'It wasn't obvious to me. Nor to Felicity. It's exactly what I mean – you do it by instinct. So don't talk to me about taking this training for daft ulterior motives.'

'But . . . you see, Eileen . . .' After a moment Barbara painfully explained her feelings over having to leave Petey. 'Felicity didn't like my attitude. I see I was over-anxious. I had no right to imagine I was so important to Petey.'

'Well, who's to say you were wrong? I don't know whether it's right to pack kids off to prep school like that in the first place, and then to play a dirty trick like not letting you see him when he came back . . . The poor mite must have been sick about it.' Eileen sipped her brandy. 'But mind you, I think you have to accept things the way they are. Right or wrong, parents think they know best for their children. I suppose if you contradicted me about Jane or William, I'd be peeved. But the fact that you think you know best doesn't make you a sort of Svengali trying to make off with somebody's offspring.'

'You're only arguing so hard because it was something Archie said. If you'd read it in a magazine or heard it on the wireless, you'd nod your head and say, "Yes, that's right – Nannies do get between parents and their children." '

'They do, I'm sure they do. But parents hire them to do just that. What I reckon is, there's a fine line that Nannies learn to draw – between the parents' involvement and their own. Archie's been sneaky in making you think you're peculiar in wanting to build up a relationship with the children.'

Barbara was sitting turning her glass round and round in her slender hands. Eileen suddenly put out a hand and touched her wrist. 'All I can tell you is, I'd trust you with my children, Barbie.'

Barbara made no reply. The question was, could she trust herself? Could she be sure she wouldn't let herself become too deeply tied in affection to the children whom she would be given?

As had happened on the previous evening, Baby William got himself tangled in his covers when he tried to turn over. His cry brought both women to their feet. Eileen moved towards the door of the sitting-room. The wail became distinguishable as words.

'Auntie Babs . . .'

Barbara drew back. 'You go,' she said to her sister.

But even after Eileen had been in the nursery for some moments the wails of distress continued. Barbara set down her brandy glass then went to join her sister. William, half-awake and half-asleep, heard her voice. He gave a great snuffle of satisfaction then subsided. The ragged breathing became regular. He fell asleep.

Both women sat side by side in the quiet nursery until they were sure all was well. It came into Barbara's mind that it was a good thing the term resumed at the training school the following week. She had stayed long enough in Eileen's home.

When she got back to the Hogarth School it was with a head full of questions needing answers. But only after the term's work had commenced did it dawn on her that there was no one to ask. It was useless to speak about her doubts to the other girls in the dormitory, although she now looked on them as close friends. They didn't face the same problems, perhaps had never even considered the points that were troubling Barbara now.

As to the instructors . . . She reviewed them mentally.

Miss Bell would tell her she was getting in a state about nothing, that being physically involved with children at close quarters would take up all her energies and she oughtn't to worry about ethics. Mrs O'Mara, as an ex-hospital sister, would say that every nurse had these thoughts and the only solution was to grow a protective shell. Miss Parrish would say her anxieties were caused by lack of vitamins and too little exercise. Mrs Stepps-Astley – well, life was hard enough without giving Mrs Stepps-Astley any darts to prick her with.

Outside lecturers came in from time to time. They had a series of talks about the Froebel methods and paid visits to the Froebel Institute. Much that was said in the conversations was of interest to Barbara, but Fräulein Bickhardt, the lecturer, seemed wrapped up in the view of the world from the child's standpoint. And what Barbara needed was someone who could see the problem from the point of view of the adult who was given care of the child.

A follower of the psychologist Jung came to begin a series on that school of thought. Barbara was all agog. At last, a fully trained expert on psychology! When he asked for questions at the end of his first talk, her hand shot up.

'Dr Bennett, you say that Dr Jung's view is that the visions he had in childhood were messages. It must be very important that people dealing with children should be aware of things like that. How close do you think we should become, in the course of caring for the children of others?'

'Now that is very interesting,' said Dr Bennett, smiling at her with kindness. 'I hope to deal with that point in a future talk. Next question?'

'Should children be guided towards painting in hopes of producing work such as Dr Jung's paintings?' asked another girl.

'Oh, indeed.' A long discourse followed on the importance of free expression, and the provision of paints, paper, brushes, aprons or smocks, and so on.

In the course of the ten talks on Jung it became clear that Dr Bennett didn't want to talk about Nannies and how they felt about their charges. He wanted to show them how to turn all their little charges into small disciples of Jung, painting mandalas and talking about their dreams every morning. 'All I can say is, it'd give kids an awful big head,' Janice remarked with complete cynicism.

'Not to mention the mess of paint sloshing about and wax crayons getting mashed up underfoot,' Agnes agreed.

'But perhaps there's something in it,' Barbara put in' She wanted to be fair to the lecturer, even if he'd shown a great aversion to answering any of the questions she had tried to put.

'Perhaps this new fellow will be better,' Agnes said, looking very doubtful. 'To tell the truth, I don't understand what they're all on about.'

Lillian closed her notebook with a snap. 'If you ask me, it's all a waste of time. There's only one way to look after children, and that is to keep them happy and healthy.'

'But didn't Dr Bennett say that happiness and unhappiness come from the psyche, not from outside sources?'

'Is that what he said?' Lillian rejoined. 'Hanged if I know. I took notes all through that course and now I can't make head nor tail of them.'

'Well, I think you're going to find it even more difficult to follow the next one. I've tried reading a bit about Freud, and I can't make my mind up – either he's mad or I am.'

'Barbara, you take it all too seriously,' Agnes said. 'Just ask yourself – are any of the parents going to ask you if you understand Freud?'

'No-o, I suppose not. But we're not going to these lectures just to be able to say we've heard of Freud if parents ask us. We're supposed to learn something from them.'

'I think it's just so they can have something to put on the exam papers,' Janice said. 'Well, come on, let's go down and listen to Henry Hall.'

Lillian looked at the timetable in the back of her notebook. 'Dr Deniz. Another foreigner. I hope his accent is easier to follow than Fräulein Bickhardt's!'

When they assembled for the psychology lecture on the morning of the following Wednesday, they found a young middle-aged man sitting at the table on the small dais at the end of the room. He stood up, proving to be a little above medium height and dressed in the pin-stripe trousers and dark jacket of the consultant. He had dark hair receding from a high forehead, a sallow complexion, a rather weary mouth, and when he spoke used fluent, uninflected English.

'Well, ladies, I have been given the charge of introducing you to the work of Dr Sigmund Freud. Before I do so, may I ask if anyone here has already read any of his work or attended any other lectures?'

Silence. Agnes dug Barbara in the ribs. 'Own up,' she whispered.

Dr Deniz turned his glance towards them. 'Anyone?'

Barbara put her hand up. 'I tried to read "The Interpretation of Dreams".'

'Tried to – and failed?'

'I'm afraid so.'

'It's only what I would expect. Let me tell you, young lady, you are in good company – many very learned men have tried to read that book and given it up. So I intend to talk to you on the basis of my own attendance at lectures given by Dr Freud, and shall quote to you from my own notes of that time. It will be easier to direct my information towards what chiefly interests you – the care of children.' He paused. 'I am right in believing that you are interested in the care of children?' he said.

This was intended as a little joke, and they all gave a dutiful murmur of amusement.

'I'll jump straight in,' Fredric Deniz said, having as he hoped broken the ice. 'I want to talk about sexuality.'

There was a faint gasp.

'That's the reaction I expected. Almost everyone shies away from speaking about sex. So I will say it again. I want to talk about sexuality. And even more shocking, I want to talk about the sexuality of children.'

A rustle of attention followed, together with some murmurs. Cynthia Albert, in the front row, was heard to utter a protest containing the words 'innocent children'.

'That is my point,' said the lecturer. 'From the view we are given through our Christian upbringing we are asked to believe that children are "innocent". I tell you, quite to the contrary, that sexual life begins in the human being almost at once. To quote the words of Dr Freud, "Sexual life begins not at puberty but in plain manifestations soon after birth".'

'That's absurd!' Janice said.

'Not at all – if you understand how the word sexual is used in this context. Sexuality in an infant consists, as it does in adults, in obtaining pleasure from zones of the body. In adults, this pleasure is most often directed towards reproduction. In infants it is directed towards something which for them is just as important – gratification.'

By now his audience was so stunned that they didn't make a sound. He talked without interruption for the next forty minutes then put his hand in the pocket of his jacket, took out a scrap of paper, checked that he had said all he meant to say at this session, and sat down. 'Any questions?' he asked.

The outbreak of words was more protest than question. He selected one or two of the more vociferous speakers, and tried to sort out their remarks. After about ten minutes he said: 'You see, ladies, you react with anger to the talk I have just given. You don't use reason, you use reproach and objection.'

'I have a question, sir,' Barbara said. 'I think it's based on reason.'

'Go ahead.'

'If, as you claim, children seek gratification, how is it that they become obedient? If a child is having fun messing about in a puddle, why should he stop when you tell him to?'

'He does so because he wants your approval. That is a very big question which I'll go into in a later talk. Once affection takes over, rather than the instinctive desire for gratification, the adult has an instrument to control the child.'

'An instrument?'

'I'll explain that next time.' A bell rang to warn students it was time to be heading for the dining-room. 'That's all for today, ladies. I hope you took notes and will have better questions at my next talk. Goodbye for the present.'

'Well,' said Janice to Barbara as he left the room, 'at least he's more to the point than the last one. Less about visions and dreams, and more about coming to the business of control.'

'Control!' Barbara cried. 'He said you used affection as an instrument of control.'

'That's a way of putting it, I suppose.'

'The man's an idiot,' Barbara said.

CHAPTER TEN

She was beginning to give up hope of ever finding anyone to whom she could talk about her doubts. In fact, she was beginning to think she was making mountains out of molehills. Everyone else seemed perfectly satisfied with the way things were at present – they were being trained to take care of children and that could only happen if the parents acquiesced in handing over their children. Where, then, was the problem? If the parents had no qualms and the children were well looked after, why should Barbara be so bothered?

The speakers who came to the training school never touched on that aspect at all. Perhaps they felt it was outside their province. After all, if you were asked to lecture to girls training to become Nannies, it was surely the height of tactlessness to ask them if they were doing a proper thing in the first place.

The lectures given by Dr Deniz became quite famous throughout the school. The first year students, regarded as too young to be allowed to attend, would ask for titbits. They could hear the arguments as they went past the door of the lecture-room.

'It's all so silly,' Barbara remarked. 'When you try to get him to say what you ought to do in such and such a case, he replies with another question – "What would be your first reaction?" or something like that.'

'Well, the thing is to get him cornered,' Janice suggested. 'Ask him something that demands a factual answer.'

They put their heads together. On the next day of Dr Deniz's attendance, when he invited questions, Barbara put her hand up. 'Dr Deniz, you recommend going beyond the immediate cause to the deeper reason of a tantrum?'

'Yes.'

'How long is it likely to take to get the deeper reason?'

'That depends on how deep the reason lies.'

'When an adult patient is in analysis, the same technique is used?'

'Yes.'

'How long does it take, on average, for a patient to benefit from analysis?'

All the girls in the audience saw him frown. 'Well . . . er . . . Some months. A year, perhaps.'

'Hm,' said Barbara. There was a slight giggle from someone else.

'I don't suggest that you should spend a year trying to find out why little Johnnie is drumming his heels on the nursery floor and refusing to get up –'

'I'm, glad to hear it,' said a voice.

'Does it strike you, Dr Deniz, that it's impractical to expect us to make use of your theories in the day to day running of a nursery?'

'By no means, Miss – er?'

'Mrs Gray.'

'Mrs Gray. You imply antagonism by your tone, and of course I'm accustomed to that. But I do assure you that if you have a basic knowledge of the origins of insecurity, fear and conflict, it can only help deal with children.'

'Do you have many children in your own practice, doctor?'

'Not many. As yet parents in this country don't bring their children.'

'No,' Barbara said, 'I thought not.'

The gong sounded for lunch. Someone in the group said, 'Saved by the gong!'

To everyone's surprise, Fredric Deniz laughed. 'And glad of it,' he said. 'Have you any idea how formidable you look, ranged in rows ready to contradict every word I say?' He bowed, then made his way to the door with the quick stride he always used.

'He isn't half bad,' Janice said, looking after him with a

calculating gaze. 'Pity he's so old. I wouldn't mind getting to know him better if he was younger.'

Barbara's conscience was pricked. Perhaps it was unfair, the way they all ganged up on him. Still, he ought to be used to it. As far as she could gather, nobody approved of Freudian psychology – and that being so, it was difficult to know why it kept being argued about so forcibly.

In the dining-room the lecturer was sitting down at the small table where the teachers ate, with Mrs Stepps-Astley at its head. As Barbara took her place on one of the students' tables, she turned her head and found by chance that he was looking in her direction. She gave him a little smile of apology, and was rewarded by an answering smile and a nod.

'Who is that girl who keeps asking awkward questions?' he asked Mrs Stepps-Astley.

'Who? I don't know whom you mean, since I'm not in the room during your talk.'

'The slender fair girl, older than the others. Mrs . . .?'

'Mrs Gray,' said the Director with some grimness. 'Is she a trouble to you?'

'Not at all. She enlivens the proceedings – not that they need that. Your students don't approve of Freud, Mrs Stepps-Astley.'

'I don't approve of Freud myself, Dr Deniz. But since a friend of mine, a very experienced and sensible child specialist, thinks Dr Freud has something important to contribute, I felt I had to give some notion of his work to my students.'

'I wish others would be as fair.' He gave his attention to the grilled chop, then inquired, 'Mrs Gray seems very quick on the uptake.'

'I believe that in your jargon she is what is called "highly motivated". She has come to the idea of being a Nanny rather later in life than most of my gels. You say she asks good questions?

'Well, she's still trying to score points off me. But she understands more than the others, I think.' He hesitated. He was trying to think how to inquire if there was a Mr Gray, but dared not. He had a feeling Mrs Stepps-Astley wouldn't like it.

The following week he asked for some written work, an appraisal of what he had said as it might be applied in their work. 'I don't expect you to write an essay,' as groans greeted his request. 'A few paragraphs, to give me some idea of whether you're getting anything you feel you can use . . .'

'Ooh, written work,' sighed Agnes. 'I took up Nannying partly because I wasn't any good at scholastic things – more suited to everyday life, if you know what I mean.'

'He doesn't want much,' Janice agreed, meaning it ironically. 'Anything we feel we can use . . . All he's done, as far as I'm concerned, is make me think every kiddie is as evil-minded as Crippen.'

'Well, I shall do him twenty lines,' Lillian decided. 'As if it was a punishment, which listening to him *is*!'

Barbara felt everyone ought to make an effort, because although she disagreed with a lot he said, she'd gathered he was quite a distinguished man. The previous weekend she and Janice had gone up to the West End to see Benita Hume in 'Symphony in Two Flats', but had separated until theatre time. Janice had gone to keep a tryst with a boyfriend; Barbara had gone into the Westminster Reference Library and after some searching in great tomes had found that Dr Deniz had had work published on the subject of psycho-analysis.

She had also discovered something which had somehow rather dashed her, though she didn't know why. There was a photograph of him and his family in one of the magazines containing an article of his: 'Dr Deniz, author of our short study of the Viennese School, with his wife and two children.' The photograph showed a quietly dressed woman and two boys, one about eleven and one about thirteen.

Well, it was none of her business if he was married. The reason she was interested in him was to see if people took him seriously. It certainly did seem he'd gone out of his way to simplify and popularize these preposterous notions about psychology.

When the written work was handed in to Fredric Deniz the following Wednesday, he put it straight into his brief case without examination. At home in his Harley Street flat above his consulting rooms, he took the papers out. As he had expected, most of the girls had done as little as possible. A few paragraphs he had asked for, and that was what he got. Few had filled the page. Only one student had done more, and it was odd that he had no sense of surprise when he looked at the name at the top of the first page: 'Barbara Gray'.

She had covered three pages of foolscap with her neat, rather girlish writing. Her main point was that Nannies had to deal instantly with nursery situations and shouldn't be made to feel guilt if they looked only at what they saw – 'To make us feel guilty will only hamper us.' Then she disagreed with the theory, on which he had spent some time, that there is no such thing as accident, that if we stumble and bruise ourselves against the furniture, we are punishing ourselves for some deep-hidden error. 'If a little child gets her hands tangled in the hair of another child,' she wrote, 'are you saying that Child 1 is really intending to scalp Child 2? Isn't the answer more likely to be that Child 1's hands were accidentally sticky with honey?'

The third page dealt with a point that no one at all had mentioned except Barbara. 'The child must be affected by the relationship which grows up between the Nanny and itself. What we don't learn, except by experience, is how to handle the need for affection. The child needs it, but so does the Nanny. Should this need be suppressed on the side of the Nanny?'

'Well,' thought Fredric to himself, 'there is an interesting girl!' Psychologist though he was he wasn't enough of a psychologist to notice that he was glad of an excuse to single her out for a chat, next time he came to the centre.

'I found your paper very helpful to me,' he said. 'Naturally I want to speak about problems the Nanny will have to face and give some deeper insight into their cause. But

I feel I can't deal with the last question you raise.'

'Which one's that?'

'About affection.'

'But surely . . . that's so important . . .'

'I can see it is, to you. I wonder if you'd like to expand that point? Give me an example of what you mean?'

They were walking in the grounds of the school, lunch was over and by rights Fredric should have been driving back to London, but he was enjoying this stroll among the rhododendron bushes.

'What worries me is this . . . According to what you teach, the relationship between mother and baby is the most important thing in the world. Right?'

'For the baby – yes.'

'But what I'm actually getting trained to do is step in between mother and baby. At the end of the first month, when the maternity nurse leaves, the Nanny takes over. As far as I can gather from the way the work is taught here, it's taken for granted that the baby will be bottle-fed – you'd say, from your Freudian standpoint, that that in itself is a mistake, wouldn't you?'

'Circumstances may make it inevitable. Go on.'

'I don't see how anybody could have care of a baby for more than a few days without getting fond of it – and you say that the baby at once begins to build up affection for the person who tends it. Right?'

'That is the thesis, yes.'

'So it has to happen that the Nanny is coming between the mother and the baby. And even with other children whom the Nanny takes over – if she sees more of it than the mother does, it seems to me the child's going to get as fond of Nanny as of its mother, or more so.'

'Why should it worry you so much, this matter of inspiring affection?'

'Don't you think it ought to worry me?'

He grinned. 'You are beginning to sound like a psychiatrist,

Mrs Gray – answering a question with a question.'

'I don't want to sound cheeky, Dr Deniz, but I really should like an answer. Don't you think it's worrying that the mother is being replaced in her child's affection?'

'If it were so, it would be worrying. But children have an enormous capacity for love – and all the better for it. They can love Nanny, and Mummy, and Daddy, and the nursery-maid, and their pony Cuddles, and the cat, and the postman, and everyone else in their surroundings who is kind to them.'

'But their chief affection will go to the person they see most of.'

'And there it is – the key to your problem. A Nanny comes into a household to care for children because for some reason the mother cannot.'

'Or will not.'

He stopped, so that she had to stop also, and they looked at each other.

'You say that,' he remarked, 'as if you think the mother should be forced to look after her child. "Or will not", you said, as if the mother were being wayward or selfish.'

'Well, I –'

'There can be many reasons why a mother will not be present among her children in their daily life. If she has a social position that requires her to be with her husband – a diplomat's wife, a Lady Mayoress – she may not have the time to deal with children. In these days, also, there are women with careers.'

'Not many.'

'More than you might think. The War brought many men back who have never been totally fit. Their womenfolk have had to take a share, sometimes a major share, in running the business that provides the income. Then there are those who simply wish to use their talents – and who can say they are wrong? And if we speak of talent, there are women who have no talent for understanding children, who simply aren't good at it. Surely it's better for someone like yourself to take over in circumstances like that?'

'Ye-es,' Barbara agreed. 'I've said those things to myself, of course. But you have to admit that mostly, people who can afford a Nanny have one because it's expected of them.'

'Exactly. And how can you hope to change the customs of the country? Rich families have always hired others to look after their children. I've never done any research on it but it comes into my mind that there's a nurse in "Romeo and Juliet" who seems a lot more important to Juliet than Mrs Capulet. I think you have to face it, Barbara – I may call you Barbara? – that that's the way things are. So it's better to have kind, efficient nurses than lazy, hard-hearted nurses – Yes?'

'I suppose so. It's just that I . . .'

'Picture yourself applying for your first post. You think about it and decide it's wrong to take it because you think the mother should look after the child. But the mother has already decided not to – hasn't she? – otherwise why is she advertising for a Nanny? So you don't take the job and she hires a hard-hearted, conventional Nanny who puts the child in the cupboard when it's naughty.'

'Oh, don't!'

'There you are, you see! You'd rather be there, doing it the right way.'

'And that's what you're in favour of?'

'The point is, is that what you're in favour of?'

'There you go again, answering a question with a question!'

They laughed, and he offered her his arm to walk back towards the house. He got into his car in front of it, she stood back to wave him a farewell. As she made her way through the hall to the back of the house where her next class awaited her, Lillian joined her. 'What did Dr Deniz want to talk about?' she inquired.

'That paper I wrote . . .'

'Yes, it was ever so long, wasn't it? I never thought you were a swot, Barbara!'

'Neither did I. Don't worry, it won't happen again.'

Before the course of lectures ended, it had become an accepted thing that Fredric and Barbara might go for a stroll and have a talk. Mrs Stepps-Astley didn't know exactly what to do about it. When she murmured to Dr Deniz that it hardly seemed suitable to single out a particular student, he replied that Mrs Gray was a very interesting girl and, after all, completely adult.

'But friendships between teacher and pupil . . .'

'Are quite common, Mrs Stepps-Astley – in fact, at university they are unremarkable.'

It was on the tip of her tongue to say this wasn't a university, but she stopped. The notion was rather flattering. She decided to see the friendship between Barbara and Fredric as that between Socrates and Plato – she'd never read any Plato but someone had once told her that it was the example of all others.

He said goodbye to the second year class at the end of his last lecture to them. 'Of course, I shall be here again next year,' he pointed out. 'There will be a different set of students in your place, while you go on to the residential nursery and the other delights that await. If I can be of any help, please feel free to come to me.'

'And that's very likely, I don't think,' Agnes said. 'Glad to see the back of him, I am. I couldn't make out what he was on about half the time.'

Barbara said nothing. The Easter break was approaching, which she'd decided to spend with her father at the cottage. The idea didn't seem to have as much appeal to her as she'd imagined when she made the arrangement.

But everything seemed brighter when she received a note from Fredric Deniz asking if she'd care to meet him in London and be taken to the opening of an exhibition of children's toys. 'I thought it might interest you to see how primitive children amused themselves,' he wrote. 'The show has been mounted by a friend of mine, an anthropologist. He would value your comments.'

Even before she replied, accepting, she was wondering what to wear. It was a pity the spring weather had continued so cold – she looked best in her Delysia dress but it was too thin.

To Fredric it was quite a shock to see her in an afternoon frock. At the school the second year students wore the obligatory dark skirt and light blouse over which they mostly had a bibbed apron, either of starched white if they were about to do nursing work or striped green and white if they were launching into cleaning or cooking. All at once, here was a slim creature in a dress of pale cream and brown, somehow cut on the bias so that it clung a little. Instead of flat, sensible shoes, the trim foot was in high-heeled kid with a little strap across the high instep.

The exhibition, in a small gallery not far from Debenham and Freebody in Wigmore Street, was opened at about six o'clock by a speech from a whiskered gentleman who said it was all very 'significant.' The Press were there to make something of it for the next day's papers. There was wine, offered with little snippets of food on toast.

'I don't know about you, but all those little nibbles are making me terribly hungry,' Fredric remarked. 'How about if we slip away and have a meal?'

'Oh, but won't your friend –'

'I've done my duty – said a few quotable things to the reporters. Come along.' Without more ado he fetched her coat and his, then marched her off into Soho.

The restaurant he took her to was French, specializing in peasant dishes. Bemused, she let him order the meal and the wine. Then, nerving herself to it, she inquired, 'Is this a place you and your wife often patronize?'

He was prevented from replying at once by the arrival of the patronne with a bottle of Les Perrieres to go with the first course. When he had tasted it and seen their glasses filled, he let a moment go by.

Then he said, 'My wife lives in Amsterdam.'

Barbara was so taken aback by this unexpected answer that

she simply stared.

'My grandparents are Dutch,' he went on. 'My father settled in England as a young man and married an English girl, and I was born here. But naturally I'd go back and visit the grandparents, and so I met Anna and we got married. But she doesn't like England. She thinks it's dirty and grubby. She prefers Holland where the housewives really know how to clean and polish.'

'Oh,' Barbara said.

'I have two sons. One is at Winchester, the other is at prep school. I live alone in a flat above my rooms in Harley Street.'

'Oh.'

'Now that I've told you all about myself, perhaps you'll tell me something that's been bothering me. You are Mrs Gray – is there a Mr Gray?'

'There is. He's my father. But what you mean is, have I a husband? No, I'm divorced.'

'Oh.'

The waitress came with the crevettes. They addressed themselves to the food. 'This is so good,' Barbara sighed. 'They cater for us at Hogarth as if we're all fifth-formers.'

'Don't you find it all rather . . . juvenile?' Fredric inquired.

'You mean because I'm obviously so much older than the rest of them.'

'If you're fishing for a compliment, waiting for me to say, older but much more attractive – perhaps I will.'

'I was going to say,' she went on with a little frown, 'that I don't enjoy being looked on as "Auntie Barbara" by the others. But on the other hand most of my time's taken up learning what I need to know about child care.'

'What happens outside term time?'

'I go to relatives.'

'In London?'

'I have a sister in London.'

She couldn't help noticing that he was pleased to hear it, and thought it was because that made it easier for him to suggest future meetings.

For her part, she had decided as the Les Perrieres was being poured that she would avoid him in future. It was a dangerous situation – a man alone and perhaps lonely, a woman who shared an interest with him and who found him sympathetic.

But by the time the coffee was being poured she'd changed her mind. True, he took a personal interest in her. They didn't talk only of generalities. But there was nothing Lothario-like about him. He didn't seem to court her or flirt with her; he treated her as someone he liked to talk with and listen to.

He couldn't have known how flattering it was. No other man had paid her the compliment of thinking her an equal. Her father loved her but thought of her as his daughter, sensible, capable, but only a woman after all. Her husband had ordered her about – not in a bullying way but without ever stopping to wonder if she had an opinion of her own. She had been pursued by Bob Dexter, weighed up by Brian Sethard, accepted as a sister-in-law by Jimmy. Only Fredric seemed to regard her as a friend.

They continued to be friends, good friends, from then on. When the summer term ended and the long vacation began, Barbara took a temporary job in a bookshop in Brighton to help out with her finances. To her delight, Fredric took the trouble to drive down for a visit two or three times, although he had his own family to consider.

They walked along the stony beach one evening, a light drizzle beading the pebbles and keeping the other holiday-makers away.

'I'm off to Amsterdam tomorrow,' he said.

'Oh yes – to take the boys to see their Dutch grandparents.'

'After that we're going to the Vosges for a holiday.'

'The Vosges – is it nice there?'

'Late summer, early autumn – yes. It rains other times.'

'How long are you going for?'

'Three weeks. Then the boys have to be back for school.'

'What do you do in the Vosges?'

'Oh, walking . . . boating . . . We have a cottage there.'

'It sounds lovely.'

'Yes.' He hesitated. 'You'll be back at Hogarth by the time I return.'

'Yes.'

'Will you still come up to London from time to time?'

'It won't be easy. I do the residential nursery work this year.'

'But you'll have days off – there are plenty of other girls to stand in so you can have days off?'

'Oh yes. I shall have free time.'

'Then . . . it's all right? We'll see each other in London?'

She didn't disagree. They wandered on for a while in silence, their feet crunching on the pebbles, the sea sighing to and fro to their left as they neared Hove.

'I wish I didn't have to go to the Vosges,' Fredric said suddenly.

She paused. 'You're not going absolutely this minute,' she pointed out with a faint smile.

'No . . . That's true.'

They looked at each other. After a moment he put his arm around her. They turned and began to walk back the way they had come with her head on his shoulder.

CHAPTER ELEVEN

The return to school was greeted with eagerness by Barbara. This was the year in which she would actually be allowed to act as Nanny to real children in the residential nursery of the school and, later, when she had proved her reliability, would be sent out on temporary posts under the aegis of the training centre.

The children who were accepted into the residential nursery were confided to the care of the school by their families. There were a variety of reasons. Sometimes there was sickness at home, sometimes marriage problems, or parents were going abroad on temporary assignment. In general the children came for a short stay, seldom more than a month although some were entered as 'three-month residents' from the outset. There were one or two who were kept for quite long periods due to unforeseen circumstances – two missionary teachers who had disappeared in the South American jungle had left their little boy, who had been at Hogarth for almost a year now while the lawyers tried to sort out what to do with him.

The third year students weren't given immediate charge of a child. For the first month of the term they had to act as nursery-maid to students who had stayed on from last year's course to look after the little residents during the summer holidays. This first month was known as the 'hand-over', and was regarded as very important for the wellbeing of the child.

It was also quite demanding for the 'nursery-maid'. The senior student was apt to be going for interviews with prospective employers, so the junior had to be prepared to stand in at any moment. There was a lot to learn, for the school's standards were extremely high and a teacher might drop in at any moment to make an inspection of the nursery.

Barbara was quite prepared to immerse herself in the work. But it was during her 'hand-over' that Janice at last came totally unstuck.

Janice's senior partner was a girl called Mabel Welsh. She was a serious, hardworking girl, but not particularly attractive to look at and apt to go to pieces in an interview. This being so, she was finding it hard to get a post despite the good report she always took with her from the school. If she had had experience in a family who spoke well of her, life would have been easier for her. But going to an interview with only a good school report, her twitchy chattering put the parents off. They had no idea that with children she was a totally different person, cheerful, easy and calm.

Janice got fed up with being kept in the nursery. During the previous terms there had always been free time at weekends but now Janice was almost always forced to stay in school. That being so, she took to going up to London on her evening off, although it was difficult to get up to Waterloo and back again by the lock-up hour of ten o'clock.

But Janice wasn't the type to be baulked by circumstances. She found herself a boyfriend in Haslemere, so that she could nip out and spend an hour or two with him after lights out. She had never had any problems getting back in again – the night porter was a kindly man.

Alas, in the natural course of events there came a night when Lowell had a toothache and went to the dentist in the afternoon. He was so unwell afterwards that he rang up and asked if he might be excused duty that night. The day porter, Timpson, agreed to stay on. He, poor man, naturally went to sleep at his post after a full day's work.

So when Janice tried to get back in she couldn't make anyone hear. The front door was locked and bolted. She dared not make too much noise in trying to summon a helper. She went off to inspect the ground floor windows but they were securely fastened.

A solution occurred to her. She would go round to the

residential wing and throw pebbles at the window of one of her friend's rooms. Alas, her knowledge of the geography of the place was at fault – everything looks different in the dark. The pebbles she was throwing hit the window of another third year student who woke in a panic thinking a burglar was trying to get in. Screams and cries brought everyone else to wakefulness. Mrs Stepps-Astley came sailing down the passage in a quilted dressing gown and steel curlers.

'Don't make such a racket, gel!' she said with indignation to the girl who had screamed. 'Do you want to wake every baby in the wing?'

'Sorry, Mrs Stepps-Astley,' stammered Peggy, 'b-but there's a man trying to g-get in!'

'Nonsense.' Mrs Stepps-Astley swept to the window of her room, looked out, saw a figure skulking off down the slope of the lawn, and sent the now wakeful Timpson after it.

He came back holding Janice by the arm. He was furious with her. He had been one of the last on the scene when the outcry arose, thus showing he had been very deep in slumber. He knew he was going to get a roasting from Mrs Stepps-Astley and he intended to put it off on to Janice if he could.

Mrs Stepps-Astley eyed Janice with her lips pursed up. 'I might have known,' she said with a nod of her grey head in its speckling of steel clips. 'Off to bed now, if you please – and *quietly*! Nannies with children disturbed, see to them at once and then retire. As for you, Nanny Templeton, I'll see you in my office at eight tomorrow morning.'

'Yes, Mrs Stepps-Astley,' Janice said, going pale.

She went to bed in the room she shared with Mabel Welsh. Barbara had seen almost nothing of all this because the baby she was nannying with Emily Parkins had set up a roar at the first cry of alarm from Peggy. She and Emily were busy. When the baby fell asleep, all they could learn from the few girls still lingering in the passage was that someone had been caught trying to climb in and it was all over.

Next morning Barbara and Emily went about their usual

tasks, getting their two-year-old bathed and dressed and ready for his outing in the pram. He was due to be collected by his parents the following Tuesday, and on the following Wednesday Emily would leave to begin her career in a private family. Barbara would then be given her first assignment in sole charge of a child or children.

Emily took little Gavin out for his airing. Barbara was left behind to tidy up the nursery. She was wiping down the surfaces with a cloth dipped in disinfectant when Janice came in, looking unusually subdued.

'Hello, why aren't you with Nanny Welsh?' Barbara asked in surprise.

'That was me last night.'

Barbara put down the damp cloth, wiped her hands on a towel, and looked at Janice in some dismay. 'Oh dear,' she said.

'You may well say. I've just had a session with the Boss.'

'What happened?'

'I've got the push.'

'Janice!'

'I suppose I expected I'd be in the soup. But it's worse than I thought. Timpson's gone all hard-hearted – he's told everything he knows or suspects and Lowell's got the sack.'

'Oh, Janice!'

'Mrs Stepps-Astley says she can't have goings-on like that in the school. I said she must know jolly well that other girls came in late from time to time and she told me to mind my own business. Then she said I could pack and leave at once.'

'This late in your training?'

'Isn't it rotten? After all the time I've put in – not to get my certificate.'

'Oh, Janice,' groaned Barbara, putting an arm round her. 'You know you've been asking for it . . .'

'I suppose I have. But I never really thought it would happen . . .'

'Have you told the others?' She meant Agnes and Lillian,

their former dormitory-mates.

'No, I came to you first. What am I going to *do*, Barbara?'

'What can you do?'

'I don't know. I thought you might think of something.'

'Let's go and talk to the others.' In rooms in other parts of the residential nursery, Lillian and Agnes were finishing off the chores just as Barbara had done. Lillian had already heard the news, Agnes was as surprised as Barbara when she heard it at first. Then her reaction was the same.

'You have been asking for it, after all, Janice.'

'Don't keep saying that! I never for a minute thought the Boss would react so . . . coldly. I mean, for all her faults, old Stepps-Astley is a realist.'

'You're saying that she knows some of the students play night-owl?'

'I bet she did it herself, when she was a girl.'

They all were silent for a moment as they tried to picture Mrs Stepps-Astley as a girl.

'You see,' Janice said, in a voice that was oddly shaken, 'I've put a lot of my life into training to be a Nanny. Contrary to what a lot of folk seem to think, I really want to do it.'

'Did you tell all that to the Boss?'

'I . . . I don't remember. I got a bit upset. I think I told her she was a narrow-minded old fool.'

'Oh, *Janice*,' they groaned in chorus.

'Well, what are we going to do about it?' Barbara inquired after a moment.

'What can we do?'

'Well . . . we could go in a body and ask Mrs Stepps-Astley to reconsider.'

Lillian and Agnes stared at her, aghast.

'Not me,' Agnes blurted. 'She's not too keen on me in the first place. She thinks I'm thick, I know she does.'

'Well, you and me than, Lillian –'

'Oh no. Oh, no!' Lillian protested. 'I'm not going into that office and tell her she's making a mistake. I want to get through the rest of my training without black marks.'

'Oh, come on,' Barbara urged, looking from one to the other with a challenging air. 'She can't eat us.'

'Want to bet?' Lillian said, shaking her head.

'I can't. Honest, I can't,' Agnes sighed. 'My Mum has made a lot of sacrifices to pay for my tuition. I can't endanger it all now – not even for you, m'dear,' she added, with a glance of apology at Janice.

'Why don't you go?' Lillian suggested.

'Me?'

'On your own. I mean, you're older, and you've got a sort of a way with you. And say what you like, Mrs Stepps-Astley has a soft spot for you.'

'She has not!'

'Oh yes she has. If any other student had got pally with Dr Deniz, Mrs Stepps-Astley would have had her on the carpet. But she hasn't said a word to you.'

'Oh . . . well, that's because . . .'

'Yes, explain it. You know jolly well it's because . . . well, I don't know why exactly. All I know is you'd have a better chance of changing her mind about Janice than anyone else.'

'Please do it,' Janice begged. 'I don't know what I'm going to do if she gives me the sack.'

Barbara backed away from the idea but in the end felt it was worth a try. She went back to her nursery, washed her hands, did her hair, and took off her housework apron. Then in her green dress, all neat and clean, she went to ask Miss Goodie for an interview with Mrs Stepps-Astley.

'Oh dear,' Miss Goodie said. 'Is it important?'

'Very.'

'Only . . . this isn't a very good day to be seeing her.'

'It's important, Miss Goodie.'

'All right.' The secretary went into the inner office then came out again. 'She can give you five minutes,' she announced.

Mrs Stepps-Astley was sitting looking directly at the door

when Barbara came in.

'Well?'

'It's about Nanny Templeton, Mrs Stepps-Astley.'

'Miss Templeton is leaving the school this morning.'

'No, please, don't send her away, Mrs Stepps-Astley. I know Nanny Templeton's been silly, but –'

'Miss Templeton.' said the Director, emphasizing the title, 'is no longer a Nanny in the sense that I use the word. She has had many chances to come to terms with the life she chose, and has failed. I have no alternative but to expel her.'

'But it's so unfair, Mrs Stepps-Astley. Other girls stay out after lights out.'

'Few, I think. I know what goes on under this roof, Nanny Gray. And if you think it had escaped my notice that Miss Templeton was leaving the premises after we were all supposed to be in bed, and returning sometimes after midnight, you are mistaken.'

Barbara took a deep breath. 'Look here,' she said, coming out into the open and addressing the Director as woman to woman, 'Janice may be a bit of a bright spark. But she's good with children, she's kept up with the class work – her private life is her own, surely.'

'Nothing of the sort!' Mrs Stepps-Astley cried, slapping the desk with the palm of her hand. 'That is exactly the point I have been hoping she would come to understand. A Nanny cannot have a private life.'

'Mrs Stepps-Astley! That isn't so.'

'Believe me, the amount of free time that a Nanny is given almost precludes it. You will see, when you go to live in a family. Employers frown on having male friends calling at the nursery so it means there can be meetings on rare occasions. Of course Nannies do get engaged and married, but it is usually a long, steady courtship, carried on under difficulty. As to rushing through a series of little romantic affairs, as Miss Templeton has done, that is out of the question.'

'But I don't think anyone has the right to say that to us,'

Barbara cried. 'Janice is the way she is – she likes to have men friends.'

'I ask nothing about what she does with them,' Mrs Stepps-Astley said. 'Although I'm not so foolish as to think she is the kind to limit herself to holding hands. I'm trying to get a quite different point across to you, Nanny Gray. Miss Templeton cannot complete her training here. I cannot allow her to go at the end of the training with the diploma of this school. She would bring shame on us, I am certain.'

'Shame? Now just a minute, Janice really cares about children. She would never do anything to harm –'

'You may be right. But I can't let Miss Templeton complete her training and then go to a family with our recommendation. To put it plainly, Nanny, the Hogarth School cannot be seen to recommend a girl who shows herself to be a tart.'

'Mrs Stepps-Astley!'

'You're shocked? You thought, perhaps, I didn't know the word – or would never use it. My dear Nanny Gray, I've lived longer than you and seen more of the world. I've seen girls use their looks to raise themselves from the kitchen to the comforts of a flat in Knightsbridge. I've seen others steal, blackmail or wheedle. The girls who go into a family by means of the nursery are probably no different but those who leave our school to start as Nannies will be expected to be a cut above the rest.'

'Janice isn't a bad girl, Mrs Stepps-Astley.'

'No, I agree. But she is self-indulgent, she is vain, and she likes men. I hoped she'd get the better of those defects while she was here, but she hasn't. Last night's escapade was a blatant example of her –'

'She only went out late for an hour or so – she just wanted to get back in.'

'And where had she been? With whom? And how fit would she be for her day's work, after getting to bed so late? And what would an employer have thought if he had caught her in the same circumstances?'

'Well, I suppose he'd have –'

'He'd have thought she was coming home from a night on the tiles. And she'd have been out the door next morning. It's no use, Nanny. I know you're fond of Miss Templeton, but she is not Nanny material.'

The way in which the last phrase was uttered put paid to the discussion. Barbara could see it was useless to argue. She turned to leave.

'Wait,' Mrs Stepps-Astley said.

She turned back.

'I suppose I expected you to come to speak on her behalf.' The carefully dressed iron grey head nodded. 'It's typical. Nanny Gray, do try to be less vulnerable to the troubles of others. You're only making life hard for yourself.'

'Is that part of the training, Mrs Stepps-Astley?'

'Alas, no. Only experience can teach that. I hope you will learn to be a little more hard hearted, my dear. You may go.'

Barbara got back to the nursery wing as the others were debating whether Janice should pack or not. They turned as she came in at the door of Janice's room. They looked at her. She shook her head.

'I did my best,' she said.

'What did she say?'

'She said you . . . you liked men too much. She said it showed you weren't "Nanny material".'

'Of course I like men! What's wrong with that?' Janice burst out. 'I'm normal, good God! But just because I like to kiss and cuddle and maybe a bit more, that doesn't mean I'm a scarlet woman!'

'No, but people who're confiding the care of their children –'

'I'd never hurt a child!' Janice interrupted passionately. 'You know that!'

'Of course we know, dear,' Lillian said, beginning to cry.

'I think the whole thing's cockeyed!' raged Janice. 'Does being a Nanny mean you have to give up men?'

She put her suitcase on the bed and began to throw her belongings into it haphazardly. Lillian watched her, sniffing.

'Men are going to be a problem, aren't they?' she muttered.

'Not to me,' said Agnes.

Barbara looked at Agnes and knew it was true. Quiet, placid Agnes was never going to want to kick over the traces. It was difficult to imagine Agnes getting in a state about anything, let alone a man. Her pulses were never going to race, her eyes were never going to fill with tears for what might have been. Sex meant nothing to her.

But for Janice it was important. Lillian too, though in a more romantic style.

And for herself? When she thought of her encounter with Archie, she was shaken. Was she going to have to say goodbye to the joys of physical love? From what Mrs Stepps-Astley said, it was implied that a Nanny must live like a nun.

Was that what she had expected when she began to train for the work?

Janice left in a taxi half an hour later. As it was by then the time for ten o'clock feeds in the nursery, almost no one was around to see her go. Barbara asked Emily's permission and was in the hall as Timpson, his expression sour, put the case in the taxi.

'I don't care,' Janice said. 'I can get a job as a Nanny without their rotten certificate!'

'Write and let us know how you get on,' Barbara begged. 'We'll be worried about you.'

'Huh!' scoffed Janice. 'I'll be having a better time than you lot, that's certain.' She waved brightly as she was driven away. Barbara waved back.

The timetable now moved on inexorably. Emily Parkins handed over her two-year-old to his parents with a sigh, but cheered up over packing for her first job. She was going to a titled family in Northumberland.

'Your "intake" arrives tomorrow,' she said to Barbara. 'What are you getting?'

'Don't know yet. The Boss hasn't told me so far.'

'You'd better give the room a thorough going-over after I've gone. Some parents look at things through a microscope before they hand over their kiddies.'

'I will, I promise.'

She began as soon as Emily had departed. She was on her knees scraping at a mysterious small spot on the lino with a knife when the summons came from the Director. She scrambled up, tidied herself, took off her housework apron and presented herself at Mrs Stepps-Astley's office.

'Ah, Nanny Gray,' Mrs Stepps-Astley said. 'Your "intake" arrives today. Two babies, a boy of fifteen months and his little sister, four months.'

'Oh,' Barbara said, delighted. She would have been pleased whatever Mrs Stepps-Astley had confided to her, would have devoted herself to a ten-year-old with just as much eagerness. But two little babies sounded like heaven.

'The parents are diplomats stationed in this country who have to go home on family business. They estimate an absence of at least three months, perhaps longer.'

'I'm to have the children for the entire time of their absence?'

'That is the plan, unless at any time you ask for a "take-over". You –'

'Oh, I shan't!' Barbara broke in with haste. 'I'll be delighted to stay with them.'

'Even over the holiday breaks?'

'Of course. With their parents away, it's important they should have continuity in their absence. Thank you, Mrs Stepps-Astley.'

'No thanks are necessary. This is part of your training. The parents will bring the children before lunch. You will have the nursery ready and after introduction will escort them there.'

'Of course. Everything will be ready.'

'Is there anything else?'

'Er . . . what are the children's names, Mrs Stepps-Astley?'

The Director consulted the papers on her desk. 'The boy is called Kung Chun-jui, and the girl Kung Chia-jen.'

Barbara's mouth came open. She sat for a moment gazing at the Director.

'You mean . . . they're Chinese children?'

'With names like those, I should think that is obvious, Nanny.'

'But – Mrs Stepps-Astley – I can't speak any Chinese!'

Mrs Stepps-Astley fixed an irate glance upon her. 'My dear Nanny Gray, neither can the children, so don't be absurd.'

Oh, of course. Fifteen months and four months. Conversation was hardly likely to be a problem with babies of that age. Barbara relaxed.

'Of course. I just wasn't thinking. But . . . what about diet? Do little Chinese babies have the same kind of regime as Europeans?'

'Mr Kung assured me when we conversed on the telephone that he wished his children to be brought up under the most advanced Western system. He is a gentleman of high intelligence and education. This is why he chose to send his children to us while he has to be away. You need have no fears on that score, he understands our methods.'

'Oh, then that's all right. Very well, Mrs Stepps-Astley, I'll go and just put the finishing touches, shall I?'

When she got back to the nursery she surveyed it with a dispassionate eye. It was comfortable, hygienic, airy, but you couldn't exactly say it was a pleasure to look at. She had heard that the Chinese were very sensitive to beauty, that their paintings were dream-like and pale, that they had special views on harmony and so forth. After some thought she went into the garden and begged some flowers from the head gardener, a crusty old man who parted with a few sprays of chrysanthemums very unwillingly.

She put the kettle on so as to offer tea to the parents. She'd heard from the other girls that parents liked to be given nursery tea – it struck an old chord with them.

At eleven-thirty she was sitting on the edge of a chair in the hall in her best Hogarth uniform, waiting for the Kungs to arrive. A handsome Rolls-Royce swept up to the front door. A chauffeur got out – an ordinary English-looking chauffeur in a uniform. He opened the door at the back. Out stepped a slender dark man of middle height in the obligatory frock coat and pin stripes of the diplomat. He moved towards the porch. The chauffeur helped out a small lady in a sable coat and tiny high-heeled shoes. She followed the man into the porch. The chauffeur hurried to ring the bell. Everyone was lost to sight for a moment while Timpson went to open the front door.

Miss Goodie hastened out of the front office to escort the Kungs to Mrs Stepps-Astley. Barbara had been bade to wait until she was summoned, but she couldn't resist slipping out to the car.

The chauffeur was standing by the door.

'Hullo,' he said, 'you the Nanny?'

She nodded.

He jerked his head at the interior of the Rolls. 'There they are,' he said. 'Poor little sods.'

Barbara stooped and looked in.

On the seat lay a basket of red-lacquered cane. On the satin pillows which padded it lay a four-month-old baby fast asleep, dark hair in a little tuft on the crown of her head. There was nothing particularly Oriental about her.

Beside the basket sat a boy in a short frock of stiff silk. One small hand held the edge of the basket. His triangular face was dark-skinned. His hair came on to his forehead in a straight fringe. His eyes really were almond shaped.

Barbara looked at him, and he looked at Barbara.

'Hullo,' she said. 'I'm your Nanny.'

He met her smiling gaze. Uncertainty flickered over his face. He made a wriggling movement – whether he was trying to scramble towards her or away from her she couldn't have said.

At that moment Mrs Stepps-Astley spoke behind her. 'Ah, getting acquainted, I see. Nanny, will you bring in the children for Mrs Kung?'

'Certainly, Mrs Stepps-Astley.'

She picked up the little boy, who allowed himself to be lifted without putting his arms up to catch hold. The chauffeur brought the baby in her basket. In the hall Mr and Mrs Kung were waiting.

'This way,' Mrs Stepps-Astley said, and led the way regally to the nursery which was to be the children's home for the next few months.

Barbara set the little boy down in the play-pen she had made ready for him on the nursery floor. There were one or two soft toys and a few bricks awaiting him. 'You've brought his own toys with him?' she inquired.

'If you will go with Mercer, he will give them to you,' Mr Kung said.

Barbara withdrew. She accompanied the chauffeur back to the Rolls, where he produced fine leather suitcases from the boot together with a box of toys. 'Look after the little beggars,' he said in a rather sad tone. 'They're going to miss their Ma. Thinks the world of them, she does.'

'Of course she does. But it won't be too long before they see her again.'

'I wouldn't bet on that,' Mercer said. 'There's a war going on out there, y'know. And they've got to find their folks before they can bring 'em south.'

'Oh . . . I . . . You mean the Japanese invasion?'

'That's what I mean, miss. The family's from the North, see, and that's where all the trouble is – troops marching across, even attacks by aeroplanes, so I hear. They haven't had word from their family for weeks now. The rumour at the Embassy is that *his* father's dead. Last they heard of her family was over two months ago, and now the Japs are all over the area. I dunno. I hope they know what they're doing.'

'I'd no idea,' Barbara murmured, taking up the box of toys. 'I thought they were just going home on a visit.'

'Some visit. Well, be kind to the poor little beggars. Good as gold, they are.'

When she reached the nursery again with the toys Mr and

Mrs Kung were coming out. Mr Kung was listening with a calm, reserved expression to Mrs Stepps-Astley's assurances that the children would be in the best possible hands. But it seemed to Barbara there was a glint of tears in the wife's eyes.

'Is there any special instruction you'd like to give to Nanny Gray?' Mrs Stepps-Astley said to Mrs Kung on a note of encouragement.

Mrs Kung hesitated. 'Chia-jen sleeps well through the night. Sometimes Chun-jui wakes – teeth are troublesome.'

'Of course. I'll look after him.'

'We shall be back as soon as possible,' said Mr Kung. 'We are lucky to be able to travel by air for part of the journey.'

Mrs Kung looked down, as if she didn't much look forward to air travel. Barbara was suddenly desperately sorry for her. Leaving her children, journeying by this new hazardous method to a country torn by war, looking for her parents who seemed to have gone missing . . . If she had been an Englishwoman Barbara would have essayed some words of sympathy, but the reserve of the two Chinese made it clear they had no wish to discuss private affairs.

'The children will be fine,' she assured them. 'I'll look after them.'

Mrs Kung raised her head. Their glances met. 'Yes,' said Mrs Kung. 'Thank you.' Then to her husband, 'We must go.'

He nodded. 'Goodbye,' he said, with a little bow.

'Goodbye,' Barbara said, uncertain whether to bow or hold out her hand. When she turned to Mrs Kung, she let instinct take over. 'Goodbye,' she said, 'don't worry,' and took the other woman's hand in a quick pressure.

Mrs Kung said something in Chinese to her husband, the only word of which Barbara could distinguish was 'Hao'. Later she was to discover that the word meant 'good', and that Mrs Kung was telling her husband that Chia-jen and Chun-jui were in good hands.

But it wasn't until later that Barbara decided to learn Chinese.

CHAPTER TWELVE

The children's names were quite beyond her to pronounce. Besides, unless she kept referring to the little name-card on the nursery door, she couldn't remember which name belonged to which. The name-card told her because they were registered there in order of age, with the boy first. But before the first day was over she'd got tired of trying to call him Chun-jui.

His baby sister reminded Barbara of a little dark red rosebud. As she was bathing her that evening she began addressing her as Rosie, which the little thing didn't seem to mind in the least. From there it was a short step to calling the little boy Robbie, and before the end of the following day they were so firmly established in her mind as Robbie and Rosie that she couldn't recall their Chinese names.

They were a joy to nurse. Although, as Mrs Kung had said, Robbie tended to wake in the night, it was only because his teeth were coming and he was in pain. He was never naughty. He scrambled about the nursery on his seat, amusing himself with his toys. He sat up in his pram looking pleased with the world.

'There now, aren't you a clever boy?' she demanded as she helped him into his high chair for lunch towards the end of his first week with her. 'Now, who's going to be a good boy and eat up his minced chicken for Barbara?'

'Baba,' Robbie said obligingly, opening his mouth.

'That's right, Barbara!' she agreed, laughing. 'I'm Barbara. Nanny Barbara. Now another little spoonful for Robbie. Robbie's hungry. Open wide, in it goes . . .'

Robbie swallowed his chicken then watched her get a refill. 'Baba,' he said, waving his hand at her.

'Nanny Barbara. And you're Robbie.'

'Baba,' Robbie said. To get her name right seemed to be enough for today. It wasn't until next day he came out with something that might have been Robbie. She hugged him and told him he was clever, then coaxed him into calling his sister Rosie. No one could have said it was a perfect pronunciation, but he was certainly beginning to talk. Within a few days he had a vocabulary of about twelve words, including her name, his own and his sister's, and such things as 'cot', 'mug' and 'din-din'.

'It's such a shame,' Barbara said in a tone of regret to Agnes. 'They're missing it all.'

'Who?'

'His mother and father, of course. He's saying his first words and they're not here to hear them.'

'Seems to me it makes no difference,' Agnes said in her stolid way, 'since they wouldn't understand 'em anyhow.'

'How d'you mean?'

'Well, the parents are Chinese aren't they?'

'Yes, but they speak English, for heaven's sake!'

'Oh, yes, I reckon they'd have to, being diplomats here. What I mean is, Mrs Thingummy wouldn't be likely to teach her kiddies "din-din" and "po-po", would she? I mean, she'd talk Chinese to 'em, wouldn't she.'

'Well, she . . .'

'She certainly wouldn't teach 'em to call themselves Rosie and Robbie,' Agnes said with a laugh. 'What was their funny names?'

To her consternation, Barbara realized she had no idea.

'But . . . that's terrible, Agnes!' she burst out. 'They're learning to talk, and they're not learning their own language!'

'Don't be daft, how can they? They're here, with you, and you have to talk to 'em in English. Stands to reason.'

'But it's all wrong!' Barbara cried. 'I don't know how you can stand there and not see it's all wrong!'

They were out with their children in the grounds. Agnes had a four-year-old girl to look after, who was now off in the sandpit making pies. Barbara had Rosie and Robbie in a twin's pram, the baby asleep while Robbie sat up at his end watching a windmill, made for him by Barbara, whirl round in the November breeze.

Agnes shook her head at Barbara. 'I can't see how it's wrong.' she said. 'And even if it is, there's nothing you can do about it.'

'But you just don't know what a . . . a maze you get into when you're a child and get in a muddle with language! I was brought up in India, don't forget, and sometimes I didn't know who I was, I had to switch about so much. The servants would chatter away at us in Urdu, and then all of a sudden Daddy would be asking us a question, and we couldn't think of the answer in English, and we'd come back in Urdu and he'd call us little ignoramuses . . . It was bad enough for me but worse for Eileen. She didn't know how to cope with England when we got here, she'd been so soaked in Indian ways.'

'Well, all that's prob'ly true, but it makes no difference to the fact that Mr and Mrs Kung wanted their little ones looked after by a Hogarth Nanny and you have to use the King's English. That's the end of it, so stop worrying.'

But Barbara couldn't stop worrying. On her afternoon off she was to meet Fredric in London for a drink, but before going to the Berkeley she visited a bookshop in Charing Cross Road. There she looked along the shelves in the language department and after much perplexity came away with a small book. It had a blue paper cover showing a Chinese gentleman bowing in a welcoming fashion and was called 'Chinese for Newcomers'.

After she and Fredric had exchanged news and settled to talk, she asked his advice about the matter of language. 'Do you think it matters if a child learns its first words in a different tongue from its parents?'

'I don't see what you mean, Barbara?'

'Well, if the parents have to go away and the baby is left with foreigners. Would it make a difference when it was reunited with its mother?'

'Of course. There's always some alienation in a separation, but if the child has to learn a new language as well as getting to know its mother again –'

'That's what I thought. I've got these two little Chinese mites, you see.'

'Chinese?'

'Yes. Their parents have gone home to try and sort out some family troubles.'

'What part of China?'

'I think it says on the documents, Liaoning Province.'

'Oh dear. That's where the Japanese are fighting.'

'I know, Fredric, isn't it awful. Mr and Mrs Kung hoped to be back in three or four months, but I can't help wondering if they might be longer, and Robbie is just beginning to learn to talk.'

'Robbie?'

'That's what I call him. He's got some unpronounceable name in Chinese. And the baby – she's not talking yet but she might begin if she stays a long while with us. She might pick it up from Robbie; that happens sometimes, when two children are close – but of course you know all that,' she said, feeling a fool to be telling such a thing to a psychologist.

'I shouldn't worry about it too much,' he soothed. Interested though he was in Barbara's work, he didn't want to waste too much of their short time together on discussing her charges.

All too soon it was train time. He saw her to Waterloo. 'See you next week?'

'I hope so. Same place?'

'And time. Unless anything crops up.'

'All right.' They kissed quickly as the guard blew the whistle, and the train chugged out.

She sat back in the corner of the carriage and in the rather poor light of the single bulb she opened her book and began to read.

'Introduction. Most Europeans arriving in Shanghai will

find that the area of the Bund is well-supplied with English-speaking servants, clerks, and business agents. Nevertheless it is an undoubted advantage to be able to understand and use a few basic words of Chinese.' Good, she thought, a few basic words.

'First,' the introduction continued, 'this book will give illustrations of Chinese pictographs likely to be seen as signs outside buildings, and if these are memorized it will be helpful in finding one's way round the city.' She turned the page. Beautiful little squiggles, very complex and well-balanced, took up the surface. She saw that they meant 'Hospital', 'Bank', 'Restaurant'. But since she felt it was unlikely she'd want to put up such signs in the nursery, she turned the page.

'Chinese,' the author went on, 'is spoken in many dialects. Mandarin is regarded as the standard for educational purposes although the various provinces have their own variations.' There followed a list of the regions. It occurred to Barbara that her two Chinese children might have been born of Hakka-speaking Chinese, since that was one of the northern dialects. But there was nothing to be done about that and in any case, 'Mandarin is regarded as the standard for educational purposes.'

She prepared to pay strict attention. Now the author was coming to the main point. 'Chinese is a tonal language. There are four main tones in which each word may be uttered: high level, high rising level, low rising, and high level falling to low.'

'What?' gasped Barbara, aloud.

The other occupants of the compartment, two elderly ladies, ceased their conversation to look at her as if she were mad.

She gave them an apologetic smile and went back to re-read the paragraph. She must have got it wrong.

But no. Worse was to come. 'The word "ma", for instance,' informed the author, 'may mean four different things according to the inflection with which it is spoken. High level, *mother*. High rising, *hemp*. Low rising, *a horse*.

And the descending tone, *a curse*.'

'Ma,' Barbara said to herself inside her head. She tried to imagine it in a high voice. 'Ma?' As if she were a very small child calling to its mother. But that was high-rising – a child calling would raise its voice.

How about the low level rising to higher? 'Ma-a', she practised. But it was no use. You'd have to say it aloud before you knew whether your voice was really rising or falling.

She read on: 'Words in Chinese are very short' (thank goodness for that) 'but are put together with rapidity in the same ways as syllables in English. The voice rises and falls with more flexibility than in an English sentence and the rhythmic pattern is more staccato. It is important not to hesitate too long in the formation of a command or request as the hesitation in itself may change the meaning of the phrase.'

Oh, great.

'The Romanization of Chinese spelling can only be approximate. There are sounds in Chinese which do not occur in English, and unfortunately as the first to attempt the task of putting down the sounds on paper were German scholars, our Romanized approximations are very imperfect.'

She closed the book with bafflement. Romanization? Germans? All she wanted was to learn a few words in Chinese so as to teach them to Robbie, in the hope that when his mother said them to him later he'd recognize them.

She turned over a few pages to find phrases for actual use. The first page she lighted on was 'In the office'. 'Bring me the Bought Ledger, the Sales Ledger, the Statement of Accounts.' 'Send a message to the shipping office.' 'Check the cargo for damage.'

No, no. She turned over. 'In the restaurant'. 'Bring me a whisky and soda, a gin and tonic, a bottle of wine.' 'I will have the roast chicken, the duck.'

Ah . . . chicken. She looked at the words: *Tsiang-ji-chi.*

'Eat up your *tsiang-ji-chi,* Robbie,' she rehearsed inwardly. But should it be a rising *tsiang-ji-chi* or a falling *tsiang-ji-chi*?

By the time she got out at Haslemere, her head was in a whirl. It was no use. She'd better start again in the morning, she was too tired to take it in at the moment.

Naturally the care of the children took up her time at first, but when she went out for her airing she'd hoped to find a sheltered spot to study and practise. Unfortunately the November weather had turned very cool so she had to keep on the move. She addressed herself to Robbie, who sat up in the pram buttoned into his thick knitted coat and cap, listening with interest.

'Hello, Robbie,' she said, '*Wai-wai, ni hao?* How are you? Rosie is very *mei-li. Wai-wai,* Robbie. Say *wai-wai.*'

'Baba,' Robbie said in approval.

'Yes, I know I'm Barbara. Say *wai-wai*. That means hello. *Wai,* Robbie. Say *wai*."

'Robbie,' said Robbie.

'Oh dear. Chia-jen, that's you. Say Chia-jen. No, hang on, that's Rosie. Well, all right, say Chia-jen. Say *wai-wai*, Chia-jen.'

But by the time they came back from their walk, Robbie was still telling her she was Baba and waving his hand towards a horse in a neighbouring paddock and calling 'gee-gee'.

Peggy dropped in during the afternoon when all the children were having their nap. This was the time when the Nannies caught up with their chores and, having done so, had time for socializing.

Barbara was walking back and forth in the nursery with the book in her hands. *'Hao tang shu tong tai bao?'* she was enunciating.

'Pardon?' Peggy said, pausing in the doorway.

'Hao tang shu tong tai bao?'

'And the same to you. Have you gone bonkers?'

'I'm learning Chinese. It's so as to say a few words to Robbie – I mean Chun-jui.'

'Honestly?' Peggy was impressed. 'Go on, let's have a bit, then?'

'Yi nu chia so wen?' Barbara said.

'I say! Agnes said you were walking about across the lawn this morning chatting to Robbie in a funny way.'

'*Ni hao,* Chun-jui?' said Barbara. *'Chin jih san hsien?'*

'Marvellous. What does it mean?'

'I think it means, hello, Chun-jui, listen to the nice song now.'

'It does? Well, explain something to me. Why does it all sound as if you're asking questions?'

'Oh, that. Well, that's because of the rising inflections.'

'Chinese is all questions, then?'

'No, sometimes there's a falling inflection.'

'But you didn't fall any inflections.'

'No, well, I may have got that wrong. In which case I may have said something quite different from what I intended because I gather it all depends what pitch you say it at. *Ni hao,* Chun-jui, *san jih chin hsien*?'

'It was *chin jih* last time you said it, not *san jih*.'

'Was it? Oh, bother.' Barbara dived for her book to check.

'I think you're out of your mind,' Peggy remarked. 'As if it isn't enough work looking after two babies full-time, you have to try to learn the most complicated language in the world.'

'It can't be all that complicated, Peggy. The Chinese speak it without any difficulty.'

'Don't be a nitwit. They learn it in their cradles. They don't suddenly start when they're grown up with a book for businessmen.' Peggy took it out of Barbara's hand. 'Measure me for a double-breasted jacket,' she read out. 'I can just see Robbie needing a double-breasted jacket.'

'But . . . well . . . I don't think it's right those little things should never hear a word of their own mother-tongue, Peggy. Fredric agrees it will make things more difficult.'

'Oh, Fredric says, does he? It's all very well for him. Can he help you learn Chinese?'

'No, of course not.'

'What's Chinese for "Eat up your porridge, there's a good

boy"?'

'I don't know. The Chinese don't seem to say that sort of thing.'

'I bet they do. But the only person who's going to be able to say it is a Chinese.'

Barbara sighed. 'Yes,' she agreed.

'Well, are you going to offer me a cuppa or must I go and scrounge one from Aggie?'

In the evening, when the children had been put to bed, Miss Bell came round on her tour of inspection. Having peered into the cupboards, turned over the garments on the airing stand, and gone into the kitchenette to check the feeding bottles, she sat down a moment to listen to any complaints or problems.

'Miss Bell,' Barbara said, 'the little boy is learning to talk. He's picking up words every day.'

'Excellent, Nanny. I needn't ask if you're encouraging him.'

'I am, of course. But Miss Bell, the words he's learning are English.'

'Well, naturally.'

'There's nothing natural about it,' Barbara replied almost crossly. 'He ought to be learning Chinese.'

'Don't be absurd, Nanny Gray.'

'I don't think it's absurd at all! We've no real idea how long his parents will be gone, and in the meantime he's left in the charge of an English Nanny. By the time he sees his mother again, she'll be a stranger – and she'll *talk* like a stranger!'

Miss Bell was about to reply that Barbara was talking nonsense. But she checked the words on her lips.

'Well,' she said after a moment. 'That is a point.'

'It certainly is! I don't want to go into a long description of my childhood in India, Miss Bell, but one of the difficulties was that my sister and I spent an awful lot of time in the company of servants who didn't speak English.'

'It didn't do you any harm, all the same –'

'But we had our father there in the house and English friends around. There isn't a single soul here who can speak a word of Mandarin Chinese.'

'That would hardly be expected.'

'I'm not saying it's expected. But you must admit it would be preferable.'

'I admit that. But since it isn't so, what do you suggest?'

'I really think,' Barbara said, although it pained her to have to say it, 'that Robbie and Rosie should be taken away from the Hogarth.'

'Taken *away*?'

'To live with a Chinese family. The Kungs must have friends at the Embassy who could take the children in.'

'Oh . . . I see . . . Well, Nanny, this is a facer, isn't it? I never met the problem before, not once in all my years of nannying or teaching others. I . . . I'll speak to Mrs Stepps-Astley about it. Yes, I think you have a point. I'll speak to Mrs Stepps-Astley.'

'Thank you,' Barbara said.

When the teacher had gone Barbara went to see if her charges were safely asleep. Rosie was lying with a fist curled by her chin, like a cherub on a cloud. Robbie was in a position he often adopted, face in the pillow and his seat in the air. She turned him and covered him up, then moved off to stare out of the window.

She'd hate it if the babies were taken away from her. But it was best for them.

Mrs Stepps-Astley sent for her next morning at a time that one of the other Nannies could look after the pram in the garden. 'Nanny Gray, Miss Bell passed on your thoughts to me last night,' she said. 'And this morning I've telephoned the Embassy and spoken to the Second Secretary. He understands the point you are making, but it appears that Mr Kung has very strong views on the upbringing of children. He thinks Chinese households are restrictive and particularly wanted Chun . . . er . . . Jun –'

'Chun-jui and Chia-jen.'

'Exactly. Wished them to be cared for here, in the absence of himself and his wife. It appears they were on the verge of hiring an English Nanny when the need arose for them to go home.'

'But surely they wouldn't have wanted their children never to hear a word of Chinese?'

'Perhaps not. I confess I am at a loss.'

'This Secretary – what did he suggest?'

'Only that we should carry out the wishes of Mr and Mrs Kung. To keep their children here.'

'I see.' Selfishly she couldn't help being glad. But she was only too aware that the problem hadn't been solved. It was only storing it up for the future.

The following day the little Kungs had visitors, a man younger than Mr Kung and one much older. These two were brought to the nursery, where they looked about with interest and some apprehension. The children were brought forward, the two men smiled, tickled Rosie, let Robbie drag at their carefully tied foulard cravats, chatted a bit in Chinese, and took their leave.

'That's a lot of help,' Barbara said to Peggy. 'I can see they meant well, and it's nice of them to bother, but what good will it do, an occasional visit from an Embassy official?'

'Isn't it better than nothing?'

'Not much!'

The following Sunday was a fine, bright day. It was just the sort of day for an outing in the country. A fine Bentley rolled up to the door of the Hogarth School and out stepped a portly Chinese gentleman with a small but stout lady at his heels, followed by four others. The ladies ranged in age from mid-twenties to a little girl of about eight.

'May I introduce self and family,' the gentleman said. 'Commercial attaché of the Chinese Embassy, Edmund Tsu. This is Mrs Tsu, and Mrs Tsu sister, Mrs Diang. Young ladies are my daughters, Nora, Susan and Kay. Kay is least in age. We come to visit children of Mr Kung.'

'How lovely!' Barbara cried, ushering them across the lawn to the bench in the sun where she had been sitting with the Kung children.

'We are much impressed by your concern for Kung children. This is a thought that Mr Kung forgot – that the babies would be learning to speak. Mr Kung is a very sci-en-ti-fic man but even scientists forget things.'

'Babies look good,' Mrs Tsu remarked.

'Thank you. I think they're very well. And no trouble.'

'Kay, rock pram. We will have talk with Nanny Gray.'

Kay, nothing loth, devoted herself to amusing Robbie, who seemed to fall in love with her at sight. When it was time for the children to go indoors and have lunch, she begged to be allowed to help. Barbara was pleased to allow it, and though the nursery seemed very crowded when everyone came in, the meal went off without a hitch. Rosie took her bottle like a lamb. They were changed and put down to take their nap while the Tsus and their relations went to talk to Mrs Stepps-Astley in her office.

'Can you come back again soon?' Barbara asked at leave-taking.

Mr Tsu shook his head. 'Work at Embassy keeps me in London. Also Mrs Tsu has social duties, and elder daughters at day-school.'

'Oh,' Barbara said, dashed. It had been so enjoyable, watching eight-year-old Kay chattering to the two little ones in Chinese, and playing with them with unending patience. 'Is Kay at day-school?'

'Kay has governess.'

'In London?'

'Yes.'

'Mrs Diang?'

'No, I live not too far off,' said Mrs Diang. 'I have a house near Guildford. Embassy property. My husband is at Rosyth for the moment – naval business.'

'I see.' Barbara hesitated. 'Mr Tsu, could I ask you a great favour?'

'Great favour should be granted to friend who does great things. Please ask.'

'Could your youngest daughter and her governess stay with her aunt in Guildford?'

Mr Tsu's round face creased in a frown. 'I do not see how that is a favour to Nanny Gray?'

'If Kay were staying nearby, she could drop in every day for an hour or two and play with Rosie and – I mean, Chia-jen and Chun-jui – and *talk* to them.'

There was a silence. Barbara caught Kay's eye and saw a spark of pleasure at the idea. But no one dared say anything until the head of the family had spoken.

For a moment he held them in suspense. Then he said teasingly, 'Youngest daughter always a trouble to household. Good excuse to be rid of her for three or four months.'

Kay threw herself upon him with a cry of delight. A rapid crossfire of Chinese followed. Mrs Tsu naturally put up objections, these were done away with by her husband, Kay seemed to be insisting loudly that she wanted to do it, and Mrs Diang from time to time threw a word of translation to Barbara.

'Mrs Tsu naturally . . . doesn't want to part – not far off, though. Mr Tsu says it's a short drive. Weekends . . . Yes, I think it's all right. I think so.'

'Please let me speak.' Mr Tsu said, waving his sister-in-law aside. 'Nanny Gray, youngest daughter will visit Kung children every day if possible, governess will bring her. This kind idea we like very much. When Mr Kung and wife return, we will tell them. We feel debt on his behalf.' He bowed to Barbara. 'Until now, much doubt in our minds of English Nanny he approves. Now we understand his view. Very honoured to know Nanny Gray.'

'Thank you,' she said, bowing.

When they had gone in their shining Bentley, Mrs Stepps-Astley turned to Barbara. 'I think we handled that rather well,' she remarked.

Barbara gave a demure smile. 'I think we did,' she agreed.

CHAPTER THIRTEEN

At the end of a four-month stay, the Kung children were collected by their parents. After the usual shyness and reserve, Robbie began on a bright prattle in Chinese. Barbara wondered if anyone would ever explain to the Kungs how this had been achieved in an English speaking school. She also longed to ask if the elder Kungs had been found in Liaoning Province and brought to safety, but there was so much dignity and punctiliousness in Mr Kung's manner that she didn't dare.

It struck her then as strange, and was often to come into her mind later. She would play such an important role in a family, and yet always be on the outer edge of its life.

The time had now come for her to do her hospital months. Every Nanny turned out by the Hogarth School was expected to be able to nurse her charges through the usual minor illnesses and to be aware when a more serious illness had arisen. The Hogarth School had an arrangement with three or four general hospitals, to take their students into the children's ward as helpers. It was accepted that the student wasn't training to be a medical nurse and wouldn't be asked to do anything more than be a dogsbody, although she was expected by the school to take note of bedside procedures, become familiar with common symptoms and generally put the experience to good use.

Barbara dreaded this part of her training. She remembered her wartime nursing, first the training in Brixton and then the Base Hospital at La Baule. She associated hospitals with suffering men, with long-term invalids and death.

Nor was her mood lightened when she presented herself at Bayswater General Hospital on the Friday requested. She asked the hall porter the way to Matron's room, was directed there, and told to leave her case with him. 'Don't you go cluttering up Matron's corridor with cases,' he warned.

The corridor outside Matron's office was like a skating rink. There was a bench outside the door, on which sat four nurses looking very scared. They muttered to each other; Barbara couldn't hear the words but guessed each was on the carpet for some dreadful crime such as wearing a cardigan over her uniform, or failing to pleat the screen curtains before threading them on the rod.

The door opened, a nurse came out looking pale. 'Next,' she said, and jerked her head at the door.

Barbara could see she was going to have to wait her turn. She took a book out of her handbag. The three nurses remaining when the next victim went in stared at Barbara as if she was insane. 'You're not going to *read*?' they gasped.

'Yes, I am.' But she didn't. It was impossible to keep her attention on the printed page – 'Rogue Herries' borrowed from Boots Library – with these three terrified young women muttering to her left.

One by one they went in and came out, looking shattered. 'Next,' the last one said to Barbara. Barbara rose and went in through the mahogany doorway.

'Now, nurse,' said the lady at the desk. Then she looked up, and was visibly surprised. 'And you are –?'

'Nanny Gray, Matron, from Hogarth.'

'Ah yes. I see. That means the disciplinary list is over for today. Sit down, Nanny.'

Barbara obeyed. The chair facing the desk was straightbacked and hard, very penitential.

'I want it understood, Nanny, that Hogarth students are welcome here.'

'Thank you, Matron.'

'So long,' Matron went on, holding up a finger, 'as they do not hinder in any way the efficient running of my wards. The children's ward in particular needs to be calm and orderly.'

'Yes, Matron.'

'I see from your particulars,' Matron said, putting her hand unerringly on the file among those ranged before her,' that you have hospital training.'

'Yes, Matron.'

'You trained at Brixton in . . . let me see . . .'

'It was a wartime training, Matron. Then I went to France.'

'Oh, yes, *wartime* . . .' Matron's tone indicated that she thought nothing at all of nurses brought in for the emergency. 'That of course is some time ago. Procedures have changed considerably since then.'

'I know, Matron.'

'But in any case you are not required to take part in any clinical procedures except under the strictest supervision.'

'Yes, Matron.'

'You will be in Children's Ward B. Sister McMahon will give you your timetable. You are in . . . ah . . . Room 34 of the Nurses' Home. Home Sister is expecting you. You may go.'

'Thank you, Matron.'

She went out. Another nurse was now sitting on the bench outside, with a sheet of paper in her hand. She cast an agonized glance at Barbara as she left. Poor child – she was someone not on the 'list', someone caught this morning in some crime and sent on 'report' with a note of her shortcoming to hand to Matron.

Well, one good thing, Barbara thought as she went to reclaim her case from the porter, they can't do that to me. But she knew very well they could do almost everything else, because although Hogarth School paid the hospitals for the training they gave their students, they received no special privileges.

That was made clear at once by Home Sister. 'Well, so here you are,' she said cheerfully. 'Another little Hogarth learner.' She looked at Barbara through thick glasses. 'You're older than most?'

'Yes, Sister.'

'Makes no difference. You still get the Hogarth Room.' She grinned and led the way up the stairs to the third floor, where she opened the door on a tiny room furnished with a bed, chair, a curtain hiding a clothes-rail, and a mirror tacked to the wall. 'Here you are. Specially reserved for students from the Hogarth Training School.'

'Oh, God,' said Barbara.

'Cheer up. It's only for three months. And you'll be so tired you won't notice it anyway.'

Barbara sat down on the chair. It creaked. 'Hogarth is actually paying for my board and lodgings, you know,' she protested weakly.

'Ducks, all the rooms are much the same. This one's further to walk and gets hot in summer and cold in winter. Otherwise there's nothing to choose among them. What did you expect, the Ritz?'

'No-o,' Barbara said, with memories of her original training.

'Right, then. You'll find the notice-board in the hall. Read the rules. Absolutely no noise after ten at night, and as little as possible during the day out of regard to the night shift trying to take their rest. Understood?'

'Yes, Sister.'

'When are you expected on the ward?'

'Matron said Sister McMahon was expecting me – I'd better get over there.'

'Off you go then. She'll give you a cup of tea. "Meal" is at six.'

The jargon came back to Barbara as she unpacked swiftly. 'Meal' was the evening meal, served in the hospital dining-room from six to seven. Anything after that was called either 'breakfast' or 'supper' – breakfast for those going on night duty, supper for those coming off day duty. Food served in the morning before nine o'clock was usually called 'early meal'. At midday came 'dinner'. It was all quite different from the schedule of a normal home and was kept so on purpose to keep the staff alert.

She found her way to Children's Ward B by direction. A probationer in a grey print dress and crumpled white apron directed her to Sister's office. She tapped on the glass door, then went in briskly when called. Most sisters, she knew, hated anything that interfered with their system. Barbara's aim was to be as little trouble as possible.

'Nanny Gray, reporting for duty,' she said.

'Who? Oh, the Hogarth girl. Humph.' Sister McMahon was a surprisingly good-looking woman, perhaps three or four years Barbara's senior. Her hair under its frilled gauze cap was well cared for, she even seemed to have a trace of lipstick. 'You're older than I expected,' she remarked.

Barbara suppressed a sigh. 'Yes, I took up the training later than most.'

'Not a bad scheme, eh? I rather fancy the Nanny life myself. One day when I've been driven too far by the bunch of half-wits who run this place . . . Suite of rooms to yourself, eh? Nursery maid to do the chores, regular time off, living with rich folk, seeing the nobs come visiting . . .'

Barbara made no response.

'This is your last year, eh? Got a good job lined up for when you finish?'

'Not yet.'

'Y'might get something here. One or two high-class parents coming in and out – make yourself known to them.'

'I don't expect to have much time for that, Sister.'

'Why not? You don't think I'm going to let you *do* anything?'

'Well, I –'

'If you imagine I'm going to let you lollop about interfering with the running of my ward, think again. This place goes like clockwork.'

'But I –'

'You can do the flowers, pick up the toys, help wheel 'em out on the balcony in good weather and wheel 'em back again. Apart from that, you're no use to me, so steer clear.'

'Sister –'

'All this rubbish about learning. What can anybody learn about sick children in three months on a ward? I've been nursing sick children for eleven years and still know nothing.'

'Sister, I'm not untrained.'

'Huh, Nanny training.'

'No, I was a nurse during the war. I'm SRN.'

For the first time Sister McMahon actually looked at Barbara. Until now she had been gazing past her through the glass panels of her office at her ward. Now she turned a sharp blue eye on her.

'Trained? Why wasn't I told?'

'I took it for granted you knew.'

'I tell you, this place is run by half-wits. Hospital management – huh! Where did you train?'

'Brixton General.'

'Awful dump. I did six months' gynie there. Well, so you at least know one end of a syringe from the other?'

'Yes, Sister.'

'And you can lay out a dressings tray?'

'Yes, Sister.'

'Well, forget all that, because I have probationers who come before you in the list of learners. But since you're so well-trained, we can use you, I'm sure. You know your way to the sluice, I take it?'

Barbara groaned. 'Yes, Sister.'

'Excellent. You'll no doubt find a pile of bedpans waiting to be scrubbed. Ward tea will be served in half an hour – that gives you time to get started. Then I expect you to be washed, disinfected, and in a clean apron to help push the trolley. Am I clear?'

'*Yes*, Sister.'

She should have held her tongue. If she had gone on as a know-nothing Hogarth student, Sister McMahon would have let her fiddle around in corners being 'helpful'. Since she had insisted on her qualifications as a trained nurse, Sister

McMahon was going to use her, but on the level of the merest probationer.

So be it. You couldn't argue with a ward sister.

The first three weeks on Children's Ward B passed by in a dream of bedpans. The sinks in the sluice never seemed to be empty of them. The clang and clatter of them were the background to almost every conversation.

There were five nurses on the day shift – two probationers, one first-year trainee, one second-year trainee, and a staff nurse. Above these reigned Sister McMahon. The ward held fourteen beds plus two side wards for 'specialling' and one private room for an exceptionally ill child – at present occupied by a five year old with a chest infection. On the other side of the staircase was Children's Ward A, and sandwiched in between at the far side was a small ward for patients who came in for tonsillectomy, usually an overnight stay.

Medical and surgical cases were nursed in the children's wards. Fever cases, when diagnosed, were moved out to isolation hospitals. The children in the two wards ranged from very sick indeed to convalescent, but when they had got to a certain stage they were packed off to remedial centres or convalescent homes.

Sister McMahon ran Ward B with the precision of an old campaign general. It was spotlessly clean, tidy, and relatively quiet. A new patient might scream and cry intermittently but he was soon exhausted. The nurses were kind, calm, and impersonal. They all dreaded visiting hours, when parents would bring back all the grief of parting and start the children crying again. Luckily, visiting was restricted to three periods – Wednesday evening from five to six, Saturday afternoon from two-thirty to three-thirty, and Sunday morning from eleven to twelve. Parents were not encouraged to visit on Sundays. 'They ought to be in church,' explained Stokes, the staff nurse. But it couldn't be denied that parents who were in work might not be able to get to see their children except on Sunday, and it was better to have them come just before lunch because then they would know they had to go as the meal trolley was brought in.

'It'd be far better for the kids if no visiting was allowed,' said staff-nurse Stokes. 'They only upset them.'

'Oh, no!'

'What d'you mean, oh no? You've seen the upset they cause in the wards.'

'But children need to see their mothers and fathers, Nurse. Otherwise they'll think they've been abandoned.'

'Rubbish, Gray. No child ever thinks in words like that. I –'

'They may not know the word, but they know the feeling.'

'If it comes to feelings, what about ours? Nobody can think we enjoy seeing the kids crying their eyes out every time the grown-ups leave. And if they didn't come in the first place, we'd all be spared a lot of grief.'

'I can't agree with that. It's better to have tears than –'

'That's quite enough, Gray,' Sister McMahon put in, coming into the kitchen to check the diets before the meal was distributed. 'You're here to learn, not to argue.'

'Fat chance of learning anything in the sluice-room,' thought Barbara, but had more sense than say it aloud.

But Sister was beginning to relent, so that during the following week Barbara was allowed to stay in the actual ward and lend a hand now and again with nursing the patients.

Her father had been intrigued at the news she was to do her three months in Bayswater General. Although he had never been in the building, it was in a main road not far from the flat they used to occupy. He used it as an excuse to come up to London for a couple of days, stay at his club, and visit his old haunts.

Because he knew nothing about hospital routine, it didn't occur to him that he couldn't visit his daughter in Children's Ward B. He walked in before anyone could stop him, or even thought to, because he had something of the air of a senior consultant.

'Well, how are things, dear?' he inquired.

'Father! What are you doing here?'

'Just dropping in.'

'You'll get me shot!'

'Oh, really? Aren't I supposed to?'

'No you're not! And in any case, I'm busy.' She was dealing with a sudden wheezing spasm which had come over a small girl, Betty, who was in for tests and observation. The child was gripping her hand desperately. She really had no time to deal with her father at the moment.

'Oh, all right, if I'm not wanted,' he said, in a huff.

'I'll see you later,' she called after him as he walked away. 'I have three hours off this evening – you can give me dinner.'

'Huh,' he said, but paused. 'Where?'

'Pick me up about six outside the nurses' home.'

'Allright, I suppose I must.' He went out looking offended.

Sister McMahon appeared at once. 'I know, I know,' Barbara said in haste. 'It won't happen again.'

'You can be sure it won't. Now come along, Gray, you've spent quite enough time with Betty.'

'But she –'

'She's settled now, there are other things requiring attention.'

'Yes, Sister.'

The short interlude with her father was rather enjoyable at first. He took her to a Corner House where they had a four course meal to music from a 'Hungarian Gipsy' orchestra. He told her things were quite comfortable in Banbury; Lily was very good at the housework though she tended to hover over him too much. He'd joined a bridge club, made some rather pleasing friendships there. They caught up on family news: Eileen had had a slight chill, Jimmy was doing rather better on the stocks and shares at the moment.

Then Barbara began to tell him about the hospital. He listened, finishing off the bottle of red wine which had accompanied their Wienerschnitzel. After a bit it dawned on her that his attention was wandering.

'I'm sorry,' she said. 'It's just that I find it all so interesting.'

'There you are,' he said.

'Where?'

'Why can't you go back to hospital work? I know, I know, you remember it as being depressing, but you've just been explaining how much you enjoy the children's ward. Why couldn't you get a job in a hospital nursing children?'

'Well, I . . .'

'You know, Barbara,' he said, the corners of his mouth going down, 'I'm not so young as I was. When you start taking posts as a Nanny, you might have to go all over the country – I might not see you for weeks and weeks on end.'

'Oh, but I'd –'

'Suppose I needed you? It'd be damn difficult. Whereas if you were in a London hospital I could always get hold of you.'

She was on the verge of telling him she had chosen her career for its own value, not so as to be handy if he needed her. 'I don't want to change horses now, Father . . .'

'Well, I think you're being silly.'

Although she argued them away, his words stayed with her. The following Sunday she had the afternoon off, and was to meet Fredric Deniz for a drive out along the Thames. When they were eating a cottage tea-room tea in Datchet, she said to him, 'My father thinks I ought to go into hospital nursing.'

'And what do you think?'

She laughed. It was so like him to respond to any opening with a question about her own feelings. 'Well, I've been thinking, Fredric. One of the things that troubles me is the need not to get too emotionally involved with the children. I've been thinking, since I've been in the children's ward it's easier to stay impersonal.'

'Is that what you took up nannying for – to stay impersonal with the children?'

'Oh, no, of course not!' She eyed him. 'That's rather clever.'

'I do my best.'

'Fredric, the way the nurses manage in the ward, they don't

get themselves tied to any one child. Perhaps it's better.'

'Perhaps it is.'

'Do you think it is?'

'I have no idea. So far as I know, no studies have been done about the effect of a hospital stay on a child. My instinct tells me the child needs to fix on some human being, and if he chooses a nurse as his surrogate mother, the nurse will respond.'

'No, they don't. They make themselves stay aloof.'

'And do you think you could do that?'

'Well – I'd have to, wouldn't I?'

'And if you could not?'

'What d'you mean?'

'Children as a rule don't stay long in hospital. If you got fond of the patients your life would be a series of griefs – meetings and partings, meetings and partings – until you got "hard". Is that what you want?'

'I don't know,' she sighed.

She would have sworn she had no favourites in the children's ward. But she had her answer to Fredric's question a few weeks later when eight-year-old Betty was discharged. The scene of tears and lamentations was wounding. Betty clung to her, begging not to be taken away even though it was her own mother who was coming for her. When at last the child had gone, still sobbing, Sister McMahon descended on Barbara like a thundercloud.

'Well, what do you think you are up to, turning my ward into a bear garden?'

'I didn't intend that to happen.'

'No, and it won't happen again. For the remaining month of your stay you will do night duty. The children will be asleep so you won't have the chance to sit with them and tell them fairy stories. I've put you on the night rota starting tomorrow.'

Barbara knew that the change-over to night shift would upset her life rhythm for at least a week, but she knew she had brought it on herself. As it happened, nights were in general quiet. If there was a crisis, it was dealt with by the staff-nurse and her probationer, Barbara being given only the menial clearing up tasks. She had plenty of time to think.

What she thought about was hospital nursing as opposed to nursery nursing. The conclusion she came to was that as she seemed fated to give affection to any child in her care, it was better to be a Nanny and stay longer with her charge. Fredric had pointed out the danger of hospital nursing; a series of griefs, meetings and partings. She would either have to grow a shell or go under, so it was better to stick to her original ambition.

She returned to the Hogarth School with a report that appeared to have no major blemishes on it. 'Well, now,' said Mrs Stepps-Astley, 'you had better have a week to get yourself sorted out, and then it will be time to send you out to a temporary post. You worked at the hospital straight through Easter, so if you wish you can take the next seven days as holiday.'

The May weather was fine. She spent the week in London, staying at a YWCA hostel for cheapness and dropping in on Eileen frequently. But more importantly, she saw Fredric every day.

The physical chemistry between them was growing more and more perfect each time they saw each other. More than that, they seemed to be in tune mentally. Sometimes he would take up a subject - one they hadn't been discussing - and she would say, 'That's just what I was thinking!' He had said to her, with a frown and a smile, that she was beginning to shake his scientific scorn about telepathy.

He took her to Lord's to watch his son's school play Eton. It was a mistake. It made the children real to her - until then she'd been able to put them to the back of her mind. But to see that rather thin, quick boy running like a deer to take a catch was to know that he was Fredric's son - a younger, slighter version of his father. And anything she and Fredric might do would harm that boy, and the brother she had not yet seen.

When Fredric went to chat to the team at the tea interval, Barbara naturally didn't accompany him. She sat in her place for some minutes. And then, with a little shiver, she went out and took the Tube back to Earl's Court and the doubtful pleasures of the hostel.

He rang her to ask what had happened. 'Did it bore you? I know cricket isn't everyone's cup of tea.'

'It wasn't that, Fredric. It was just . . . I don't know. I suddenly felt I didn't belong there.'

When she got back to the Hogarth School at the weekend, Mrs Stepps-Astley came to her room. 'Well, Nanny, your next training-stage is ready. I've had a request for a young Nanny to help one in residence. It's a two-week post in Sussex. Can you be ready to go tomorrow?'

'Of course, Mrs Stepps-Astley. I only need overnight to starch and iron some collars and cuffs.'

'Nanny –'

'Yes, Mrs Stepps-Astley?'

'I know you'll do us credit.'

Barbara was met at Lewes station by a chauffeur-driven Lancia. 'Let me take your luggage, Nanny.'

'Thank you,' she said, pleased at the good manners he showed. Some house staff, she had heard, made it a point to put the Nanny in her place from the moment she arrived.

He deposited her at the side entrance of a large mansion, mainly Queen Anne with Georgian and Victorian additions. As she stepped out of the Lancia, a horde of children poured out. 'Oh, here she is! Oh, she's little – Nanny Iles would make three of her!'

She was taken hold of, pushed, escorted and otherwise moved into the house. There, one of the eldest children, who seemed to be about twelve, said in a commanding tone, 'Now, off we go to see Nanny Iles!'

They all marched up the stairs. At a count, Barbara thought there were eleven children in the band. They hustled her to the nursery floor, along a passage, and threw open a door at the far end.

On a padded armchair near the window sat a very fat old Nanny, rocking a cradle with her foot while she read from a picture book to a small child sitting at her feet. It was so much like a posed portrait that Barbara drew back, expecting a practical joke. But the old lady raised her head, looked at her through old wire-rimmed spectacles, and said in a gentle voice, 'Nanny Gray? Do please come in. Now, children, you must all go away and let me and Nanny Gray get to know each other.'

'Aw, Nanny . . .'

'Which of you is commander today?'

'I am,' said the twelve-year-old boy who had taken charge as they marched upstairs.

'All right then, Ronald, please take the regiment off for outdoor manoeuvres. Return at eleven-thirty.'

'Eleven-thirty ack emma,' said Ronald saluting. He shepherded the others out, picking up the toddler from Barbara's feet as he went.

'Good heavens,' Barbara said, 'is it a school?'

'No, it's all the Crittenden Clan. Fifteen in all.'

'One family?' Barbara queried, aghast.

'No, no, child, don't look alarmed.' Nanny Iles smiled, and her foot began to rock the rocker of the cradle without her even seeming to think about it. 'Those children are cousins – sisters and brothers, cousins to each other. They're here for the wedding anniversary of Mr and Mrs Crittenden, grandchildren of that marriage,' She gave her head a little shake, and the starched cap on her hair slid about. She put up a hand to anchor it. 'Over fifty years I've been a Nanny, and never yet learned to keep my cap on straight!'

'Fifty years! You mean that the Crittendens – Mr and Mrs – were your babies?'

'Well, Mr Crittenden was. Ralphie . . .' She smiled to herself. 'Little rascal. Still, I made a good job of him and he's done well – Lord Lieutenant, he was, for a bit. This here is a family gathering for the anniversary. Half-term, you see. A chance to get the kiddies here. It's for me, really,' she added fondly. 'I like to see 'em again when I can.'

'You . . . How many of those did you nurse?' Barbara asked.

'Miss Rose and Miss Lucia and Master Ronald and now of course little Emily and Baby here – Baby Bertram, he's three months, he's Miss Julia's boy.'

In the two weeks that Barbara spent at Crittenden Manor, she never did get straight who was who nor which set of parents belonged to whom. It was the happiest two weeks she had ever spent. It seemed to light up all her ideas of what it meant to be a Nanny.

Nanny Iles was old now, and not so active as she had been. Therefore, for this reunion of the family, she had asked for a younger Nanny to help. There were in addition two nursery maids and a house-maid who could be called upon. It was necessary to have so many in charge, for the children were continually being put into party clothes for another celebration at some house or other, or at home in the Manor. They would get themselves in a mess and have to be tidied up, but Nanny Iles never seemed to be perturbed.

'That's what they're for,' she remarked to Barbara. 'To get in a mess and learn what things do to you, and other children, and grown-ups. Childhood's for learning and having fun.'

'But don't you think you're lucky in living with parents who don't mind a bit of dirt and untidiness?'

'My dear, I brought up Mr Crittenden. Naturally he follows my way, doesn't he? That's what Nannies are for – to lead children along the paths of good sense towards being grown up.'

They had many conversations in the quiet nursery after the children had gone to bed. One thing stayed in Barbara's mind, a slogan uttered by Nanny Iles. 'Love 'em and let 'em go, that's what I say.'

'But isn't it hard, Nanny, letting them go?'

'Bless you, girl, they never go, not really. They come back to you, and something of them always stays with you even when they're not there.'

'But in the end, Nanny, they don't belong to you. And you're left with nothing.'

Nanny Iles patted her hand. 'That's just being silly,' she said. 'I'm still here, aren't I? Still in the middle of them when most women have nothing. I mean, mothers of a family don't have as much as I do, now do they? As to who they belong to . . Children belong to themselves. A mother has to acknowledge that at last when her birdies leave the nest. No,' and she nodded so that her cap slipped about, 'love 'em and let 'em go. That's best for all.'

Barbara returned to Hogarth School exhausted and yet exhilarated by this experience. She felt she had learned something invaluable for the future. If she could do as much good in the world as Nanny Iles, she would have nothing to complain of.

The Director of the school tapped her papers with a smile when Barbara reported. 'Mrs Crittenden speaks well of you,' she said. 'You can use this as a reference when you go for a post.'

'Oh, how kind . . . But I hardly ever saw her!'

'No, but Nanny Iles clearly approved of you. Not that I would go too much by that, you know, Nanny Gray. Nanny Iles is a bit out of touch with modern child care theories.'

'Hm,' Barbara said, but managed not to start an argument.

'Now, for your last posting before you go out to a permanent situation, I have a different assignment. I think you may enjoy this rather more.'

That seemed impossible, so Barbara merely adopted an expression of polite interest. 'You are going to Lord and Lady McDemmott,' said Mrs Stepps-Astley, 'who have three children. The boy is the eldest and is of course normally at school but will be with the family for the summer holidays. Their Nanny prefers not to go with them to their country house but takes her annual holiday at this time instead. I think it will suit you because Lady McDemmott is something of an intellectual.'

Barbara almost laughed. 'You think I'm an intellectual, Mrs Stepps-Astley?'

'Not exactly – that would be most unsuitable. But I think you are a thinking gel. I said to Mrs O'Mara only the other day, Nanny Gray is a thinking gel. And as Lady McDemmott is a thinking woman . . . . A very fine family, you know. Most of the west of Scotland is McDemmott land, I believe.'

'Oh . . . then . . . when you say "Country house" – am I going to Scotland?'

'That is my understanding. CragApp, the ancestral home. In advance of the shooting, I presume to supervise the preparations for the 12th. You will join them at their home in Belgrave Square. The butler, Bowers, telephoned to say you are expected.'

'Tomorrow?'

'Dear me, no, they are travelling tomorrow. No, Nanny, you had best get packed straight away, if you wish to have a chat with Nanny Pemerson before she goes on her holiday. You are expected for nursery tea.'

'Thank you, Mrs Stepps-Astley,' Barbara said meekly and went out without more ado. Once in the corridor she all but scuttled to her room to pack. If she was to arrive in time for nursery tea in Belgravia, she'd have to get a move on.

The butler, Bowers, greeted her gravely when she rang the bell. 'Nanny Gray? Be so good as to leave your luggage here. It will be taken to be put with the rest for tomorrow's departure. You have your overnight things?'

'Yes,' Barbara said, holding up an attaché case. But Bowers didn't attempt to relieve her of that as he led the way to the stairs. Here a chambermaid appeared.

'Take Nanny to the nursery, if you please,' he said, and stalked away.

The maid sniffed. 'He always gets like this when the missus gets ready to go north. Delusions of grandeur, it's called. He'll have the whole place in his charge until September. Makes him get majestic.'

She led the way up three flights of stairs to the nursery floor. The nursery door was open. A voice called, 'Come in, Nanny, the tea's just brewed.'

Nanny Pemerson was a small, shrewd-looking woman of about forty. She waved Barbara to a chair at the table. Two children were sitting there eating sardine sandwiches. The boy, a bright-looking, fair-haired ten-year-old, stood up as Barbara came to the table. 'How do you do, Nanny,' he said with charming politeness. He gave his sister a nudge. She, aged about five and as yet with no sign of her brother's good looks, got up and sketched a curtsey. 'How do you do, Nanny,' she mumbled with her mouth full. The baby, who looked about two, waved a spoon from his highchair.

'That's a good girl, Verdie. Now sit down and finish your sandwiches so you can have some cake.'

'Verdie?' Barbara repeated.

'Short for Verdant. And this is Sylvan,' said Nanny Pemerson, with a nod at the ten-year-old. 'And baby is Folly – that's short for Folium.' Seeing Barbara's surprised look she added, 'It means a leaf. Their father is a botanist – Marcus McDemmot – you've heard of him?'

'Er . . . no . . . but then I don't know anything about botany.'

'He writes books,' Sylvan volunteered. 'He's writing a book about the ferns of the Highlands.'

'Now, Master Syl, please attend to your plate. Children should be seen and not heard.'

Syl returned his attention to the sardine sandwiches. Nanny Pemerson poured tea for Barbara then began one of those conversations over, round and past the children which Barbara had noticed was common among Nannies.

'I'm off this evening. We'll have a quick run-through their clothes before you pack them. You're not taking any of Syl's treasures so make sure he doesn't sneak them into the trunk when you're not looking. Verdie's vests are all too small for her but you'll be able to buy some in Oban – that's if you can get

Mummy to wait an hour or so before going on. Verdie doesn't like wool vests but don't pay any attention to that, wool next to the skin is best.'

'Yes,' Barbara said, dazed already. 'Perhaps I'd better make a little list of things to remember, since you're going this evening?'

'Nanny always goes to her sister's,' Syl put in. 'She "can't abide" the Highlands.'

'And who has still got sardine sandwiches on his plate?'

'Syl has,' he replied, in a tone of mockery that was almost adult. 'Isn't he a naughty boy?'

'That's enough, Mister Clever-coat,' Nanny said in reproof. 'Any more of that and who won't get any cake?'

'I don't want any cake anyhow,' Syl burst out. 'Stupid old jam sponge!'

'Very well then, if Mr Clever-coat has finished his sardines he may get down from the table.'

Syl jumped up and removed himself. Barbara thought that Verdie's eyes followed him with a glance of longing. 'Perhaps Verdie could get down too?' she suggested.

'What, with two sandwiches still untouched? I should think not, Nanny.'

'But perhaps they're a bit excited about going on holiday tomorrow.'

'Holidays are no reason for acting silly. Who's going to eat up her sardine sandwiches then?' Nanny Pemerson inquired, pushing Verdie's plate closer to the child.

Verdie gave a great sigh and applied herself to the sandwiches.

'Them as doesn't finish their food are rebuking the Lord's goodness,' observed Nanny in a pious tone, then said on an entirely different note, 'Been at Hogarth School then, I gather?'

'Yes, I'm just finishing.'

'Never had that sort of thing. All right if you can afford it but I learnt all I need to know working with children. Eat up now,

Folly, there's a treasure.' She replaced a wandering piece of sandwich on the toddler's plate. He took it, munched for a moment, then threw it down. 'Now, now, we must eat it all up before we have our cake.'

In the end the children finished and were variously dismissed. Verdie went into the night nursery to find a doll, Folly was set down on the floor with a wooden train.

'We'll go and sort out those clothes then. I want to take you through all that and get going – I'd like to reach Cromer tonight.'

Barbara went with her to the linen cupboard where they sorted out the items to be packed. Nanny Pemerson wasted no time. Barbara, who had had a mental list of questions to ask about likes and dislikes, never got the chance.

One question she got in before Nanny Pemerson departed to put her own clothes in a suitcase. 'Tell me, Nanny – what's it like at CragApp?'

'Oh, the children adore it,' Nanny said. She then closed her lips in a way that seemed to imply, 'I prefer not to discuss it.'

'From what Syl said, I gather you don't like it?' Barbara persisted. 'You have been there?'

'Once,' said Nanny Pemerson. 'Of course, it suits some people. But I must say I prefer Cromer.'

She hurried off. Barbara returned to the nursery with a worried frown. But there was a lot to do – the children had to be made presentable for the visit to the drawing-room before dinner, at which point she would meet the parents.

Lady McDemmott looked over big horn-rimmed glasses at her as she came in. 'And who are you? Oh, it's the Hogarth girl! I'd quite forgotten. Nanny . . . er . . . ?'

'Gray, my lady.'

'Nanny Gray, of course. Marcus, here's the stand-in.'

Lord McDemmott turned from a table where he had been stacking books. 'Ah. Splendid. How d'you do. Well, children, you've a nice new Nanny for the holidays, eh?'

'Yes, Papa,' the two elder children said glumly.

'Righto then. All packed up for tomorrow, are we?'

'Nanny Pemerson has shown me what has to be packed, my lord.'

'Fine, fine. Early start, of course. Sit down, Brutus,' he added as a large Great Dane suddenly hove into view from behind the sofa. Brutus took a look at the scene, yawned, and disappeared again.

'Don't mind dogs, I hope?' inquired Lord McDemmott.

'Er . . . no . . . I quite like them.' She hesitated. 'Is Brutus coming with us?'

'Of course. Wouldn't dream of leaving him. Would we, old boy?'

The Great Dane made no reply.

'All right then. Anything else to say to Nanny, my dear?'

'What? Oh. No, I don't think so. Off to bed, little ones, so as to be fresh and ready to go in the morning. Goodnight.'

They came to her one by one. She bestowed a kiss on each. Folly made a grab at her glasses. 'Naughty, naughty,' she said with great tolerance. 'There we are then, Nanny. Pack them off to bed. We want to be ready to go first thing.'

'Yes, my lady. What time, exactly?'

'What time, Marcus?'

Lord McDemmott stopped counting the books. 'I know there's one missing,' he said. 'I'll never manage if I miss one out. What did you say, my dear?'

'What time is the train, darling?'

'Six o'clock at Euston, my love.'

'Six o'clock. That means breakfast at five, Nanny, so off to bed with them all.'

'Yes, my lady,' Barbara said faintly, and shepherded the children out.

She began to have an inkling why Nanny Pemerson always backed out of these occasions.

CHAPTER FOURTEEN

The journey began badly and ended worse.

They piled into two cars at five-thirty in the morning, Lord and Lady McDemmott and four dogs in one, Barbara and the three children together with the luggage in the other. They were in good time at Euston, but it took much expenditure of energy to get everything and everyone aboard. The dogs, in particular, set up a mourning when they discovered they had to go in the luggage van. There was Brutus the Great Dane together with Ciar, a terrier belonging to Lady McDemmott, and two Pomeranians called Rusty and Trusty. There were four trunks, two suitcases, two guncases, a flat box containing materials for water colours, and two large crates full of books.

They had a first class carriage to themselves. Verdie became train-sick about an hour after they left Euston and had to be taken to stand by the open window in the corridor. Syl ran off in the opposite direction and had to be brought back from four carriages away, extremely displeased because he had found the mail van with its cages which he proposed to climb.

A capacious picnic hamper had been stowed in with them by the chauffeur, but dispensing drinks to children on a rocking train was no easy matter. At lunchtime Lord and Lady McDemmott went to the restaurant car, but it was deemed more suitable if the children ate in the carriage, so Barbara unwrapped cold chicken and ham, set it out on bakelite plates, and coaxed them to eat. Syl did so, then escaped while Barbara fed Folly and watched Verdie. Verdie was sick soon after lunch. Syl was brought back from along the train by an irate passenger who said the boy had made an aeroplane out of the crossword page of his newspaper. Folly went to sleep, Verdie asked for a story, Syl escaped again.

They reached Oban at nine o'clock at night. 'Thank God,' Barbara said, preparing to wake her sleeping charges. And to Lord McDemmott, 'Which hotel are we going to my lord?'

'Hotel?' Lord McDemmott said, surprised. 'Who said anything about a hotel? We're going on the boat now.'

Barbara was too tired even to gasp in dismay. Porters appeared with their luggage, Syl and Verdie staggered to their feet and fell out of the train hollow-eyed, Barbara picked up Folly and off they went. A sort of little bus was awaiting them. They were all helped aboard. A few minutes' drive brought them to a quay where the cold salt air had the effect of thoroughly waking Syl. 'We're in Oban!' he shouted, charging off down the jetty.

'No,' cried Barbara, with visions of him falling off the end and into the sea. But when she had made such speed as she could to catch up with him, she found him leaping aboard a boat.

It appeared to be a small steamer; she could smell the steam-coal. Lights flickered on her decks. Many hands helped them get themselves, the dogs and the baggage on board. 'If ye'd like to go below, miss?' said a kindly voice. She was helped down a small flight of steps edged with shining brass, into a long saloon with leather-covered cushions along both sides and a mahogany table in the middle. Syl was already there, kneeling up to look out of the window. 'Goodbye, Oban,' he was chanting, 'goodbye, goodbye!'

In an astonishingly short time the vessel seemed to be edging out from the quay. Lord and Lady McDemmott came below, having stopped to have a word with the skipper. It dawned on Barbara that they were the only passengers. She took a moment from the business of holding on to the excited Syl to look around her. This was a private steam yacht!

'Well now, Nanny,' said Lady McDemmott, 'I'll just show you your cabin.'

'Cabin?' Barbara said.

'You're next door to the children. Quite handy, really. This way.' She went through a doorway.

Aghast, Barbara followed her. There was another little flight of steps then a passage. Four doors opened off it. 'This is yours,' Lady McDemmott said. 'Little ones next door, so you see if they wake, you're on the spot. I think you can let Syl stay up another half hour or so – he always takes a while to settle after we come aboard.'

'Er . . . Lady McDemmott . . . is it worth putting them to bed? I mean, how long is the trip? Are we – crossing a loch? Or what?'

'Oh goodness,' Lady McDemmott said with a merry laugh, 'we're going across to the island of CragApp. It's a five hour passage if you're in a hurry, but we always ask Lowrie to take it easy, for there's no point in arriving in the middle of the night. No, no, you've got time for a good night's sleep. We'll get there by about six tomorrow morning.'

'I see. Thank you, my lady.'

Verdie had more or less fallen asleep on the sofa-bench of the saloon. Syl was still gazing out of the window at the dark waves. Barbara quickly undressed Folly, changed him, and put him to bed. For Verdie she arranged a simple change from outdoor clothes to petticoat and knickers. She slipped her into the bunk-bed and covered her up with deft movements that didn't rouse her. Even Syl went unprotesting to bed.

As for Barbara, it wasn't so simple. In the dim light of her cabin she took off her shoes, unbuttoned her collar and took it off, slipped out of her thin worsted uniform dress. Further than that she wasn't prepared to go. She lay down on the low bunk in her cabin. The room seemed to sway about. A strange sound kept coming and going, like little men running hard along the deck and back – the sound of timbers stretching as they met the swell of the waves.

After about an hour, the pitching and rolling became much worse. They had come out of the shelter of the coast of Mull and were nosing out into the waters of the Inner Hebrides.

Barbara's forehead began to be damp with sweat. Her

stomach seemed to be lurching about. She regretted the high tea she had eaten in the train's dining-room, of smoked haddock and buttered scones.

She leapt off the bunk, staggered to the door, fell up the stairs and out on deck. The night air smote her face. She gulped it in. She felt better. Her stomach seemed to settle.

Then she smelt that wondrous aroma that can only be found on a steam yacht: hot engine oil, coal and ash, steam, metal, tar and rope. She gave a groan and ran to the rail.

Just in time . . .

She wasn't seasick all night. Just after midnight her protesting stomach became quiet. She crawled into bed and slept. When she opened her eyes it was to know that the launch had ceased moving. She knelt up on her bunk and looked out of the porthole. In the mists of the early morning she could see a vague outline of hills and trees beyond a sandy beach. This, presumably, was CragApp.

She hurried next door to see if the children were all right. If they had cried in the night, would she have heard them as she hung over the side heaving her heart out? But they seemed fit and well. Folly was sitting up on his bunk chatting to himself with satisfaction, Verdie was still sound asleep, and Syl was already dressing himself.

'We're here,' he said eagerly, 'come *on*!'

The *Heather Maid* edged into the quay, a wooden erection. A group of men in dark blue sweaters and coarse serge trousers waited to catch ropes and moor her. Luggage was quickly taken ashore and loaded into a cart pulled by a plump pony. Barbara came ashore with Folly in her arms and one hand holding Verdie. Syl darted ahead, to jump into the trap parked by the beginning of the sandy track that led up the slope and into the trees.

It was a governess cart harnessed to a donkey. It took Barbara back to her childhood in India. She clambered in after Syl, helped Verdie up, and settled herself and the children for the journey. Lady McDemmott mounted beside the driver of the cart. Lord McDemmott waved them on. 'I'll walk up. Want to take a look at that hollow by the big rock, see if that fern's managed to overwinter . . .'

Barbara took up the reins of the governess cart. She saw Syl eyeing her with interest, waiting to see her make a fool of herself. 'Come on then,' she said to the donkey, slapping the reins on its rump, 'gee up!'

To her astonishment, the donkey started ahead.

'I didn't know you could drive a governess cart,' Syl said, impressed.

'Neither did I! But I've seen it done. I used to be driven about in a gharry when I was a little girl in India. Has the donkey got a name?'

'Daisy.'

'Come on then, Daisy – hurry up!' She glanced at Syl. 'Do you know what Daisy says?'

'You mean, hee-haw?'

'No, no – she can say a piece of poetry. It goes like this:

'Up hill urge me not,
Down hill hurry me not,
Along the level spare me not,
And in the stable forget-me-not.'

'I like that!' cried Verdie. The rest of the journey to CragApp Castle was spent in learning the words of the old rhyme of the Horse's Prayer.

CragApp really was a castle. A little bridge led over a stream to a great paved forecourt, then the way led through a granite arch into a smaller court. Here an old man came to take the reins of the governess cart and lead it away after Barbara and the children had stepped down. 'Where's Himself?' the old man inquired over his shoulder as he went.

'Who?'

'He means Papa. Walking up,' Syl informed the servant.

'Oh aye. I micht have known it. In ye go, then, Mrs Moffat's waiting for ye and your parritch is a' ready.'

'Er . . . what is ready?' Barbara asked.

'Porridge. He means breakfast really. Come on, I'm starving.'

He ran ahead into the huge hall, stone-floored and stone-walled. At the far end a great fireplace glowed with a log fire, necessary although the June morning was growing warm. The place felt chill and damp. Barbara glanced about. The old man had vanished. She heard the cart with the luggage and Lady McDemmott clatter into the courtyard, then Lady McDemmott bustled into the room. 'Chalmers! Chalmers!' she called. 'Come and see to the luggage.' And then in explanation to Barbara, 'The place is so big, you see, they don't really know we're here unless we yell for them.'

Big was scarcely the word. Further exploration during the day led Barbara to think of it as vast. The hall into which she had stepped from the courtyard was the old hall of the original castle, with a gallery above it and rooms opening off. But behind it was what was called 'The Auld Hoose', now unused and closed up, while to each side of the hall new wings had been added, the first by a rich McDemmott of the sixteenth century and the second by an ambitious McDemmott of the eighteenth century. It was the latter which was now used as a family residence. At the top of this, Barbara and her charges had their establishment.

It was so far from the kitchens that there wasn't the slightest chance of food arriving in the nursery hot or even warm. Mrs Moffat, the cook, made no efforts in that respect. She was quite taken aback when Barbara asked if she hadn't a hotplate or a *bain-marie* on which she could send the meals.

'Och, I'm having nane o' they forrin things in my kitchen,' she said with scorn.

The staff for the castle seemed minimal. There was a butler called Chalmers, the cook Mrs Moffat, a silent girl called Effie who seemed to do the fires and the sweeping, the old man Donal who looked after the stables, and a lad, Charlie, the odd job man. There were other people on the island, whom Barbara met on her outings with the children, but they seemed to have their being in one or two stone cottages a little to the east of the landing jetty and were concerned with the keeping of the steam yacht or the catching of fish.

But the children loved it. They recovered from the fatigue of the journey within twenty-four hours. Syl and Verdie set off at once to explore on the morning of the second day, to check that all their favourite places remained the same. Barbara completely lost them for over two hours, and was pleading with Donal to help her find them when they showed up again quite unconcerned.

'Where have you been?' she scolded. 'I thought you were lost!'

'Oh, don't be silly, we couldn't be lost on CragApp,' Syl said airily. 'Anyway, we haven't been far – just looking for the bogle and all that kind of thing.'

'The what?'

'The bogle . . .' He gave her a surprise glance. 'You mean you don't know? CragApp is haunted.'

'No it isn't,' she replied in automatic rejection of possible nightmares. 'There's no such thing as ghosts.'

'Yes there is. Verdie's heard it – haven't you, Verdie?'

'Yes, I have, it's a sort of thudding thing. And there's a kelpie, too,'

'What's a kelpie?'

'It lives in the stream. The kelpie of CragApp. Everybody knows about it.'

'Well, I don't,' said Barbara, 'and what's more I don't want to. There's enough in the world that's good and interesting without inventing frightening things.'

'Oh, the kelpie isn't all that frightening,' Syl said. 'It's sort of like a little horse. It comes up out of the stream near the beach. You'll see it perhaps, if you're quiet.'

'No I shan't,' Barbara assured him. 'Come along now, come and wash your hands, it's lunch time.'

But there was no denying that Castle CragApp was just the sort of place to be haunted, if there were such things as ghosts.

At night there were strange sounds from the old part of the building. Barbara told herself firmly that it was only old beams contracting, old stones settling, but she didn't altogether believe her own assurances.

She and the children went bathing most afternoons after their nap and when the shallow water by the shore had warmed up enough to make it bearable. Syl had been astounded when Barbara, after the first visit to the beach, announced that in future she would come into the water with Syl and Verdie.

'You mean you can swim?' he said in surprise. 'Nanny Pemerson can't.'

'Well, I can do dog-paddle.' She hadn't thought to pack a swimming costume, but got one delivered by the post boat when it called from Oban. Most things could be obtained if you sent a message by the outgoing boat and went to collect it from the incoming boat, which called twice a week.

It was on one of their swimming parties that they had their encounter with the kelpie. It was a sultry day, warm and humid with thundery clouds threatening overhead. By four o'clock the light was quite poor, and though it was still early Barbara decided to get the children dressed and head for home.

They were turning to paddle ashore when suddenly from the waters of the brook there came a disturbance.

'It's the kelpie!' screamed Verdie.

True enough, in the grey light a head could be seen emerging from the pool of quiet water on the far side of the boulders at the top of the beach. Barbara clutched Verdie to her and began to run towards Folly, who was sitting on a rug on the sand.

The head disappeared in the waters. Barbara reached Folly and snatched him up. There was a wailing sound from the pool, and the head re-emerged. Was it a horse's head?

Yes it was. No it wasn't. It was the head of Brutus the Great Dane, and he was whining because he had just missed the fish he had snapped at.

Barbara collapsed on the sand with a little yelp of laughter.

'There you are, you see!' she cried. 'It was the dog!'

'But you believed it was the kelpie, didn't you?' Syl challenged. 'You said you didn't believe in it!'

'No, well, Brutus looked sort of funny in this half-light. But if you hadn't talked about a kelpie I'd never have thought it was anything else but a dog swimming.'

'Well, I believe in it, and so does Verdie – don't you, Verdie?'

'Yes, I do,' Verdie said loyally.

'And she believes in the bogle too, don't you?'

'Yes. I heard it. It goes thud-thud.'

'It's only a tree branch knocking against a window or something.' Barbara said. 'Come on now, let's get home before we get soaked.'

'But we're wet from the sea,' Syl pointed out.

'So we are. Well, let's get home anyway, because it's nearly tea-time.'

They weren't difficult to persuade. Truth to tell, the light was eerie. A great storm was coming, anyone could see that. They gathered up their paraphernalia and set off up the path to Castle CragApp.

Barbara and the children saw very little of the parents. Lord McDemmott seemed to spend almost all the daylight hours crawling about the island on all fours looking at ferns through a lens. Lady McDemmott sat in a wooden summerhouse surrounded by books which, when Barbara stole a peep at them, turned out to be all in French and poetry at that – Lady McDemmott was translating Baudelaire. The only occasion on which the family came together was the 'mother's hour' after nursery tea, when Barbara had to take the children to the drawing-room for inspection. The encounter seldom lasted an hour; after a few inquiries about how they were amusing themselves and whether they were being good, conversation seemed to languish.

On this evening, Verdie volunteered, 'We saw the kelpie but it was only Brutus swimming.'

'He's a bad dog,' said her father. 'He keeps running off to amuse himself. But he does love CragApp so – he's not a town dog, really.'

To Barbara's way of thinking that was only too true. How they coped with him in Belgravia she couldn't imagine.

The storm broke as they were chatting. Lord McDemmott explained to Syl how thunder was caused by the air rushing together when lightning had split it apart, but although it sounded very scientific it didn't seem very reassuring when they took themselves off up the great stone staircase to the nursery floor.

'You're scared,' taunted Syl to Verdie.

'No, I'm not, *you're* scared.'

'I am not. Thunder's only clouds colliding, Papa says so.'

'You're scared of the bogle. You put your head under the pillow so as not to hear it go thud-thud.'

'I don't.'

'You do!'

'Now, now, children,' soothed Barbara. She started baths and bedtime early, and sat with them for longer than usual reading to them from *Heidi.* At last they settled; Folly was already asleep, too young to be perturbed by alarms about bogles and kelpies.

What brought Barbara awake in the middle of the night she couldn't quite tell. But she sat up in her bed, and was aware of a tiny sound from the night nursery next door. She swung her feet out, found her slippers, pulled on her dressing gown, and hurried in.

Verdie was sitting on the floor just inside the door.

'What on earth are you doing there?' Barbara asked, picking her up.

'Listening for Syl,' said Verdie in a trembling voice.

'Syl?' Barbara glanced at the bed he should have been occupying. In the glimmer of the nightlight she could see it was empty. 'Where is he?'

'Gone to catch the bogle.'

'What?' Barbara was taken aback, then alarmed. 'When did he go?'

'I . . . don't know . . . A long time ago. Ages. I woke up and heard the bogle, and I woke him up and said "Listen", and he said he was going to show me he wasn't afraid and went to find him.'

'Oh, *no*.'

'I think the bogle's got him,' faltered Verdie, and burst into tears.

'No he hasn't,' Barbara said. 'There's no such thing. He's just hiding somewhere so you'll get worried. I'll go this minute and fetch him back to bed.'

'No,' cried Verdie, seizing her dressing-gown, 'don't go! Don't leave me! The bogle will get me!'

'There's no such thing as a bogle,' Barbara repeated. 'And I must find Syl, Verdie. It's the middle of the night. He ought to be in bed.'

'I'll go with you,' Verdie said, holding on tight to the dressing-gown. 'We'll go together and find him.'

There seemed to be no alternative. Even if she rang for Chalmers to come and look after Verdie while she searched for Syl, it wasn't at all certain the butler would hear. The bell system in the castle seemed to be as old as the rest of it – it didn't work properly.

'All right then, where was Syl going to look for the bogle?'

'The Auld Hoose, of course. That's where it lives.'

'Come on then.' Barbara went into her own room to collect the oil lamp from her bedside table, turned up the flame, and they set off.

It certainly wasn't an enjoyable journey along the gallery of the great hall to the door at the back that gave entry to the Auld Hoose. This door was kept locked but the key hung from a hook by its side. Tonight, however, the key was in the lock and the door opened when Barbara pushed it. She walked forward into a stone passage, her bedroom slippers making no sound on the flags. Verdie whimpered and hung on to her.

'Syl?' Barbara called. 'Syl, are you there?'

'Y-yes, I'm here,' came a muffled voice.

'Where? Where are you, Syl?'

'I'm in the room at the end, Nanny.'

Verdie grabbed Barbara. 'Don't go, it's the bogle pretending.'

'It's Syl, don't you know his voice? Come on.'

They hurried down the passage. The door at the end was closed but not locked. However, age and dampness had caused the wood to warp so that it wouldn't budge until Barbara had thrown her weight against it a dozen times. It creaked open – and there was Syl sitting on an aged wooden bench with a pocket torch illuminating the area around him. He had been trapped when the old door swung closed behind him.

'Oh, Nanny!' he cried, and came hurtling towards her to bury his face in her skirts.

She put an arm around him, then told him everything was all right and they must get back to bed. She gave him the lamp to carry so that he would feel important. He led the way, and with Verdie hanging on for dear life they went back through the long passage and the door to the gallery, up the stairs, and into the night nursery.

'There's something in the Auld Hoose,' Syl whispered as she tucked him up at last. 'I heard it, bumping about in the room below.'

'Nonsense, it's nothing,' Barbara soothed. She sat in the night nursery until both children had gone to sleep.

She herself slept badly. When the first rays of the sun lit up her room, she was broad awake. 'Bogles!' she said to herself crossly. 'There are no such things!'

She got up, dressed quickly, and retraced her steps of last night. In daylight it was much less fearsome. The place was dismal and dank, but it had no powers to alarm her. She stood in the room where she had found Syl, and looked about her.

To her amazement and consternation, she heard a bumping sound just below her.

She gave a gasp and clutched at herself with her own arms, as if to guard herself from attack. Then she took a hold of her wits, and listened.

True, she could hear a bumping sound, a thudding sound. But there was nothing supernatural about it. It came from below, and seemed loud and unnatural because it was coming from an empty room.

She went back to the gallery, and down into the main hall of the castle. After some thought she went outside and worked her way round the walls until she came to the point on the ground floor of the Auld Hoose which ought to be below the room on the first floor in which she had been standing.

There was a row of sash windows here. And one of the sash-cords had broken so that the upper half of the window had fallen down. To the casual observer it wouldn't be noticeable – but the window was open at the top.

She went to Lady McDemmott's summer-house and came back with the chair from it. She stood on the chair and looked in at the window.

There, lolling on the floor, was Brutus.

The bogle of the Auld Hoose was unmasked. Brutus, left to roam at will all over the island, had discovered that he could leap in at the window when he wanted to. He was supposed to sleep in a kennel in the courtyard but that apparently didn't please him. When it took his fancy, he jumped in at the ground floor of the disused Auld Hoose and made himself comfortable.

And that was the explanation of the bumping heard by Verdie. The great dog, landing after his leap, was no small weight. The sound echoed in the empty room. And Verdie slept in the bed nearest the window, so that the sound carried to her sharp little ears.

Barbara made a great adventure out of unearthing the lair of the bogle. She made the children gird themselves with weapons – a toy sword, a gun from a cowboy outfit. They marched in formation round the castle and then she boosted them up one after the other so they could peer in at the window and see the room. By that time Brutus had departed to chase the gulls on the beach, but he had obligingly left a bone on the floor.

Syl was delighted. 'Brutus the Bogle, Brutus the Bogle,' he carolled. And of course now that they knew he was the culprit it wasn't long before they actually saw him padding round to the window and leaping in. Once you know the explanation, it's amazing how easy it all seems.

Although from then on the children and Barbara were on the best of terms, life on CragApp became a little harder. The fine warm weather had disappeared with the thunder storm, and though from time to time the sun shone there was much rain and too much wind for pleasure. It wasn't surprising that the baby should be fretful and sniffly. The castle was chilly even when the fire was glowing brightly in the nursery.

Barbara put him to bed after a light meal and a good warm bath. But next day he was worse. His temperature kept rising and he developed a short, painful cough. 'Folly, my love, I think you're quite poorly,' she told him about midday, and covered him up while she went in search of Chalmers.

'Chalmers, where is the nearest doctor?'

'A doctor? Ah, dearie me, I'm thinking the nearest is Tyree. What for do you ask?'

'I'd like one to have a look at Master Folly. How do you fetch him?'

'We send a boat for him, Nanny. But there's nae chance o' that, with this gale blowing. It would be madness.'

'But, Chalmers, it's quite important to have the doctor call. Surely there must be some way?'

'Not at all, Nanny, not at all. If the weather's bad, you canna cross between the islands by any manner of means. And this wind'll no' change for three-fower days.'

And there was no telephone. Barbara had established that when she wanted to order her bathing suit and Verdie's new vests from Oban. The only means of communication was the post boat, and the post boat wouldn't be running until the weather improved.

'Is there anything I can do, Nanny?' Chalmers said, for once volunteering to put himself out. He could see Barbara was worried.

'No, thank you, I don't think so.' She went back to the nursery. Perhaps she was being alarmist. Babies often ran temperatures and then got better within twenty-four hours.

But she didn't like the cough.

By evening, when it was time for 'mother's hour', she knew she had to impart her fears. She got Syl and Verdie ready, and then said to Syl: 'I want you to take Verdie down by yourself tonight, Syl, and tell Mama that I need to speak to her. Ask her to come upstairs, will you?'

Syl, proud to be given this task, took hold of his little sister by the hand and marched her down in her best blouse and skirt to be viewed by Lord and Lady McDemmott. It seemed a long time before the nursery door opened and they reappeared, with their parents bringing up the rear.

'Well, Nanny? Something up?' inquired his lordship.

'Run along and get ready for your bath, children,' Barbara said, and when they had gone darting into the bathroom to enjoy the pleasure of letting peat-coloured water cascade into the great claw-footed bath, she waited a moment. When she knew they were busy, she said, 'I think the baby has pneumonia, my lord.'

'What? Pneumonia? How could that be?'

'I don't know. He hasn't been himself for a couple of days but today he's got a cough and he's really not well. I hear from Chalmers that there's no way of getting a doctor.'

'Well, no . . . Do you really think it is as serious as that?'

'If you'd like to come with me –'

'No, no, I leave that kind of thing to you,' his Lordship said, backing away. 'You know whether the little chap's sick or not.'

'Will you come, my lady?'

'I . . . suppose so.' Lady McDemmott followed Barbara into the night nursery, where Folly was tucked up in his cot.

'His temperature is high, and his breathing is very shallow. As you can see, he's very flushed.'

'Ye-es,' said Lady McDemmott doubtfully. She leaned over the cot and surveyed her son through her horn-rimmed glasses. She laid a hand on his forehead. 'Yes, he's very hot,' she agreed. 'But it's probably just a summer cold.'

'I wondered if there was anyone on CragApp who has medical knowledge, my lady? Any of the men ever been on a ship where they acted as orderly, or any of the women been nurses?'

'Not that I know of. They're a fishing community. Oh, I think you're making too much of it, Nanny. Just keep him in bed for a day or two. I'm sure he'll be all right.'

Barbara realized that Lady McDemmott didn't want to think the baby was ill, because if he was, there was nothing to be done about it. She was about to argue with her, but checked the words. What was the use? There was no one to nurse him but herself, and perhaps it was better not to have the mother alarmed and interfering.

'Very well, my lady,' she said. 'But just in case, I'd like to keep him away from Syl and Verdie. It will mean someone else will have to look after them. Can I ask for Effie to help me?'

'If you think it best, but she's not very bright, I'm afraid.'

'She'd be better than no one, my lady.'

The children were put to bed and Barbara made a game out of moving them into the day nursery to sleep. She spent the night on a chair in the night nursery. There was no doubt the baby was very ill indeed, his growing restlessness turning into momentary convulsions, and the cough growing worse.

Next morning Barbara took the two older children into her confidence. 'I want you to find Effie and bring her to me. She's going to look after you for a day or two, because Folly needs me specially. You can be a great help by being good, and doing whatever I ask. Will you do it?'

'Of course,' Syl said, standing up straight.

'Course we will,' agreed Verdie.

Effie was rather pleased at being promoted to nursery-maid. Syl ordered her around shamelessly but, mindful of his promise to Barbara, played no tricks. They went out on walks with her, well-buttoned into their rain coats and sou-westers, or played hopscotch in the great hall, or read to Effie out of their storybooks. She went along with all their suggestions, and was painstaking over their meals and their baths.

The weather continued absolutely wild. The fishing boats had not been out for four days. But Barbara had ceased to think about the hope of a doctor. She was engaged in a struggle to save Folly McDemmott despite the lack of medical advice.

In any case, she had seen pneumonia before. She knew there was no treatment except minute attention, determined efforts to keep the temperature down, and prayer. By and by the fever would break; this almost always happened on an odd-numbered day from the outset – the fifth, the seventh, or the ninth. She prayed it would be the fifth, for Folly was so small that the fever would burn up his strength if it went on long.

She sponged him regularly, held him when the rigours seized him, tried to comfort him through the nightmares of delirium. She dripped honey and lemon juice between his lips, and tiny amounts of beef tea prepared and actually brought while still hot by Mrs Moffat.

'Lassie, you're worn out,' said the cook. 'Let me take a turn at watching the bairn.'

'No, he might wake and need me.'

'But I'll be here.'

'He'd expect to see *me*,' said Barbara. She knew Mrs Moffat wanted to help, but she had no nursing experience. She wouldn't know what to do when Folly screamed and arched in terror in his delirium.

The children were as good as gold. They went to visit in the drawing-room each evening, made polite conversation, and came back again to put themselves to bed. Effie tidied up after them, then told Barbara when they were in bed. She would hurry in to tuck them in and say goodnight.

They never asked if Folly was getting better. They knew they would see the news, good or bad, on Barbara's face.

The wind began to abate. It had been blowing for four days, as Chalmers had foretold. Barbara sat in the night nursery listening to it, and jerked her head up to find she had been asleep in her chair.

Asleep? How long? She looked at the watch on her dress front. She'd slept nearly five hours. And the baby had not wakened her? She almost fell out of her chair, to lean over the cot, afraid that the worst had happened and Folly had died while she was asleep.

But the baby was breathing more deeply. His flushed colour was less noticeable. She put out a hand and touched his cheek. It was not so hot. He stirred under her touch and opened his eyes. 'Nana?' he mumbled, and fell asleep again.

The improvement held. At daylight his forehead was cool, he woke for more than half an hour and knew where he was. That evening Barbara left him with Effie keeping watch, so that she herself could accompany the children down to the drawing-room.

'Well, Nanny,' said Lady McDemmott, blinking at her through her glasses, 'so there you are. Come out of your self-imposed exile, have you?'

'I'm happy to say, my lady, that the baby is much improved.'

'There,' said Lady McDemmott to her husband, 'I told you it was only a summer cold.'

On the following day it was possible to send to Tyree for the doctor. He examined Folly, clucked in concern over the sounds he heard on his chest, but on the whole was inclined to nod reassuringly. 'He'll need looking after for a bit,' he said, 'but he'll do, he'll do.'

'I was terribly afraid it would turn to double pneumonia.'

'Was Lady McDemmott worrying?'

'Oh no,' Barbara said, looking down.

'That's good. No need to worry her now with the news that you were struggling alone with a very serious case.'

Barbara didn't say, 'I don't know why not! *I* worried, why shouldn't she?' Instead she nodded agreement.

'You know the drill - plenty of rest, keep him warm, build up his strength. I'll send a linctus over with the boat, to keep his chest easy. And he'd better have Virol, three times a day, just an eggspoonful. Keep an eye on the brother and sister - it's an infectious disease, after all, but you seem to have done a good job keeping the baby in isolation.'

'Thank you, Dr MacIlroy.'

Lady McDemmott spoke to the doctor before he left. 'It will be all right for our guests, won't it?' she inquired. 'You know they're here for the Twelfth.'

'Quite all right,' he assured her. 'The children will be out of the way in the nursery in any case, but I've told Nanny to keep them quiet, just to be on the safe side.'

'Splendid,' said her ladyship. 'It's a nuisance having all these people descending on us every year, especially when I've still so much work to do on the last ten poems . . . But after all, that's why we come north. It would be too tiresome to have to put them all off, wouldn't it?'

'Quite so,' said the doctor.

As the governess cart bore him away to board the boat at the jetty, he glanced up at the windows on the top floor of the Georgian wing. That was where the Nanny had conducted her fight for the life of little Folly.

Too tiresome if she had lost the battle and the shooting party had had to be cancelled on account of a funeral . . .

CHAPTER FIFTEEN

Before she left London with the Clan McDemmott, Barbara had had time only to scribble a few lines of explanation to Fredric. He had written to her at CragApp, regretting that he hadn't seen her before she left but making plans for her return.

He would be taking his family to the Vosges as usual at the end of August, but would be back in London by September. Barbara was able to assure him that, according to all she could learn, the McDemmotts would stay on the island for about two weeks of grouse-shooting, so she would be in London again by the end of August.

A batch of Fredric's letters was delayed by the gales. When they arrived, they put a plan to Barbara. She had to be at the Hogarth School on a day early in September for the ceremony in which the students were given their certificates. She was due to come to London with the McDemmotts by the end of August. There were a few days' leeway.

'Let us for once think of ourselves,' begged Fredric, 'and go away together so that we can have some time to ourselves. I have a friend in Hereford who has a cottage above the Wye, where we could be alone with no one to spoil things. Say you'll come, Barbara.'

The next letter in date order gave details of train times to Hereford and planned how he would hire a car and pick her up at the station. The next pleaded with her to reply: 'You don't answer my letters – have I offended you by putting forward the idea of a holiday alone with you? If I was wrong, forgive me. But at least write to me. I can't bear your silence.'

She wrote at once to explain that the mail had been held up by gales, and accepting completely the idea that they should go away together. She had sensed that the time was coming when they must make up their minds, either to commit themselves to each other or to draw apart. She knew there were obstacles; Fredric was married, with two young sons who could be damaged by dramas in his marriage. But she didn't ask him to bring things out in the open with his wife, to ask for a divorce. She remembered how much it had hurt her when Archie asked her for a divorce. She didn't want to inflict that on another woman. Nor did she want to harm his two boys.

But she had a deep longing to be close to him. There was warmth, deep affection and tenderness in their relationship. But she knew there could be passion too. She needed to know how much they meant to each other in the physical sense. She wanted to have the joy of love given and received.

She nursed the little boy with infinite care, and when the time came on the 27th August to return to London, she insisted that it must be done in easy stages. They made the crossing to Oban, but stayed there overnight before going on. Lord McDemmott and his wife insisted on travelling by day because they hated train sleeping accommodation and preferred to sit reading and occasionally moving to the restaurant car. But Barbara demanded overnight sleepers for herself and the children. She took them aboard the train at six o'clock on the Tuesday evening, and unpacked them all in good condition at nine next morning at Euston.

Folly was quite well and ready to be handed over to his own Nanny. But Nanny Pemerson was delayed in Norfolk by family troubles of her own. She telephoned from a public phone box to Lady McDemmott, to explain she couldn't return for a few days yet.

'But it's no problem, Nanny, is it?' Lady McDemmott pointed out. 'You can stay on a few more days.'

'But I –'

'I telephoned the school. They don't expect you back until the 10th September for the Founders' Day ceremony.'

'No, but –'

'In any case, we've no choice, have we? Someone has to look

after the children and especially Folly, after being just a teensy bit poorly. So we'll take it as settled, shall we?'

'Yes, my lady.'

There was no way to get in touch with Fredric. He was off in the Vosges Mountains quite unaware that their plans were going awry. But there was still a chance that Nanny Pemerson would be back in time for her to get to Hereford.

But the days passed and it became clear Nanny Pemerson would not be back by the date when Barbara was expected to be in Hereford. She telephoned from Cromer direct to Barbara in the house in Belgrave Square. 'I'm ever so sorry, Nanny Gray, but my mother has died. I can't leave my father just yet and there's the funeral and all – you understand.'

'Of course I do.'

'My sister's coming to stay with Dad after the funeral. That's next Saturday morning. I reckon I should stay Sunday – anyway, trains from Norfolk are that bad on a Sunday it'd take me all day to get back. So I'll arrive on Monday. You can hold the fort until then?'

Why shouldn't she say, 'The nursery-maid will have to take over on Friday because I'm expected elsewhere on Saturday'?

She couldn't do it. She couldn't deliver Folly into the hands of an inexperienced girl. The baby was well, but not so fit that he didn't have his ups and downs. Her conscience wouldn't let her leave him to anyone except his own Nanny.

'Very well,' she said, with a voice that she determinedly kept steady, 'I'll hold the fort.'

She tried ringing Fredric's Harley Street flat in hopes someone could take a message, but it was empty until he himself returned. He was going direct from Dover to the cottage in Hereford, as she understood it. There was no way of contacting him. She didn't know the address in Hereford.

On the Saturday when she would have been travelling westwards, she took the children for a walk in the park. It was the first day of September, a fine warm day of yellow sunshine. Folly sat up in his pram taking an alert interest in all that was going on around him. Syl raced about, rejoicing in the last few days of freedom before he was returned to prep school. Verdie trotted at Barbara's side, holding the pram handle, chattering about the birthday party she was going to the following week.

Barbara walked along, listening, nodding, smiling. It was no use letting herself think her heart was broken. Hearts didn't break that easily. But she hated the thought that Fredric would go to the station to meet the train, and she wouldn't be there . . .

Nanny Pemerson arrived back on Monday about midday. She had lunch with Barbara in the nursery, then when the children were having their nap she told the sad story of the bereavement, complete with details of all the wreaths at the funeral. 'And my Uncle Meredith, that's worth a small fortune, he only sent evergreens. Evergreens! Old skinflint!'

Then it was Barbara's turn to describe the events at CragApp. 'Huh,' sniffed Nanny Pemerson, 'I can't abide that place, I really can't. Nothing will ever get me to go there, I don't care how many years they do it. It doesn't surprise me in the least Baby was poorly. Nasty damp dark place! I wonder he didn't catch his death.'

'The doctor up there said to watch his chest through the winter. He's on Virol three times a day.'

'Oh yes, very nourishing. Perhaps I'll give him a touch of Parrish's Chemical Food too.'

'If the family doctor here agrees with that.'

'Oh, pooh, shan't ask him. What do they know? I'll look after Baby, don't you worry, Nanny. Well, I suppose you're all packed up ready to go, are you?'

'More or less.'

'Need any help?'

'I don't think so, thanks.'

'Oh . . . well . . . I'm to give you this.' Nanny Pemerson held out an envelope.

'But . . . all arrangements about pay go through the Hogarth School –'

'No, this is for you, personal.'

Barbara opened the envelope. Inside was a piece of headed notepaper with the words. 'For Nanny Gray', written in the handwriting of Lady McDemmott. And a five pound note.

'Oh, but that's . . . I mean, I don't expect to be paid extra just because Folly was ill and I –'

'Oh, it's not that,' Nanny Pemerson said with a dimissive wave of her hand. 'They always do it, for every holiday Nanny. Nothing special for them, you see.'

'I see.' Nothing special. Well, perhaps they were right. She had come to look after their children, and that was all that she had done, in fact.

She got the butler to call a taxi and was taken to Waterloo Station, where she checked her suitcase into the Left Luggage office. Then she passed away an hour or so in window-shopping, and had tea. She didn't want to get to Harley Street until after the hour at which the doctors and surgeons finished appointments for the day.

It was after seven when she rang the bell at the heavy black-painted door of the suite of rooms. There was a delay, then the lever at the top was pulled so that the catch on the door was released. She pushed it open and went in. When she got to the foot of the marble staircase, she looked up the well of the stairs. Looking down from the top was Fredric's dark head.

'I thought it would be you,' he said. His voice echoed in the empty building.

She toiled up the stairs. He came down to meet her halfway. 'What happened?' he inquired.

'Let me get my breath,' she panted, 'and then I'll tell you.'

When she was seated in the sofa in his flat with a weak whisky and soda, she met his eyes.

'I couldn't come,' she said. 'The other Nanny was delayed getting back, and I just couldn't leave the children.'

'I see.'

'I just couldn't leave them,' she insisted. 'The baby had been very ill. You do understand?'

'I understand,' he said, 'that it points the way of our relationship.'

'What does that mean?'

'It either has to go forward and blossom, or it dies. You had a choice to make on Saturday, and the way you made it shows your inner decision.'

'No!' she cried. 'I wanted to come. Don't blame me for deciding against it. I had no choice but to stay.'

'Really? There was no one else you could have put in charge? In a house full of people, there was no one else?'

She hesitated. 'No one . . . I could trust.'

He sat silent for a long moment.

'What are you thinking?' she asked.

'I was at a lecture once when Freud was asked about the difficulty of making up your mind when you had a difficult choice. He said, "I recommend you toss a coin." The student was horrified. He protested, "But suppose it comes down the wrong answer?" And Dr Freud looked at him and replied, "If it is the wrong answer, then you know which is the right answer, do you not?"'

She shook her head and jumped up. 'Don't explain it all away by mumbo-jumbo, Fredric! I *couldn't* come!'

'No. You *didn't* come. You could have come if it had been the right answer. But the children were more important.'

'Are you blaming me for that?' she burst out, indignant.

'I'm not blaming you. I'm facing the fact. The children will always come first, with you. It's the way you are.'

'But . . . but, Fredric – I really do love you!'

He took the glass from her hand and drew her close. 'And I love you, very much. But nothing is ever going to come of it.'

'Oh, don't! You make me feel so . . . so . . .'

'So defeated? Never. In a way, it's the opposite. You've won. You know what you really want to do.'

'But I've hurt you. I never meant to do that.'

He took her into his arms. 'I'm not hurt. I don't deny I was disappointed when you didn't come, but . . . in a way . . . it didn't surprise me.'

'Because of what Freud said about "the right answer"?'

'It's always been a problem for you, Barbara. And always will be. Choosing to spend your life with children isn't going to protect you from feeling . . . attracted, shall we say . . . to men. I wonder if you realize how hard it's going to be, always putting yourself last?'

'Don't,' she said, clinging to him. 'I'm not built to be a martyr, Fredric. I don't know whether I've done the right thing, taking up this role in life. Perhaps I should back out now, while there's still time.'

He let her hold him tight for a moment, then leaned away a little. 'That was just panic talking. You know you're doing the right thing. You wouldn't have struggled so hard to get this far if you weren't sure.'

'Fredric . . .'

'Yes?'

'Promise not to answer a question with a question?'

'Are you asking me to commit myself?' he inquired.

They looked at each other and smiled at the question-and-question passage of arms. Then she said, 'Do *you* think I'll be a good Nanny?'

'You want my honest opinion?'

'Oh, Fredric! Please. Don't tease.'

'I think you'll be the best,' he said, and she could tell from his expression that he meant every word.

She sighed. 'It's just that . . . at this very moment . . . I have a lot of doubts.'

'That's natural. Anyone who doesn't doubt himself is a megalomaniac. It's this business of questions again, my dear. You question yourself, and perhaps all you get in reply is another question – am I sure I'm right? I'm asking myself that now, Barbara. Perhaps I should have said I think you'll regret being a Nanny. If I'd said that, perhaps I could persuade you to stay now, and we'd go to bed together, and I'd feel I'd won. But what would I have won? My own satisfaction at the expense of a lot of regret on your part.'

'And so far we've done nothing to regret – is that it?'

Instead of replying, he kissed her. It was a deep, quiet kiss, full of emotion but without passion. 'I suppose you'd better go now,' he said. 'Knowing you as I do, I can't imagine you don't have something you're supposed to do next.'

'Well . . . I am expected at the school. They know I finished with the McDemmotts this afternoon.'

'Exactly. So you'd better run along now, my love.'

'Fredric, I . . .' She didn't know what to say.

He shook his head at her. 'It's all right. We'll see each other again, I've no doubt. I even wish I could be at the training centre next week when you go up to the platform and get your diploma. But that would hardly be proper in those hallowed halls, would it – your would-be lover watching you receive the final accolade.'

'Shall I let you know where my first job takes me?'

'I hope you will. Come along, I'll see you out.'

He went downstairs with her and opened the heavy door. She stepped out into the cool evening air.

'Goodbye, Fredric.'

'Goodbye, Barbara. Good luck.'

She smiled and nodded. She walked away feeling she had thrown away something of great value, but knowing Fredric was right. Her choice would always be to put her children first.

She was lucky enough to get a taxi in Wigmore Street. Even as it carried her to Waterloo to claim her luggage, her thoughts were moving forward to next week, to the great day.

The day when she would walk out of Hogarth School a fully trained Nanny, with a world full of children waiting for her.